I0674071

Fanny's Destiny

Micki Smith

Avid Readers Publishing Group
Lakewood, California

i

PREFACE

This story belongs to Fanny; her life in the midst of an evolving new country. I first met Fanny through a fan and pair of shoes in the state history museum in Montpelier, Vermont, back at the end of the 20th century. Standing there wondering who in the world Fanny Allen might be, a voice inside my head clearly said, "You will tell my story!" There was no avoiding the command. For the next half decade I traveled Vermont researching old records, reading histories, journals, and standing on a mountain top awaiting a visit from the Great White Stallion. When my enthusiasm waned, Fanny prodded and poked from the Beyond. It's taken almost two decades to share Fanny's story. I'm proud to know Francis Montresor Brush Buchanan Allen Penniman and delighted she chose me to share her intriguing story.

All characters in this historical novel are real with the exception of Onncie, Cooper, his wife Sarabella, Emma, and Maggy the doll, who are figments of the author's imagination.

BACKGROUND

British King George III issued land grants in the New World to favored supporters. Since little was known about these areas, two such grants (the Duke of York grants and Hampshire or Wentworth grants) overlapped. Heated dispute went on for some time not just for land ownership but because those in the Duke of York grants favored the King while those in the Hampshire grants yearned for freedom from British rule. The Allen brothers (Ethan, Ira, and Levi) and the Green Mountain Boys were instrumental in resolving this conflict—first by establishing the disputed territory as the Republic of Vermont that in 1791 became the 14th state in the newly founded United States of America.

Significant Locations in the Life of Frances Montresor Buchanan Allen Penniman

NEW FRANCE

St. Lawrence R.

MAINE
(Part of MASS.)

Lake Champlain

③

N.H.

N.Y.

①

②

Portsmouth, 1624

Salem, 1626
— Massachusetts Bay

MASS.
Boston, 1630

④

Hartford, 1636

CONN.

New Haven, 1638

Plymouth, 1620

Providence, 1636

R.I.

Long Island

N.J.

••••• Disputed area between Duke of York's grant and the Hampshire Grants. 42 miles wide at the bottom, 120 miles wide at the top.

① Westminster

② Sunderland

③ Burlington

④ Scoharie

iv

Prologue

The Truth of Fanny's Lineage

John Montresor unconsciously rubs his leg as he limps through the dust of Schoharie's main street. The wound he received at Cumberland Gap has healed, but the aching continues, a condition he mostly chooses to ignore. His slightly gimpy stride in no way detracts from his brooding good looks. Indeed, the impediment adds a glamorous arrogance. At 19, John Montresor, in his scarlet English uniform with gilded buttons, excites the fantasies of many Schoharie young ladies.

The young officer turns right into the wide, gutted lane between the tavern and the town meeting house. Montresor would prefer a quick stop at the tavern. A neat, pint of rum would fortify his resolve, but alcohol on his tongue was a sure deterrent to his mission. Instead, he continues his stride past the dry goods store with its dangling sign, past the schoolhouse, and past the schoolmaster's own sturdy frame house and barn. Montresor walks another quarter mile out from the last building at the edge of town before he stops. Nonchalantly, he turns his muscular torso to gaze back along the lane and seeing no one, turns left to cut across the field towards the woods. Once Montresor is safely past the low growth and into the sturdy trees, he works his way back towards town. He moves slowly, quietly; listening as he picks his way through the mature oaks and maples skirting the underbrush wherever possible. Mostly, he hears the sound of his own pounding heart.

Montresor removes his scarlet coat, folds it neatly and tucks it under a large, pungent laurel bush. He adds his black, rolled brim hat to the stash. Moving to the wood's edge row of brush and saplings, Montresor studies the meadow and orchard behind the schoolmaster's barn. The sun is midway from high noon to dusk and there are few shadows. He will have to move carefully and swiftly in the tall meadow grass. The schoolmaster, James Schoolcraft, still has two hours at his work. Anna Schoolcraft, the schoolmaster' wife, Montresor knows, is attending Mistress Beaufort's quilting bee and afternoon social. Montresor calculates he has about an hour to be with his Catherine. The thought of her fresh, young face and emerging nubility spurs him to action. He makes his way to the barn.

Catherine giggles as John Montresor climbs the wooden ladder to the loft. John aches to kiss her, run his hands along her small breasts, taste the sweetness of her mouth. With great physical control, John takes Catherine's small, fine hands in his and pulls her gently to the hay. "My love," he whispers passionately. Catherine leans into his body, just barely touching his chest. Her yearning is every bit as strong as her lover's but fear of her father's wrath and her brothers' fury remain between the two.

Catherine's father, James Schoolcraft, is a proud and prominent man in Schoharie, New York. He had been a soldier for the English long before young Montresor was born. James' army career had ended in 1704 with a wounding at Blenheim where he had fought for the English along side the Palatines in the great War of the Spanish Succession. Taking advantage of his engineering skills and his camaraderie with the Palatines, James came to the new world, America. He had worked his way from Boston to Albany where he began surveying for England's interests in New York. He'd married Anna Christina Kemerer whose family had received a Palatine land grant from Good Queen Anne. When their children had become school aged, James Schoolcraft decided that if the younger Schoolcrafts were to become successful in this new country they must learn to speak English rather than the German spoken in central New York grants. He opened the first school in the region teaching in English rather than German. As schoolmaster, James Schoolcraft demanded behavior above reproach from his many children.

Catherine was the youngest and most willful. At 15, she had endured many harsh punishments for her stubborn exuberance and knew what lay ahead if Papa discovered her trysts with the handsome Montresor.

John gently pushes Catherine from him and leans back against the mounded hay. "Catherine, there's something that needs discussion between us." John speaks quietly, his eyes focused on Catherine's flushed face. "Soon, I must leave to rejoin my regiment.

My orders call me back south, to the city, the first of August. We're to prepare the troops to oust the French. That means I leave within the fortnight.

Catherine feels the breath going from her. She can't inhale new air to fill her lungs. Her chest hurts; her heart sobs yet she makes no sound. Tears wet her cheeks and John lifts her apron corner to wipe them away. "Come with me," he whispers and kisses her damp cheeks. "Come with me, my dearest Catherine."

Catherine gasps for air. Her heart pulses erratically; her head throbs. Has she heard correctly? "Oh, John. You'd really take me?"

John Montresor nods and pulls the girl to him. He'd committed himself. He'd done it. His hands begin to roam Catherine's body, stopping periodically to caress a soft curve or toy with a tress curling in the heat. Catherine rolls to her side beside John and presses her hot flesh against his coarse shirt. Her hips search for his and begin undulating to a new rhythm heretofore unexperienced.

"No!" she almost shouts, sitting up quickly. "No, we mustn't."

"Come with me, Catherine. In New York we'll live together as husband and wife."

Oh, how Catherine wanted to go; to see the thriving new city she'd only heard about. To be with her beloved John; to make gorgeous babies with him. Mama and Papa would never allow it. There was no time for a proper courting, for posting the bans. Propriety was a must for the Schoolcrafts. Running off, unmarried, to a strange city with the town rake definitely fell outside the parameters of good manners. Unthinkable. But letting John Montresor leave Schoharie without her was even more disastrous. Catherine feels as if the devil is struggling for her soul. The contest is really no contest at all. Catherine opts to run away, to follow her love into adventure.

John and Catherine plot their departure in every moment they can claim together. Feigning illness, Catherine stays in the room she shares with her sisters, packing what little she possesses. Slowly, a few at a time, she wraps two spare dresses, her chemises, and linens she's been working on for her hope chest. Catherine holds her old stuffed doll to her face. It smells of childhood summers and winter smoke, of tears long since spent and of nights at the small window watching the moon. "I can't leave you, Maggy," she weeps to her treasured toy. "My story lies in you." Opening the last of her packages, she stuffs the doll in the folds of a precisely hemmed sheet and carefully reties the string. Catherine stashes the few packages under the eaves, praying they'll go undiscovered.

Finally, the day comes for their departure. After breakfast, Catherine kisses her mother on both cheeks, bidding her an unusually energetic farewell for the short trip to the dry goods store. She hugs her oldest sister, Margaret, an additional moment and steps out in the dooryard for the last time. As she walks by the schoolhouse Catherine can see Papa through the window, pointer in hand, emphasizing some unknown factor on the slate board. She waves and blows a kiss. "Goodbye, Papa, goodbye. Just before the tavern, Catherine stoops to brush an imaginary something from her skirt and steals a surreptitious look up and down the lane. Seeing no one paying her any attention, she darts into the tavern's ice house where, long before sunup, she'd stashed her meager parcels.

Catherine hadn't realized she was so brave. Holding her chin forward, she steps confidently onto the public wagon that will carry her to the Hudson River pier. John would be waiting for her, he'd promised, out of view of the wagoneer. They wanted no one to connect their simultaneous departure. John had moved from Schoharie three days prior to Catherine's leaving. A close coincidence, yes but there was nothing obvious to connect the two lovers.

Catherine's thoughts dart from past to future as the wagon bumps and jostles over the ruts. The wagoneer's shouted encouragement to the two sweating horses barely reaches Catherine's consciousness as she indulges her fantasies. The journey is but a moment impinging on her musings. The driver deftly brings the wagon to a halt and dismounts his seat to assist his passengers. True to his word, John appears from behind the dock office, grabbing Catherine's arm, pulling her to him. The two share their first public kiss.

"Hurry, dearest. If we miss this skiff, there isn't another for three days." John gathers up Catherine's packages and guides her along the wharf to the boat.

The voyage down the Hudson challenges the young couple's vicissitude. Wind and rain pound at the small boat. The biscuits and cheese Catherine has brought from home roil in their stomachs. Just south of Poughkeepsie the skiff pulls to shore for an unscheduled stop. The unusually rough waters endanger the journey and the captain wisely waits out the storm under protection of the giant cliffs. The respite is welcome and Catherine begins to ask about their future. Where would they live? Would they have a house or just rooms? John smiles, stroking his lover's cheek. "We'll see m'love. Not to fret, we'll see."

Four days later, their journey ends in the city called New York. The disheveled pair disembarks and walks the length of a wharf reeking with rotting fish and damp sailcloth. John hails a lorry and hands Catherine up the single step. He leans forward and with authority directs the liveryman to a west side address. "Where is that, John?" asks Catherine.

"My father's house, dearest."

"Oh!" Catherine seems surprised. She'd never thought to ask if John had parents, or siblings. Or any relatives for that matter. How little she'd bothered to learn about her husband-to-be. John's hand caresses Catherine's thighs and she becomes more intent on her physical sensations than on the city she is passing through street by street. The heat is overwhelming but she attributes it to her personal flush.

The lorry stops before a stately, painted wood house with a large brass doorknocker. Catherine fixes her gaze on that shiny request for admittance not yet knowing she will gaze up at it in the future with great longing and painful anger.

"Wait here, m'love." John offers her a seat on steps leading to the imposing front door. "I'll go in and speak with the Major."

"So, his father's a military man," muses Catherine as she waits in the heat. Minutes pass. Catherine removes her bamboo fan from the tapestry handbag in her lap. Her legs are sticky with sweat and she stands, shaking out her full skirt. "How did I get this dirty?" she mutters. She bends and brushes dust from her hem. Swishing her fan with agitated vigor, Catherine begins to pace in front of the house. Movement at the window catches her eye and she looks up to see a gray haired man move away from the glass. "How I must look," exclaims Catherine and returns to her seat on the steps. Bells in the nearby steeple chime another hour passed.

John Montresor opens the big door and walks down the steps to Catherine. "Come, my sweet. We'll find lodging elsewhere." No further conversation ensues between the two until they alight from their lorry onto a street of small, two story, unpainted houses. Prevalent odors tell Catherine they are again near the wharf.

John leaves Catherine standing at the corner while he moves from house to house, making inquiries. "Madam, do you have rooms to let? May I ask your fare?" After conversation at the fifth house, John enters the doorway and disappears.

Catherine trembles as a group of rough looking, sullen men push past her, some smelling of rum, others just smelling. Catherine tucks her packages beneath her skirt and fixes her eyes on the door of the fifth house. At last, John emerges from the house and trots towards her, smiling.

"I've found a room. Come see if it suits you, m'love." John laughs as Catherine lifts her skirts to gather up her belongings. "How quickly you adapt to the city, my Catherine." The two walk to the fifth house and climb the three steps to the door.

"Catherine, meet Mistress Haupt."

The frightened, young woman from upstate drops a curtsy but not her eyes. "Mistress," says Catherine with an almost imperceptible nod. Her gaze scans the meager parlor furniture arranged against the wall, the floor at the corners, the candle sconces on the wall. No signs of dust. The room smells fresh, though a faint trace of lye aroma hangs in the closed room. No heavy cooking odors waft from the nearby kitchen. "You keep a fine house, Mistress," speaks Catherine, smiling at last.

"Danke." Mistress Haupt replies solemnly. "Come. I show you da room." The landlady leads the way up the narrow, unpainted stairs and down a short, dark hall toward the rear of the house. "I rent only two rooms. This is the largest." Mistress Haupt unlocks the door with a key from the ring on her apron sash. She ushers Catherine into the room. John follows, remaining silent as Catherine takes in the furnishings.

The room is simply furnished; a poster bed, a trunk, one wooden chair with arms, a small table with blue crockery bowl and pitcher. Catherine crossed the room and bends to look under the bed. Good, the chamber pot is clean and un-cracked. Straightening, she says to no one in particular, "Ah, the pot is covered." Catherine walks to the single window and pushes aside the muslin curtain. Rooftops meet her gaze, the first almost within touching distance. She shifts her feet just slightly and there, in a narrow slit between rooflines, Catherine gets a tiny glimpse of water, the horizon broken by a rocking skiff mast.

Catherine turns to the landlady and speaks softly. "This is quite sufficient, Mistress Haupt. If Master Montresor and you agree on the rent, it is settled." Catherine swished her dusty skirts past the landlady, through the door and into the hallway before turning with a question. "What meals are served, Mistress?"

John answers quickly, "Mistress has included dinners for you in her weekly rent."

Before Catherine can digest the significance of the singular 'you', Mistress Haupt continues, "I serve promptly at one o'clock except on Sundays when it's half after the hour."

John again intercedes. "The mistress does allow bread and cheese in the room."

"At the first sign of crumbs that draw varmints or bugs, the privilege is denied," interrupts the landlady. "I inspect the rooms thrice weekly. Any signs of lice or disorder that might dirty my house, you will be asked to leave. I have enough trouble keeping the wharf rats at bay. It is understood, ya?" Mistress Haupt extends her hand toward John Montresor an adds, "That will be two weeks, in advance, sir."

Financial transactions completed, Mistress Haupt takes a single key from the ring on her apron and hands it to John. "One key. If you lose it, you pay for a new one or stay out of the room. Ya?"

John accepts the key, nodding. Taking Catherine's arm, he leads her into the small room and closes the door. Immediately, he pulls her to him, and his long repressed desire becomes apparent. "I've waited so long, Catherine. So long for this moment." He moves toward the bed guiding Catherine with his body. His kisses move from her lips to her neck and his hands undo the tiny buttons down her bodice. Catherine moans softly and falls back on the bed bringing John down on top of her. Somewhere, thrust into the back of her mind is the notion that she is not yet married to this man who is fumbling at her corset strings. Her passion keeps the thought locked just beyond reach. Quickly, the fact loses all significance.

Catherine awakens and studies the room. Her left hand rests on John's rhythmically rising chest; her head on his outstretched arm. As she turns quietly so as not to wake her lover, Catherine realizes she is sore. Her breasts ache. Her thighs are sticky. The smell of fresh blood rises to her nostrils. "I must clean myself," she thinks, then wonders, "Where do I get fresh water?" Catherine gathers her clothing from the floor and omitting her undergarments dons her dress. She straightens her hair with her hands as best she can. Taking the crockery pitcher, Catherine opens the door and goes in search of water.

Now fully dressed, Catherine sits in the chair studying the man in the bed. The intensity of her scrutiny reaches John and he rolls over and blinking several times, opens his eyes. His smile reflects memories of his recent passion and he reaches out to Catherine. "Come, m'love. Sit beside me, here," he murmurs, patting the bed.

Catherine remains in the chair, unconsciously straightening the folds of her skirt. Her eyes focus on her lover's face, but she does not smile. "When will we be wed, John?"

John rises on his elbow and pats the bed again. "Come here, Catherine, and we'll talk. Come on, right here."

Catherine rises and moves toward the bed. She is determined not to fall again under passion's spell before she has her answers. "John, did your father not like the look of me?"

"Dearest," he murmurs, reaching out and pulling her to sit beside him. "The Major will come to treasure you as I do. Perhaps it will take time, but it will happen. How could he not love such a beautiful creature as you?" John reaches to pull her prone but she resists.

"The Major claims it is inconvenient at this time to add another woman to his household. You see, he's entertaining a lovely lady himself. He suggests that two such jewels in the parlor and the kitchen at the same time will bring only doom. I agree. Besides, I want you all to myself, m'love." John caresses Catherine's arm, bending to place soft kisses strategically from wrist to shoulder. "I'll come every day after regimental drill dismisses. Kiss me, sweetest."

Catherine rises and walks to the window before speaking. She pulls the curtain aside and stares at the little bit of river in the distance. "I repeat myself, John. When shall we be married?" Catherine is willing her hands to be steady, her head still, and her eyes dry. It takes extraordinary effort that nearly exhausts her in the seconds it takes John to reply.

"First, we must have a proper home, m'love. That takes pounds I don't currently have. I plan to ask the Major for a generous wedding gift when an appropriate moment arises. 'Til then, you must make do with these lodgings. It won't be long, I promise."

"*I* must make do? What about you, John?" Catherine continues her steady gaze toward the river. Hearing no answer, she turns and glares at him.

"Darling Catherine. Don't be sad. This is only temporary. In the meantime, the Major insists I keep quarters at home. It is my home, you know." John rises from the bed and walks naked toward Catherine. "I think of you as my wife, sweet Catherine. So what do a few weeks matter before the bans are posted?"

John's reawakened desire is obvious and Catherine's resolve weakens. The two temporarily discard discussion of their future and return to the bed.

This time, when Catherine wakens, the room is dark and the other side of her bed empty.

The weeks unfold into mid-August. John visits the fifth house on Amsterdam Street almost but not every night. He usually brings bread, cheese, and apples when he can find them.

Occasionally, a smoked fish wrapped in oily paper. One such evening, John remarks with no particular preamble "I have grand news, m'love."

Catherine's heart quickens; she stops chewing a bit of cheese in mid bite. "Oh, John, you've found us a house!"

"Well, not quite that good, dearest!" John bends forward and kisses Catherine's flushed earlobe. "The regiment has been posted to Nova Scotia." Hearing his lover gasp, he continues quickly. "The 'good' part is that we'll not be leaving until late October—though why we're going to that godforsaken part of the world in winter, is far beyond my comprehension."

"Will we be married before you leave?" Catherine refuses to voice her deepest fears. She could not bear to hear them spoken aloud lest her thoughts become reality.

John's visits become less frequent. Catherine offers to help Mistress Haupt with the cleaning. The landlady doubts that a boarder should be involved in the minutiae of housekeeping but realizes physical activity might ease the doldrums of waiting for that arrogant officer who pays the rent. Frequently, when Mistress Haupt is cleaning the upstairs hallway, she detects faint sobs from under the last doorjamb. She seems so refined, that pretty lady from the north. Every day, she takes an afternoon stroll up and down the street never going further than the corner to the west or the intersection to the east. "Tsk, such a shame," the landlady thinks.

Mistress Haupt invites Catherine to help with the laundry and often they share an afternoon cup of tea now. They learn of a shared Germanic heritage and frequently their conversations lapse unnoticed into their native language. Occasionally, when it is obvious that John will be absent of an evening, Catherine accompanies Rosel (they have come to use their given names between them) to a nearby pub. The short walk, down to the corner and over two streets, is safe enough. There's always some sailor or working man willing to buy them a pint and the time is spent pleasantly. One evening, strolling arm in arm on their return from the tavern, Catherine expresses a worry about her reputation. Rosel giggles, "that missy from up the River Hudson, is an issue well beyond its inception!"

One evening in mid-October, John and Catherine are lying together on her bed. John places soft kisses on her eyelids, murmuring the gently, appreciative words that follow lovemaking. In that same personal whisper, he speaks into her ear. "The Major is giving a farewell dinner for me on Friday next. This is the last time I'll see you before I leave for Nova Scotia." Catherine feels the warm breath caressing the few wisps of damp hair along her cheek. Seconds pass before her brain supersedes her heart and she hears the truth of John's words. Anger arises in her breast. How cruel he waited for such a vulnerable moment to spew his awful message. Catherine jerks to a sitting position and yanks at John's hair. With all the strength of raw fury she pins his head to the pillow and forces him to look at her.

"The Major has not seen fit to invite me? Your little wharf whore might dirty his fine carpets?" Now that her rage is finally unleashed, she cannot retract its rampage. "Damnation on you, John Montresor! What is it you expect me to do while you're off shoving the French into the ocean? I'm tired of this dank, little room. I'm tired of wondering if you'll soil your shoes tonight with fish guts and gutter slop."

John tries to caress her cheek but Catherine yanks her head away. "Don't try that tactic with me, you ass. I'm slow about getting your sly tricks, but the message has become quite clear. How dare you treat me so!" Slowly, Catherine releases her grip on John's hair. Her anger, momentarily spent, she dissolves into tears. Disconcerted, Catherine is embarrassed at her outburst, but even more abashed at her own stupidity.

John seizes the moment to climb from the bed and pull on his clothes. He paces the room, scowling. Certainly, he's not plagued with remorse. Such self-indulgence is long past. His honor as an officer in His Majesty's army does demand some action however. John moves to the bed and places his fingers on the softly sobbing Catherine.

"Dearest Catherine." His powerful hands gently trace the tears down her cheek, his fingers seared by the burning heat of her flush. "Duty is my honor. You knew this must happen; we've talked of it often enough." He reaches inside his waistcoat pocket and withdraws several pound notes. "Take this, Catherine. Ten pounds is all I have. I'll send more when I can. Please know I love you." John kisses her forehead, barely brushing her damp skin. "I'll come as soon as I return to New York. Trust me, loveliest." He rises, tugs at the back of his waistcoat, dons his hat, and strides to the door. Catherine hears the latch click and then fading footsteps in the hall.

Rosel and Catherine spend many hours reliving the debacle and discussing Catherine's need to earn money. Each conversation repeats the last, occasionally a new idea arises, getting added to the routine. On the Friday of the Major's dinner party, Catherine has decided she will arrive unannounced and demand to be included. Rosel attempts to discourage this tawdry plan but fails.

Catherine dresses in the finery she's been saving for her wedding. Rosel, still protesting, curls and pins her hair. Catherine opens the trunk and runs her hand carefully along the side, among the linens in search for the pound notes John has given her. Her fingers touch a familiar treasure. "Maggy," exclaims Catherine as she pulls the doll from the trunk. "Oh, Maggy," she says, holding the bedraggled toy to her breast. Tears burn at the edge of Catherine's eyelids but she refused to let them fall. Rosel has dusted her face with powder and Catherine will not ruin the look with silly tears. She places Maggy on the pillow, then kissing her own finger gently touches the doll, transferring the affection.

"I'm ready. Wish me luck. Let's hope I can find a lorry on this godforsaken street." Catherine swishes down the stairs, and out the front door. Thirty minutes later, she steps from the lorry in front of Major Montresor's fine house. She climbs the steps, and reaches for the big, brass knocker. She cannot. Her bravado has evaporated. What was she thinking? Insane? Have I gone insane? Catherine can neither touch the doorknocker nor withdraw her hand. She freezes in time, in this terrible moment of disgrace and despair. At last, thank god, she is able to relax her arm and retreat down the steps. Catherine crosses the street and stands looking at the lit window of Major Montresor's parlor. Wigged gentlemen and well-coifed ladies move about, sipping some unknown libation. John, her beloved John, moves past the panes, stopping to kiss a lady's hand. Suddenly, Catherine heaves. Vomit spews from her mouth. She does not bend in time to save her skirts. She reels at the smell of it and staggers back to lean on the railing of this anonymous house. Her degradation is complete. Soiled and exhausted, Catherine turns and starts her long walk through the alien streets of New York.

The tower clock chimes three times as Catherine turns the corner onto Amsterdam Street and sees the familiar door of the fifth house on the left. Light glows behind the curtain in the parlor window. Hardly able to lift her arm, Catherine inserts her key into the lock and stumbles through the door. The sound wakens Rosel asleep over her mending. She rushes to Catherine's side and half carries, half drags her to the parlor chair.

Rosel cleanses her friend's face and brings hot tea before speaking a word. "Things did not go as you'd hoped, I gather," she says at last. Between sobs, Catherine chronicles her mortification outside the Major's house and at the assault of rude words hurled at her as she walked the streets in search of the only home she knew in the city.

"How did you find your way back?" asks Rosel.

"I just walked until I smelled rotten fish!" Catherine, too exhausted to reveal more detail, allows Rosel to help her to bed.

In the weeks that follow, Catherine stays in bed more often than she rises. The chamber pot become a frequent repository for her vomit—a situation Catherine attributes to her despair. Rosel encourages her friend to think toward the future and not to the past. After all, the rent has expired and Rosel cannot afford to lose the income. She suggests Catherine write her family for funds or perhaps to come carry her home.

"I wrote Papa the very first week I was here," Catherine reveals. "I wanted them to know I was safe and happy. He never responded. I cannot write now that I've fallen into bad times. What will he think?"

Rosel was one to be pragmatic. "Your papa's already done all the thinking he's going to do about you and come to an opinion. I suspect that opinion would case you pain. You've nothing more to lose. Write another letter. In the meantime, I must rent your room. We'll make a bedroll for the parlor floor that you can open at night. There's a wee bit of room in my shrunk, enough for your dresses, I think.

Catherine convinces the pubmeister at their favorite tavern to hire her as a barmaid. She works long hours into the night for little pay. The constant noise of rowdy patrons gives Catherine headaches and the bodily odors keep her nauseous. She drags herself back to Rosel's each night and falls into her bedroll. Rosel often tiptoes in to check on her and finds Catherine snoring, clutching Maggy to her chest.

One morning over tea, Catherine confides to Rosel. "I have not bled for four months. I must be carrying John's child though I notice no swelling."

"Have you heard from your father?" asks Rosel, knowing full well Catherine has not. You must go home to Schoharie. Meister Braun will not keep you on at the pub when he knows you are with child."

"I can't," Catherine weeps. "I cannot bring more shame to my family."

"Love overcomes shame." Rosel rises and puts her arms around Catherine's spare shoulders.

No letter comes from James Schoolcraft. The winter of 1759-60 is particularly cruel. Freezing dampness invades everything and is barely kept at bay by the small fireplace in Rosel's parlor. Catherine huddles in front of the flames, absorbing what heat her thin body will hold. Rosel's prediction becomes reality; Catherine is without work. Food is scarce and only through Rosel's continuing generosity does Catherine have anything at all to eat.

By mid-March, the cold abates somewhat but the dampness lingers. Catherine hardly notices. She spends most of her days lying in her bedroll in the parlor, hugging her old doll. Rosel coaxes her to eat the broth and porridge she prepares. Occasionally, there is a root vegetable to add to the gruel. Catherine's eyes have sunken into her face. Her pale skin has become even more ashen. She speaks seldom and only to the doll. Rosel and Catherine no longer share conversation. The baby inside Catherine is making itself known. Rosel sees movement in the small mound under Catherine's skirts.

April sun begins to warm the air. Fresh breezes stir the few budding trees on the street and Rosel props open the front window in hopes of catching a breath for Catherine. Rosel is just poking a pan of cornbread into the beehive oven beside her fire when she hears Catherine scream out.

"My god, the devil himself is punishing me," Catherine cries. She jerks her frail knees toward her chest and then just as quickly straightens them again. She is rigid with fright.

Rosel runs to her asking as she crosses the floor, "Is it the baby? Is it time?" When no answer is forthcoming, Rosel places her hand on Catherine's abdomen and feels the taut muscles quivering. She lifts Catherine's skirts and the prone woman weakly bats to push her away. "Be calm, Catherine. I must look or I can't help you." Rosel hums softly hoping to quiet the agitated young woman.

"I'll birth the devil. I know it," sobs Catherine. "'Tis to be my punishment."

"Quiet, liebkin." Rosel, in her concentration drops into the more familiar German.

Labor is long and Catherine too weak to be of much help. Just after dusk, Rosel pulls a tiny baby girl from between Catherine's emaciated legs. She bites the umbilical cord, knotting the end, and wipes the newborn clean. Having wrapped the baby in a blanket she has knit over the winter, Rosel places the frail child in her mother's arms, half expecting neither of them to survive.

Catherine manages a weak smile. She studies her daughter a moment and then raises her gaze to Rosel. "Her name is to be Frances Montresor. Fanny, I'll call her." As if the pronouncement has drained her last bit of strength, Catherine drifts off into a sleep from which she's never to return.

Rosel is ill prepared for Catherine's death. She is distraught at the loss of her friend, and distressed with a whimpering, sickly infant she can't possibly care for. She posts a letter to James Schoolcraft in Schoharie.

Master Schoolcraft. Your daughter, Catherine, died yesterday after borning a daughter whom she named after the father, John Montresor, who is on regimental duty in Nova Scotia. Fanny, the wee one, is in my care but I have not the means to provide for her. I would go to Mr. Montresor's family but since Catherine and John were not married, they do not acknowledge Catherine's existence. Please advise me promptly on your wishes. [signed] Mistress Rosel Haupt, Catherine's landlady and friend.

Seventeen days later, Rosel opens her door to face James Schoolcraft. "Mistress Haupt?" he asks.

Receiving a nod, he continues, "I'm Catherine's father. This is her older sister, Margaret. May we come in?"

Rosel ushers them into the parlor. Margaret's eyes search the room at the sound of a weak whimper. There, by the hearth, she sees a small bundle. "May I?" she asks Rosel.

Margaret gently rocks the baby in her arms as she listens to the details of the last months that Rosel offers. She looks down at the tiny face and coos, "Fanny, Fanny, my little one."

James Schoolcraft arranges room and board for the next few days while he goes about some business. Margaret and Rosel tend little Fanny, relinquishing her only to the wet nurse who comes four times during the day. The two women talk, evasively at first, about Catherine's life in New York. Rosel likes Catherine's 27-year-old sister, seeing the same intelligence and determination. She notes, too, how loving Margaret is with Fanny. It is a good sign.

On the third day of their stay, James Schoolcraft returns to the boarding house with a pronouncement. "Margaret, put on your finest gown. We're having dinner tonight with Colonel Crean Brush." Turning to Rosel, he continues, "I trust, Mistress Haupt, you will continue to care for Fanny while we are out. I promise we will return before midnight."

That night, when the Schoolcraft's return, Margaret's flush bespeaks her excitement. Arrangements have been solidified between James and the widower Brush. The Irishman will follow in a fortnight to Schoharie. There will be an honorable wedding for he and Margaret. Fanny's adoption by the couple is the final line in the agreement.

Two days after the Schoolcraft's departure up the Hudson, another knock comes at Rosel's door. She opens the door and straightaway spits vehemently. John Montresor drops his eyes to watch the spittle dribble down his waistcoat.

"She's dead, you wretched bastard! They've taken away your baby daughter. You'll not get a chance to lay your treacherous hand on that wee girl." Rosel slams the door. "Ha, the last I'll see of that scum."

Chapter 1
Fanny's Destiny

THE STORY

The Debut Years
1772-1775

"C'est bon. . .tres bon, ma Cherie," cackles Crean Brush. "You are much improved in your French grammar. Your recitation is impeccable, my dear."

Fanny curtsies and takes her seat at the oversized dining table draped with starched white napery. She dips her flushed face slightly toward the plate, as manners dictate. Guests return to their chattering and Fanny dares to lift her lids just enough to catch a glimpse of Mother Margaret. She is rewarded with a twinkly wink and the slightest upward curve of her adopted mother's tinted lips. Margaret never breaks pace in her conversation with the guest at her left.

Fanny picks up the ornate, pewter spoon furthest to her right, settles it in her delicate fingers and begins dipping the back edge against her soup bowl. "Potato again," she thinks. "Can we serve nothing but potato? So déclassé! Embarrassing." A most imperceptible wrinkle rises above her right eyebrow. *Pouting is unbecoming and brings premature lines to the face.* Fanny can almost hear her mother scolding and keeps quietly sipping at the detested broth.

Nine guests dine tonight, a special occasion in honor of her twelfth birthday. Usually, on party nights, Fanny's dinner is brought to her room by the maid. Not long ago, Mother Margaret decreed to Crean that their beloved daughter was now old enough and sufficiently mannered to sit at table with guests. Tonight, however, is a test of this theory. What better debut than a formal dinner in celebration of your very own birth. "So, why is everyone ignoring me?" Fanny frets silently.

1

The houseman and the maid are clearing away the meat course before Fanny draws sufficient courage to raise her head and glance around the table. Her father, holding court at the foot of the table, notices his daughter's perusal of the guests and raises his glass in salute. "To our lovely princess, on the verge of becoming a lady!" The chattering stops, everyone turns to Fanny. "Hear, hear!"

Fanny's lightly rouged cheeks—*a little is enough for someone just twelve warned Margaret*—darken a tone as a blush rises up her neck to join the tinted powder. With a grace beyond her years, Fanny lets her eyes roam from face to face before she nods slightly and smiles. "Thank you, each of you, for your wishes." Fanny drops her eyes demurely.

"You've raised her well, Margaret," comes a stage whisper from the woman seated next to her mother. Fanny cannot help but overhear and knows that beneath the polite gesture lies more to the thought: *for a bastard child.* Mother Margaret and Papa Crean had long ago decided to be honest with their ward. Fanny knew that Margaret was really her aunt and that Crean had agreed to adopt her to fill the hole left in his heart by the young daughter he had left behind in Ireland. The years had proven to Fanny that indeed her adoptive parents loved her beyond measure and she more than reciprocated that affection   A loving family erases the stigma of illegitimate birth, but the world can be less forgiving.

New York's socially elite were a small world within this new and burgeoning country. They were a wealthy group, pushing to be even wealthier. Their homes, their wardrobes, their pedigrees were impeccable. Their manners, while charming on the surface, rotted at the underpinnings in the slightest whiff of gossip. And they were, almost invariably, English.

The Brushes lived in the midst of this society. Crean, a renowned jurist, had been commissioned in the King's army to oversee British rights in the Colonies. Though Irish by birth and conviction, Crean had been opportunistic enough to pledge himself to England's expanding empire. Possibilities for reward were unlimited.

Crean's alliance with Margaret Schoolcraft not only enlarge his opportunities in the northern Yorker grants but unexpectedly brought him a great and tender love. His agreement to take on the bastard child of Margaret's dead sister had been merely a concession in his haste to add to his coffers. It was a decision he never regretted. Margaret proved barren and the beautiful little Fanny filled their hearts with joy and pride.

Margaret managed her household with tact and firmness. Crean long ago had relinquished the ledgers to his wife and only perused them at Margaret's periodic insistence. Funds were plentiful but Margaret was not a spendthrift. She negotiated boldly with tradesmen gaining their respect with her honesty and forthrightness. She hired her own seamstress noting to Crean that having the woman in their employ allowed constant oversight. The end product would be superior at a lesser cost.

Margaret's insistence on kindness was the foundation of their home. "Kindness costs nothing," she often intoned. No matter the turmoil outside their walls, there was to be peace, tranquility and thoughtfulness in her domain. Fanny frequently tested the limit.

Fanny's reverie is interrupted by a whisper in her right ear, "Is all this table talk boring you, Mistress Brush?"

She smiles at the wigged gentleman in the blue silk frock coat. "Oh, no," she whispers back. "I don't listen." Fearing his smile would turn to laughter, she quickly continues. "Papa talks so often about the politics and Mother Margaret shares all the gossip with me before I sleep. That way we can strut about, be silly, and poke a little fun." Seeing her inquisitor's smile broaden, Fanny adds in the same breath, "Oh, but we're never unkind!"

"Never?" The gentleman's eyebrow raises a question mark.

Fanny's eyes widen and she shakes her head sternly enough that her curls flip in complaint.

"How dull," he exclaims, his twinkling eyes bespeak his amusement.

Crean's laughter draws attention to the foot of the table. Fanny turns to see her father resting back in his chair, wine glass slightly raised in mock toast. "Here's to the man who brings that scoundrel to his knees." Those who had been listening joined the toast, "Hussah! Hoorah!" Crean pushes back his chair and struggles to his feet, goblet poised in pronouncement. "A toast to His Majesty, King George."

All rise to join the toast. Fanny holds her own glass safely over the table lest she splash wine on her new silk gown. Crean, more than a little drunk, continues, "Here's to our governor, His Excellency William Tryon, who will pay the pounds resting on Ethan Allen's dirty, hanging head.

As the toasting concludes, Margaret's laughter draws attention toward her end of the dining table. "Ladies, I hear politics gnawing at the air. It's time for us to excuse ourselves, I believe, and gather in the parlor. Come, Fanny darling, you must join us and recite that little Latin poem you learned this morning." Mother and daughter lead the ladies from the room.

"How clever you were, Crean, to push through that legislation in assembly last fall." Capt. Bamforth leaves his place and takes the seat just vacated next to Crean. The host raises his glass accepting the praise. The captain continues, "With that bounty restin' on his head, Allen's own men will turn on 'im. Things'll be settlin' down in the Grants before long. I'm thinkin' of buyin' up some of those shares myself."

"Good thinking, Captain. His Majesty bestowed 10,000 acres upon me for my Service. I'm mighty grateful for his generosity, indeed I am." Crean drains his goblet and continues. "I've purchased another 20,000 and am looking to buy yet 30,000 more by year's end."

"You two can try the wilderness if you like. Me? I'm staying where the business is—here at the port." Walter Buchanan's shipping partnership controlled more than 60% of the ships coming and going in New York harbor.

"Don't be too short sighted, Buchanan," counsels Bamforth. "As soon as the Grants draw settlers, there'll be more business in the north than you ever dreamed of."

Chapter 2

Margaret picks up the little bell from the corner of her writing desk and shakes it absentmindedly. Her thoughts are focused on her ledgers until she hears the swishing skirts of her maid approaching. "Onncie, light the tapers, please. The light's beginning to fade and I want to finish my accounts."

Onncie dips her head just slightly and her knee drops less than an inch of curtsy as she moves to do her mistress' bidding. Crean had given Onncie to Margaret as a wedding present and a strong bond had formed between the two women over the past twelve years. Onncie was not her real name; her baptism name was the same as her mistress' but she'd been called Meg as a child in Ireland. Crean had indentured Meg, paying for her arduous ocean journey. It seemed fortuitous that Meg's arrival in the New World coincided with Crean's newly arranged marriage. Yet it was Fanny who created Meg's new name. Meg often muttered to herself half in English, half in lilting Gaelic. She has a habit of repeating the word *honestly* as a string of genteel invectives or, just as equally, as a burst of excitement. Early in Fanny's vocabulary growth, *Onncie* became the word spoken to applaud Meg's presence. The doting parents soon found themselves calling "Onncie!" instead of Meg and the transformation became complete around the time Fanny turned two.

Onncie was almost twelve years younger than Margaret. The young Irish woman admired her mistress and the two grew quickly to respect and trust one another. Onncie was a surrogate mother to Fanny when Margaret was involved in the social season. Indeed, the nanny and various tutors over the years knew that a word from Onncie was as good as one from the mistress. This did not make her popular in the nursery and she was viewed as uppity among the other servants. Onncie's indenture had expired at the end of ten years but she had no reason to leave a situation as comfortable as the Brush's. Crean offered her a small salary and

5

a bigger room were she to stay and so the transition occurred with only a little notice.

"Master Brush be returnin' soon?" asks Onncie as she lights the last taper in the stand.

"I suspect so, Onncie. He's been gone a fortnight now. You know how he hates being away for long periods." Margaret looks up from her books and smiles at her maid. "Such a homebody for a man!" She chuckles softly. Margaret rises and walks to the window, pulling back the lace as if to look for Crean. "Let's open the windows, the stench should be less this time of day." Margaret moves aside to allow Onncie to unlatch the large windows. "We need some air in here. I hope this May heat isn't forecasting a brutal summer. I think Fanny and I will dine in the garden this evening. Tell Cook to set a simple table by the lilacs, if you will."

"Do you wish Nanny to join you?" Onncie waits by the parlor door for an answer.

"I think not, Onncie. My cherub will soon be discarding the need for a nanny and she needs more practice on table talk."

"On politics is what she means," thinks Onncie to herself as she walks quickly towards the kitchen. "And, there's no better tutor than Mistress Margaret in that arena."

Margaret softly closes the door to Fanny's room, listens for a moment with her ear to the wood, then turns and walks swiftly down the stairs and to the parlor ablaze in candlelight. Onncie rises from the chair as she enters and moves to leave.

"I'll be off to bed now, ma'am. If y'll not be needin' me." Onncie drops a brief curtsy and momentarily awaits any further instructions.

"G'night, Onncie. I'll be fine now; nothing more for this evening.

Margaret takes a seat near the open window and pulls her quilting frame to her knees. Quilting is a mindless task but one requiring precision. None is more careful than Margaret in her stitching but her mind is free to wander while her fingers push the needle evenly through the taut fabric.

"There are more and more signs of discontent," she sighs as her mind focuses on burgeoning complaints against the English rule in the colonies. King George is something of a fool but he's right in making his claim in the territories. After all, who's moved in to tame the wilderness? The English, that's who." In a political lapse, Margaret's emptied her memory of the Palatine establishment upstate and, indeed, forgotten the Huguenot's own interest in New Amsterdam, now called New York after the Duke's huge land grants. Her prosperity and her safety lie in allegiance to the British crown. Margaret's mood darkens as she recalls dinner conversations among the powerful men at whose tables she and Crean sit. There is much grumbling and small but increasing acts of subversion around Buchanan's docks and warehouses. Captain Bamforth tells of pilfering at the barracks; missing arms and supplies. They speak of those who stand up in the taverns and complain about the taxes; those who spend their last pence on a pint and forget in their stupor who paid for their labor. Margaret's fingers shove at the needle and her shoulders rise and stiffen from the tension of her thoughts. She pushes at her quilting frame almost knocking it to the floor. "I need a break from this tedium," she speaks sharply to the empty room.

"Tedium, m'love?" chuckles Crean as he crosses the threshold toward his wife.

"Crean!. I didn't hear you. When did you come?" Margaret rises, quickly moving into Crean's stout embrace. She lifts her face for the passionate kisses they still share after all these years. "Who would have thought an arranged marriage could produce such love," Margaret smiled in her mind. Aloud she says, "Come, sit with me. I'm anxious to hear what miracles you have wrought this time. Were you successful?" She drops to the small, upholstered settee and pats the space beside her.

Crean sits, his eyes searching Margaret's face, wondering at how few lines she has on her fair skin. He reaches his hand to touch her cheek, his fingers tracing along the edge of her hairline. "There are priorities above my financial successes. Let us tend to those before I tell you of my newest plans." He rises, pulling her gently with him. The two walk, arms around each other, to their bed.

Physically spent but intellectually stimulated, Margaret and Crean talk of latest land purchases in a Grant area called Westminster. "It's a disputed area, Margaret, but with the King's proclamation in favor of the Yorkers, the New Hampshire Grants will simply become invalid. It's a good investment, of that I'm sure." He strokes Margaret's tousled hair, kisses her flushed forehead and continues talking. "I've got 60,000 acres now; signed on the final 20,000 just four days ago. Now, don't be angry m'love, but I've contracted for a house to be built."

Margaret rises on her elbow and looks at this man whom she calls husband. "Angry? Crean, could I ever be angry with you?" She lays a finger on his smiling lips. "What will we do about Fanny's coming out? Is there opportunity for her in the wilderness?"

"Oh, Margaret, we'll keep this house. New York's season provides visibility. My enterprises rely on my presence here and in Boston. These contacts will be invaluable if are to survive these next years. Grants, though, require making use of the land in a profitable manner. Building and occupying a house fulfills this proviso. Besides, and this is uppermost in my schemes, the land will become Fanny's dowry and your inheritance. Someday, it's value will buy you the world, m'love." Crean bends over, blows out the candle flame, and rolls back into Margaret's arms. Soon he snores softly, while Margaret's thoughts race with plans for the new house. Earlier political fears have been superseded by the excitement of fresh adventure.

Chapter 3

Fanny peers out through the stained curtains in the stage-coach window. The trees rush by creating a smeared image of greens and brown. Her eyes wander to the coach's interior. Dust sits in every crease; the aged leather on the seats is worn and horsehair is poking through in little gnarls here and there. Onncie's chin has dropped to her bodice and short puffs of breath escape her lips, making periodic, ragged snorts. Mother Margaret's bonneted head rests against the coach wall, her hands relaxed atop her drawstring purse. Fanny wonders how they can sleep with all the bouncing and jolting. The thinly padded seats offer little comfort as the coach slams into yet another huge rut in the earthen highway leading north. The vehicle's creaks and groans create a cacophony hard to ignore and the crack of the driver's whip emphasizes the ragged, disjointed syncopation. The noise obliterates any signs that another lorry loaded with dry goods, furnishings, and supplies follows close behind. Mother Margaret has exercised her best skills at provisioning for the new house and remained adamant about goods and people arriving simultaneously. Besides, with all the political unrest these days, Margaret would provide no opportunity for petty thievery.

Fanny releases her tight grip on Maggy and places the doll in her lap. "Who'd think a girl ready to come out would be talking to a doll, eh, Maggy?" whispers Fanny, straightening the doll's skirt. "Here I am thirteen years old, off to the wilderness for months and I bring a doll!" Maggy stares up into Fanny's face, faded painted eyes unblinking. "You're not much on opinions, are you, Maggy girl. But I need y' just the same. What was my mother like?" Fanny clutches the doll back to her chest, the motion powerful enough to evoke the escape of a small, almost breathless gasp. The doll remains mute while Fanny's imagination searches again for a vision of her biological mother. There are no real images of Catherine and Mother Margaret's words are not overly descriptive;

more often than not, brief and only in response to Fanny's direct questioning. Pretty. Fair. Shapely. Quick at her lessons. Loving. That's the word Fanny holds onto time after time. *Loving.* "She would have loved me. She *did* love me." Fanny hugged the doll more tightly. "She must have loved you too, Maggy."

They would stay only a few months at the new house in Westminster, just long enough to get settled and to escape the oppressive summer heat that settled in on New York. Their return to the city in September was imperative. Fanny's portrait was to be painted in readiness for her formal debut. Margaret had decreed Fanny's ball would be the most elegant of the entire Season. Invitations were already in preparation. The silk for her gown has been selected and the seamstress instructed on design and construction. Fanny and Margaret had spent many hours discussing, planning, and fine tuning the upcoming event. Crean had laughed at their enthusiasm and industry. He was absent more often these past months. Business in Boston had been demanding and Crean traveled the post road between the two major cities four times in the last year. "This fancy affair of yours is costing a great deal of money. I need to work harder everyday just to pay the bills." He'd ruffled Fanny's hair as he'd spoken and given her a quick hug to let her know he was teasing. Still, Fanny remembers having felt a twinge of guilt.

"Well, Maggy," Fanny speaks again to her doll. "At least I'm free of tutors for the summer!" Fanny's attention is drawn again to the view outside as the coach perceptibly slows. A crude but sturdy log house appears suddenly amidst the trees. A small, curly haired child waves from the tidy dooryard. The coach window frames another house, then a barn. The team's gait adjusts to a slow trot and the coachman shouts some indeterminable words from his lofty perch. Margaret raises her head and adjusts her bonnet. Smiling at Fanny, she reaches over and pokes Onncie just hard enough to wake her. The maid, groggy from sleep stretches her stiff limbs and leans over to peer out the window.

"This it, Mistress?" Onncie asks.

In response, the stagecoach comes to a halt and Fanny moves quickly to open the door latch. "Papa! Papa Crean!" The

10

young woman leaps from the still vibrating vehicle, avoiding the step altogether. Father and daughter meet; Crean twirls Fanny around, her skirts flying, petticoats in full view of an admiring dispatcher.

Crean deposits his ward on the ground and moves to greet his wife. He raises her fingers to his lips, "m'love," he whispers and gently, sensuously moves his thumb across the back of her hand. Then, he turns to assist Onncie's descent.

Fanny eagerly pivots on her softly shod toe as she takes in the town around her. There's a new cooper since their last visit a year ago, but still no dry goods store. Oh, and there's Stephen Bradley's fine house on the square, just south of the county court house. Papa Crean and Mister Bradley often meet for business and political discussion. Papa says Bradley serves the best sherry in the Grants but keeps his finest furniture in his own quarters. Papa doesn't even mind that Mister Bradley flirts outrageously with Mother Margaret. Fanny turns full circle and finds Papa Crean giving directions to the lorry driver. "Take the first lane to the left, up the hill. Our drive is the first to the right. You'll see it. We'll be along momentarily in the shay." Crean touches his hat brim with his forefinger and the lorry driver coaxes the tired horses into a trot.

Fanny's first glimpse of the newly completed house leaves her slightly breathless. There is some small disappointment at its lack of grandeur but the setting is spectacular. As the shay draws to a halt at the end of the long, dirt drive, Margaret and Fanny step from the carriage without recognizing they are doing so. Both are enchanted, each for her own reason. Fanny takes in the lush trees, the gentle slope of the hillside into which the house is built. The carriage shed and barn are attached to the main building, opening onto a meadow filled with wild flowers in every conceivable color. As travel weary as Fanny is, the urge to run through the field is palpable and she consciously restrains herself. Fanny reaches out to take Mother Margaret's hand as if to anchor herself against her own desires. Here on these hills is the freedom Fanny could never have in New York.

Margaret gives Fanny's hand a quick squeeze and immediately begins talking excitedly. "The windows are set symmetrically—perfectly! They define the house. Come quickly, we must see the inside." Even as she speaks, Margaret is pulling her daughter up the two stone steps to the triple hinged door. Crean and Onncie stand back, watching. Just as the two women reach the front door, it opens majestically, as if by magic. Both stop instantly. A sturdy, young man, perhaps eighteen, steps from behind the door. He's dressed in simple broadcloth leggings with a matching vest over a white linen shirt.

"Madam," the man speaks through a barely visible smile and offers no bow. "Welcome to your new home."

Fanny and Margaret turn to see Crean laughing audibly. He takes leaping strides to join them, putting an arm around each. "I just couldn't tell you about Cooper. We wanted to surprise you and we've certainly succeeded." Crean ushers them into the front hall and begins introductions. "Margaret, m'love, this is Cooper our houseman, caretaker, stable master, and whatever else we might need in the way of services. Fanny, say good day like a proper young lady."

Fanny extends her hand, palm down, saying, "Good day, Cooper." She's both intrigued and displeased that Cooper's eyes stay fixed on her own. There is no deference in his manner and this unaccustomed demeanor in a servant sets her a spot off center.

Introductions complete Crean leads them on a tour of the house. Cooper moves out to help Onncie with the baggage stowed in the shay.

The house is simple compared to their city manor. There are four, square rooms on the first floor bisected by a wide hallway. Each room has its own fireplace and windows on two walls. The kitchen is an addition off the back end of the hallway connecting the main house to the barn and carriage house. The stairs are set to the right of the hallway with a beautifully polished banister leading upward. "Cooper says we'll be sorry in the winter that I didn't enclose this staircase." Crean comments as he leads the women to the second story. "Says northern winters suck all the heat out of your bones and y'need every bit of help y'can get to trap the heat where y'want it."

The upper floor is a simple repeat of the lower rooms without moving out over the kitchen. At the back end of the hall, a narrow set of enclosed, winding stairs goes both up and down. Up leads to the attic loft which Onncie will occupy; down ends just outside the door to the kitchen. Long ropes, hooped at intervals to the walls act as steadying guides.

"Which is to be my room?" asks Fanny as she skips up and down the hall, anxious to claim her very own space; equally as anxious to be done with all this and get outdoors to run through the meadow.

Cream and Margaret exchange some secret signal with their eyes and Margaret takes over the tour. "Fanny, we thought you'd like this room the best," entering the room situated on the front, northeast corner of the house.

Fanny almost knocks over Margaret in her excitement to enter her room. She dashes from one window to the other, looking out each frame. "Look, oh, look. There's the meadow," she exclaims as she presses her face to the north window. "And, the river," as she stares toward the east. "It's just perfect, too perfect," she bubbles as she hugs Mother Margaret enthusiastically. Returning to the front window, Fanny glances down toward the shay just in time to see Cooper quickly avert his eyes from her direction. A strange, delicious feeling surges through her body.

"We eat quite simply here in the grants, Mistress Margaret," Stephen Bradley raises his goblet in a toast as he speaks. "Here's to your presence, if only for a few months. You and Fanny will add a certain element of. . .of *joie de vivre* to our factious community."

Fanny giggles and Margaret almost imperceptibly raises her eyebrow in discipline. Fanny lowers her face, covering her mouth with her fingertips.

"You are *most* gracious both in your hospitality and your flattery," smiles Margaret. "I could hardly call this sumptuous meal 'simple'. Your cook is to be complimented."

Crean joins the toast and turns the conversation to his favorite topic. "This bickering will soon come to an end Stephen. The New York Grants are true and accepted. Wentworth and his partisans will retreat, mark my words. That band of hooligans led by the Allen boys will be driven north. We'll see no fighting here."

"You speak like a Yorker, my friend. But let me warn you, there is change coming and best you choose your sides carefully. There will be war, I predict, within three years; already there is movement to ready for this. You know that yourself. You've spoken of the Committee of Correspondence and their poll on the pulse of independence. Don't ignore the signs, Crean. You could find yourself squashed."

Crean, sipping his sherry, keeps his body neutrally relaxed. The fingers of his left hand rest easily on the tabletop. He's slumped slightly in the chair as he awaits Stephen Bradley's next words. New information is critical to Crean's role in the Crown colonies.

"There is basis for Wentworth's claims. His New Hampshire Grants are as valid as the Duke of York's. It is only a few million acres between Lake Champlain and the Connecticut River where they overlap. Many have bought grants from Wentworth in good faith and have moved out to tame this wilderness. Allen and his Green Mountain Boys want only to protect what they perceive as their rights."

Crean sits forward in his chair. "The power sits with York, Stephen. Don't forget that."

"But, for how long, Crean?" For how long? There is much Whig sentiment here in Westminster even though many have ceded to the Tories. If the Colonies ignite the flame of dissent and war breaks out who will come out on top? If the choice is between the Crown and their land, what decision do you think the settlers will make? I know where I stand and I suspect there are many like me. Again, let me warn you, consider carefully your own stance."

Crean decides to goad his friend into giving more information. "You've been listening to that crude oaf, Allen. He acts only to protect his own interests. He'll hang for his actions with that bounty on his head."

"Crude and loud he may be, but his mind is honed and his actions are tempered by brother Ira who speaks more quietly. Between those Allens and their cousin, Remember Baker, there's knowledge and leadership. Ethan is a good leader for all his faults. And, whichever side you straddle, Ethan Allen is to be tolerated. He serves a purpose and hear that true, Crean."

"Do you think he'll lead this territory against the Crown?" Crean leans back again in his chair and lifts his goblet to his lips waiting for his host to continue.

"You act like a spy for the king, my friend." Bradley smiles, taking measure of his neighbor. "The Allens are more interested in settling the wilderness and making a fortune in the process than fighting the king."

Fanny folds and refolds her napkin as the men spar at their politics. Her mind wanders to Cooper. He had joined her in the meadow this very afternoon. She'd been lying on her back in the midst of the multihued wildflowers, reading Plato—having promised her tutor to keep at her Latin while she was in the Grants. Cooper's approach had been slow and silent and Fanny had been truly startled when he spoke.

"You're a reader," as much a question as a statement. "May I sit beside you?"

Fanny had felt the flush rising in her neck and she risen quickly to a sitting position. She had closed her book and placed her hand over the title on the cover. Her voice had a peculiar tremor when she spoke. "Please, do sit," she'd said. They'd spent the next few minutes trying to find things to say. Fanny had settled on talking about the flowers around them. She'd asked what names the locals had given them and Cooper's replies had been knowledgeable. He'd pointed out the blue Cohush, the green Pettymorrel, and Fanny's favorite, deep purple Angelica. Fanny had been both relieved and sorry when the young man had risen to return to his duties.

"Gentlemen," Fanny's attention returns to the table as her mother speaks. "You will excuse my interruption, but the hour calls us to return home. Mister Bradley, you have been most gracious, as always." Margaret rises and extends her hand to Fanny. "Crean, will you escort our lovely daughter?" She has wisely and effectively ended the evening.

"Ah, we have gone on, haven't we?" laughs Stephen Bradley as he offers his arm to Margaret. "Despite it all, you do know you are welcome here at any time. It is an invitation valid forever, Mistress Margaret. I am, indeed, a man of my word."

Chapter 4

Fanny sits among the wildflowers, her precious paint pots beside her. August is coming to a close and there are not many days left to her stay here on the hillside, overlooking the river. She studies the lavender stalk in front of her, dabs her brush daintily into three of the paint colors and touches the brush to paper resting on a plank in her lap. The result is remarkable like the live flower before her. Changing brushes, she adds a stem, then some highlights to the petals. Fanny sits back, surveying her work, looking first at the picture and then at the plant. Satisfied, she takes her finest brush and strokes a few notes at the bottom of the sheet, ending with the date, August 20, 1774.

Fanny's concentration is such that she fails to hear the approaching footsteps and is startled almost upsetting her pots, as Cooper drops down into the high grass beside her.

"Let me see," says the young man, reaching to take the paper from her lap. He studies the painting as carefully as she had done moments before. "You are much improved, Mistress Fanny. I would know this is a delphinium, were I to see it in the dark of winter."

Fanny's embarrassment mingles with pleasure as she busies herself covering her pots and cleaning her brushes. Cooper is so close he surely feels the heat coming off her skin, a condition not solely attributable to the August sun. In an attempt to recover her composure, Fanny speaks, eyes focused on her work. "In the city, there are no flowers growing freely. There's just mud mostly, and lots of dust in the dry months. Oh, there are kitchen gardens with herbs and some flowers, but nothing wild and free."

"Rather like the people, eh?" comments Cooper. "Restrained and with a purpose set by another."

Fanny turns to look at her companion's face. "Are you wild and free, Cooper?" asks Fanny, surprised at her own audacity.

Cooper drops back into the grass, raising his arms in order for his hands to form a pillow beneath his head. He's quiet a moment before responding. "Much like a young fox, I suppose. I don't like being cornered." Cooper stops speaking and rolls to his side. His gaze fixes intently on Fanny's cerulescent eyes as he continues. "I am free to move about as I wish. I can choose the forest or the meadow in any season. But, I'm smart enough to know there are certain hen coops into which I cannot prey."

The barely disguised innuendo makes Fanny bolder still. "Cannot the jingling of Papa Crean's coins distract you from your wildness?"

"Only to a point," smiles Cooper. "There is a moment when even a fox must choose between the risks of catching the hen and a hungry night of running freely through the trees."

"Are you talking about me or about politics?" Fanny's attention focuses steadily on the young man's lucent eyes.

"Both, I suspect," laughs Cooper. "You let no one else get out in front, do you, m'lass." He reaches out and takes Fanny's hand. "You must know by now, that I'm a Whig and have little respect for the Tory."

Fanny quickly pulls back her hand; haughtiness envelops her body. Cooper interrupts her movement to speak. "Please, understand I do have respect for Master Brush. He is an honest and generous man or I wouldn't have come into his employ. But our politics differ and on that I cannot waiver. We must move out from under the King's heavy, erratic thumb. He cares little for what our life is like here on this side of the ocean. He cares only about the monies he can gain from our hard work." Cooper rises to his knees as he continues. "Right now even as we talk among these peaceful meadow flowers, they are polling the people. Asking who is for separation and who is against."

"Who is asking?" Fanny's face is intent and a slight fear creeps into her eyes.

"That group in your city—a funny titled lot. They call themselves the Committee of Correspondence, I think. Listen to me, Fanny." Cooper again takes hold of Fanny's hands and continues. "Tories aren't likely to rejoice at the vote. They chance to lose too much. I fear there will be blood shed before all is done."

"You are the one who should be careful, talking like that. The King's troops will suppress any acts of separation from the Crown. Remember, I hear such conversations all the time and we will not take kindly to the likes of you." Fanny yanks her hands free and rises to her feet. Cooper stands beside her.

"As you will, Fanny." The passion falls from Cooper's voice and he speaks neutrally. "Beggin' your pardon, Mistress Fanny. I shouldn't have been so bold. Perhaps we shall have a different perspective on this conversation a year from now. Here, let me help you carry your pots to the house." Cooper bends to pick up the paints and brushes, starts toward the house leaving his back to Fanny's stare.

Fanny hesitates. Her chest tightens and an unexplained tear drops from her lashes. She grabs her painting and follows Cooper's path through the meadow grass.

Chapter 5

Onncie removes the pale pink silk dress from its perch on the bedpost. "Step carefully, Mistress Fanny. Don't catch the hem." Margaret holds firmly to Fanny's arm as the young woman steps daintily in to the gown. Onncie's fingers deftly begin working the tiny buttons through the delicate loops, starting at the bottom, several inches below the waistline, and ending at the neckline. Margaret steps back and enjoys the vision her daughter.

"Magnificent! Perhaps I've a mother's pride, but you are truly the most beautiful young woman in all of New York. In the Grant, not just the city."

Fanny twirls on her stockinged tiptoes, swishing her skirt from side to side. "I'm even more grown up than my portrait," she giggles.

Onncie reaches out to straighten the ruffles on Fanny's sleeves. "Mmmm. This bow seems a little loose," as she fusses with the ornament on the decidedly low neckline at Fanny's nubile breasts. Onncie takes a threaded needle from her bodice and quickly takes a stitch here and a tiny tuck there. She tugs on the flowered bow, then steps back to admire her handiwork.

Fanny turns toward the door as she hears a knock. "Papa? Is that you?"

Crean walks into the room, his hands behind his back. "A vision of loveliness!" He stoops to place a gentle kiss on his ward's forehead. He steps backward for another look. "Margaret and I have a little present for you, Fanny dear." Crean hands her a cloth covered, small box.

Fanny flips open the tiny metal clasp with her fingernail and lifts the lid. "Oh!" The young woman looks first at Crean and then at her mother. Her delicate hand lifts a glimmering necklace from the box. "Oh!" Fanny holds the blue sapphire necklace up to the light. "Where did you get this? It's too extravagant to have come from the colonies."

Crean puts an arm around his wife, pulling her close. "I knew she'd like it, Megee, dearest." Margaret blushes at his private endearment for her.

"Papa got it all the way from London. Here, let me fasten it for you." The smaller stones encircle Fanny's neck, the larger stone fastened at the center rests lightly on her chest. The delicate gold filigree glitters equally with the jewels.

Sounds of carriages arriving filter through the small window. "It's time, my dearest Fanny. You are about to become a woman of society," grins Crean.

The three adults leave the room assuring Fanny that Onncie would return to prepare her for the grand entrance down the stairway.

Fanny paces the room. Her cheeks bloom with the blush of excitement. She stops beside her bed and reaches for her beloved doll. "Maggy, can you believe it. I'm old enough to be presented. Oh, I wish you could go with me but wouldn't that look silly!" Fanny pulls the doll to her chest. "You will always go with me, Maggy. I will never, ever be too old to need you." Fanny places the doll against her lace bed pillows and goes to the door in response to Onncie's whispered call.

"It's time, Mistress Fanny. It's time." Onncie's eyes fill with tears as she executes last minute adjustments to Fanny's gown and hair.

At Crean's signal, the chamber quartet plays a quick triumphant. The room grows silent and all eyes center on the staircase. The musicians begin an energetic rondo and Fanny takes her first step down the polished stairs. Margaret, standing at the bottom, gives a slight lift to her lips, a silent reminder to smile. Fanny raises her chin imperceptibly, smiles coquettishly, and continues descent to the waiting guests.

Crean greets his ward as she reaches the last step and parades her through the admiring crowd. He stops here and there to make formal introductions and when they reach the far side of the large room, the musicians begin an elegant waltz. Crean speaks loudly enough to be heard by the guests, "Mistress Frances Montresor Brush, may I be so honored to have this, your first dance?"

Fanny curtsies, dropping her right knee almost to the floor, her skirt murmuring a lush whisper as it drapes to the bend. Smiling broadly, she replies, "Indeed, Master Brush, it would be *my* honor." The two move through the crowd, heads high, perfectly in time with the music, circling round and round. At last the music stops. Crean holds his daughter's hand to his lips then turns to his guests. "It is now my added honor to present Mistress Fanny to Captain John Buchanan for her second dance."

Fanny looks at her father unable to conceal her surprise. Margaret steps from the surrounding guests, curtsies to her daughter then turns to Crean. The two begin to dance and there is nothing left for Fanny to do but curtsy and move in the Captain's arms.

Chapter 6

"Crean, I do think it much safer if I take Fanny to Westminster." Margaret sits by the fire, quilting at her round frame stand. "The street ruffians get worse each day. I'm afraid to take Fanny out in the carriage. You'll be occupied by Assembly and won't even miss us."

Crean looks up from the papers on his desk recognizing a hint when he hears one. "Dearest Megee, you know I miss you each moment we're apart. How could I not?" He's satisfied with the faint smile that tickles Margaret's lips and returns to his papers.

Crean ponders Margaret's increasing anxieties over the political turmoil rumbling through the streets and alleyways of New York. He knows his trips to Boston leave her pacing the floors in his absence. Onncie has told him of Margaret's sleepless nights. His own fears are growing. The Whigs in Boston, Lexington and Concord hold open meetings that grow larger each session. He no longer carries more than personal currency on his trips but sends funds by coach packed innocuously in crates marked *dry goods* or *household*. Perhaps Margaret is right; it would be best to send the two of them north for the rest of the Season. Besides, having the women in residence would discourage any possible Whig move to claim his holdings.

Rising from his desk, Crean moves to stand beside his wife. He places his hands lovingly on her shawled shoulders, unconsciously massaging her back with his powerful thumbs. After a moment he speaks, "You're right—as always, Megee. I think it would be better to have you in the north country. I'll post a note to Stephen Bradley and have him tell Cooper to make the house ready for your arrival."

"Fanny will be devastated to miss the rest of the Season. The Buchanan gala is just a fortnight away. We can leave after that. That gives me time to prepare the household and will quiet the likelihood of Fanny's uproar."

"A ruckus to be avoided for certain," laughs Crean.

Crean pulls a chair up beside Margaret, placing his back to the lusty flames in grate. "I sense our Fanny is not overly fond of Master John Buchanan. What would you think, Megee?"

"She seldom mentions him after an evening out and when she does it is not kindly. She dislikes his wanting to occupy her entire evening and giggles about her ruses to embarrass him. She thinks him arrogant and ill mannered; a trait I've not noticed in the young man."

"Well, he can be something of a braggart," smiles Crean in mild defense of his ward's observations. "Walter has approached me about young John formally courting our Fanny."

Margaret tucks her needle into the quilting, and pushes aside the frame. "These are unsettled times, Crean, and Fanny is still young. Can we not wait another year before we consider such an idea? Though it's a good match, I dare say. The Buchanan holdings would provide well for our girl."

Margaret and Crean sip sweet mead as they watch their daughter dancing a grand waltz. The Buchanans claim the slot for the midseason ball and this year they've outdone themselves with elegance. Fanny is flirting outrageously with young Hosiah Johnston as they twirl around the floor. Finally, the music stops and Fanny delicately mops her forehead with a lace handkerchief she's removed from her low-cut bodice. Hosiah extends his arm, letting Fanny place her hand just above his cuff buttons, and he guides her over to her parents. He bows deeply to Margaret and Crean and then to Fanny.

"A lovely dance, Mistress Brush. I'm only sorry you have no more room on your card."

Fanny drops a quick curtsy, smiles at her admirer, and then lets her eyes roam the room. Across the crowded room, John Buchanan catches her eye and nods. Fanny gives only the slightest tilt of her head in return, but it's enough to bring the besmitten young man scurrying across the floor.

"Oh, posh! He's coming." Squeaks Fanny as she turns her back to the crowd and looks pleadingly at her mother. "I think I'll swoon," she giggles and pulls her handkerchief from its hiding place and presses it to her brow.

"You will not, young lady!" Crean pulls Fanny's arm down and turns her around all in one motion. As the same instant both he and Margaret are distracted by the approach of a tall, handsome gentleman dressed in the finest satin and linens. The exchanged looks between husband and wife hold restrained panic. Crean quickly steps forward between Fanny and the approaching man.

Fanny is disconcerted by the change in Crean's demeanor and turns expectantly toward her mother.

"Master Brush," says the gentleman as he bows.

"Sir," Crean replies tersely.

"Your ward is attracting much attention, this evening. I've come to beg a momentary claim to her charms." He turns to Fanny, smiling, "May I have the honor of this next dance, mademoiselle?"

"Her card is quite full for the evening, but your attention is appreciated," says Crean in obvious dismissal.

Not to be easily thwarted, the gentleman speaks directly to Crean, "I will entice her next escort with Mistress Margaret's hand. Surely you will admit your wife is the second most lovely woman present this evening. No young man would dare to reject such a privilege of dancing with either of the Brush ladies." Turning to Fanny, he adds, "may I have the honor?" He clicks his heels smartly together and offers his arm to the confused young woman.

Fanny glances at Crean, raises her eyebrow offering the silent questions, "who *is* he?" By the time Crean recovers his composure, Fanny is stepping lightly to the music, led around the circling dancers by the brash interloper. Margaret whispers, "It was bound to happen, Crean. Society is too small to prevent it.

"Sir, you certainly know my name," laughs Fanny as she tilts her head back to look into her partner's eyes. "It is only fair, I know yours. You've not been to any of the other balls."

"No, you're right. I've been absent these past months, away on duty with the King's army."

"And your name? You've not told me your name," persists Fanny.

"Colonel John Montresor, at your service, Mistress Fanny."

Fanny's gasp draws the attention of those dancing close to them. Her legs sag and the Captain supports her as she swoons. Margaret rushes to her daughter's side, Crean right behind her. The three help Fanny across the floor, out the door; where they seek asylum in the parlor. The whispers follow them until Crean closes the paneled door.

Margaret uses her handkerchief as a fan inches above Fanny's face. Crean pours brandy from a crystal carafe on the carved mahogany sideboard and lifts the goblet to Fanny's pale, trembling lips.

"Damn you, Montresor! Could you not have done this some other way?" hisses Crean, his eyes afire with anger.

"I mean no harm. Nor do I seek any claim. But I do have a right to introduce myself to my own daughter." Montresor slips into a high backed, velvet covered chair and drops his hands limply between his knees.

"You could have given us warning, sir." Margaret indignantly steps in front of the seated man. "We could have prepared her. You are as cruel to your daughter as to her mother!"

Fanny hears these words as if in a dream. She struggles to recall what brought her to this couch. "Why can't I focus?" Slowly, she recognizes the voice of that man, her. . .her father. Her eyelids weigh a stone; she can't force them open. The room blurs; she cannot take the dizziness. She must. Hesitantly she pulls herself upright, unnoticed by the three across the room.

"Mother Margaret," pleads Fanny.

The three whirl around to face the young woman on the couch. Margaret races to her daughter and kneels before her. "Fanny, Fanny, I am so sorry."

John Montresor stands and walks towards his daughter, stopping a few inches from the couch. He turns and paces the rug, back and forth, back and forth. No one speaks. The captain pulls a side chair up before the sofa.

26

"Frances. . .Fanny, I too apologize. It was callous of me to present myself in such a public manner. Truthfully, I was frightened of a private meeting." The captain wrings his hands, unable to continue speaking. All three Brushes remain silent, offering the agonizing man no mercy.

"I needed to tell you, Frances," stutters Montresor, "t-to t-tell you that I didn't mean to neglect your mother—or you. I didn't know about you until I returned from Nova Scotia. . .and Catherine, your mother was already dead and you were given to— t-to y-your parents.

Crean reaches down and takes Margaret's hand, protecting her from what might be next. "You have NO rights, Montresor, no rights to Fanny."

"I claim none, sir. Hear me out," pleads the colonel. Turning to Fanny, he continues. "You have a family, a family who has taken good care of you. This is obvious. I, too, have a family; a daughter whom I name Frances Margaret, a child but seven years old. I named her after you, Frances. It is the only link I claim to you."

Fanny, eyes focused on the colonel's face, pushes herself to her feet. Margaret reaches out to steady her. Angry thoughts rush through Fanny's mind. Another thought stops her short from vocalizing her rage. "He knows my mother. He can tell me about my mother." Aloud, she stammers, "What was she like? My mother."

All three look at Fanny, surprised at her question. Montresor reaches out to take his daughter's arm and leads her to the settee. Both sit.

"Tell me, please, about my mother. Was she beautiful?"

"Very beautiful. Your eyes remind me of Catherine; they do." Montresor strokes his daughter's cheek. "Your mother was full of laughter—and, kindness. Yet, she was strong, strong enough to come away with me regardless of the consequences. Sadly, she paid dearly for such bravery." He pauses to wipe a tear from Fanny's face. "I am so very sorry for what happened. I had no idea. Truly, I was devastated to learn of her death.

"Tell me more. Please."

"She had a doll she loved. She brought that doll to the city when we ran off together. She talked to that doll like it was human. Shared all her secrets with it."

"I have that doll now—the only thing I have of my mother's. I, too, talk with her."

Montresor waits a moment before continuing. "Catherine would have been a fine mother, Fanny. She was so full of love."

Fanny reaches for Margaret's hand. "It must be a family trait. Mother Margaret overflows with love. I want to go home now. Please."

Crean bows to the Colonel. "You've quite unsettled us, sir." Turning to Margaret, he offers his arm. "We shall go now, Margaret. Fanny."

Montresor watches after them. He walks to the window and stares into the night. His shoulders shake and a sob escapes his throat.

† † †

Even Cooper's presence hasn't been enough to raise Fanny's spirits during the long, dark winter months. Margaret and Onncie had cajoled, scolded, teased, and thought up countless games in attempts to rouse Fanny from her gloom. Stephen Bradley's intimate dinner parties brought out the innate politeness and charm of Fanny, but the spark was absent. The small social events in Westminster exhausted her, and she remained listlessly in her room for days after each attempt at sociability.

Early in March, Onncie and Cooper return from a day's trip to Brattleboro with fresh supplies. The 15-mile journey was necessary because no one had yet opened a general store north of that village. Their shopping had also procured much gossip. Onncie is anxious to reach home and share the news with Mistress Margaret. Cooper insists on stopping first at the courthouse.

"It's here, Mistress Onncie." Cooper begins to read from the posted notice, "King George, III's Cumberland County Court convenes on March 14th, Judge Colonel Chandler presiding. Judicial hearings consist of a murder trial and such other business as shall come before the King's tribunal."

"Hurry, you scamp," scolds the anxious Onncie. "Mistress will want to know of the news."

While Cooper unloaded the shay, Onncie hurries into the parlor ready to burst with gossip.

Margaret and Fanny sit by the fire. Margaret's needle diligently moves in and out of her embroidery; Fanny's eyes are transfixed on the flames. The older woman looks up as Onncie bursts open the closed door.

"What is it? You look a-fright!" Margaret motions her maid to join them by the fire. "Or is it gossip?" laughs Margaret putting aside her handwork. Fanny focuses blankly through the interloper into furies.

Onncie, leaning forward in her chair, chatters animatedly. One story runs into the next and Onncie pauses only to answer some question Margaret interjects. Fanny hears but a jumble of words, unable or un-wanting to grasp any theme. A fury burns within her that makes the flames in the grate seem like mere sparks; a fury that obliterates all else. Fanny hugs her doll tightly to her chest, in a motion all too familiar these past months.

A knock at the parlor door gains the attention of all three women. Onncie takes a deep breath to refurbish momentum to her narrative but Margaret raises her hand to stave off any continuance. "Enter, Cooper."

Cooper strides across the room to stand in front of Margaret. He does not wait for an invitation to speak. "Mistress, I would ask for two days away. It is most important for you and for me that I go."

"For me? And you?" Margaret's eyebrows jump into arched crescents.

A flittering of interest lights Fanny's eyes. She drops Maggy gently into her lap. This meager change in Fanny's demeanor does not go unnoticed by her mother.

"Mistress, I must go to Chester before Court is to convene."

"You *must* go?"

"Indeed! It is imperative!" Cooper continues looking into Margaret's questioning eyes.

"I'll need more information than that before I can grant such permission," counters Margaret, reaching for her handwork as if to begin dismissal.

"Mother, hear him out." Fanny keeps her attention on Cooper.

Cooper seizes the opportunity that surprise has given him. "Mistress, the Whigs are gathering at Chester—at Colonel Chandler's place—to convince him not to hold the King's Court. Such a session would be in direct defiance of the Articles of Association agreed upon in our October convention."

"Why, indeed, should I be interested in such business?" Margaret pushes her needle idly into her embroidery.

"Ma'am, the Judge does not heed the people's wishes. The High Sheriff has beaten and jailed those who demand their rights; rights given them by the Continental Congress and by our own vote here in Cumberland County. Those in other colonies are proceeding under the new Articles but New York continues to ignore the decisions."

"And, why should we relinquish *our* rights as Yorkers?" Margaret asks though she knows full well the impact of this question. Not waiting for an answer, Margaret continues, keeping her needle going in and out of the fabric. "You say this will affect me. I think not. Crean, as a barrister, assures me the Judge's decision to hold Court is true and binding for the King."

"Mistress, you are fully aware that many of us here in the north country have signed for separation from the King. Here, there are far more Whigs than Tories." Seeing Margaret's eyes jump to his face, he continues, "Meaning no disrespect, but if there is trouble, you may be in danger. I have pledged my honor to Master Brush that I will care for your safety. I cannot do so unless I know what is happening. I must go at once."

Margaret focuses her attention seemingly on her handwork. She remains quiet, pondering the information. It is Fanny who breaks the unsettled silence.

"Mother, it is this of which Master Bradley speaks so passionately. Isn't it best we know the situation? Then, if there is violence, Cooper can help us."

30

"I brought you here to avoid such insults but it seems we cannot escape this abomination even here in the northern Grants. Very well, Cooper, you may go at once."

Cooper bows slightly and turns to leave the room. Margaret's words reach him from the rear.

"You will return by evening's meal two days hence." It was an order, not even slightly a question.

Fanny rises to follow Cooper. Onncie starts to rebuke the young woman, but Margaret raises her hand and gives an almost imperceptible shake of her head. Margaret speaks after Fanny has closed the parlor door behind herself. "Let her be, Onncie, it's the first sign of life we've seen in her in months. A mere distraction, I'm sure, but if it provides even a little excitement for Fanny, we should be grateful."

"I think perhaps there is something to fear," remarks Onncie, rising to poke at the waning fire.

"Balder rot, you ninny," exclaims Margaret. "If there's trouble the High Sheriff will protect us. Perhaps we should invite Judge Colonel Chandler to sup with us while he's in town. He and Crean have done business together." A slight tremor in her sewing hand is the only sign of the concerns rising in Margaret's heart.

Cooper stood at the edge of the crowd in front of Colonel Chandler's Chester house. The paunchy judge had come out to his front steps in response to the crowd's verbal summons. His stance borders on arrogance, his gaze scanning the throng defies any possible insolence. The two men who appeared to be Whig leaders had been trying to dissuade Colonel Chandler from holding the King's court.

"In the present state of affairs, perhaps it would be better not to hold court," states the judge attempting to quiet the crowd. "But there is a murder case which is necessary to try. After that," concedes the judge, "if it is not agreeable with the people, no other cases will be held."

"Aye. Fair enough, but the Sheriff has sworn to attend with his armed posse," shouts one frontiersman from the midst of the gathered. "We want no bloodshed."

"Nor do I," returns the judge over the grumblings in the crowd. "There will be no arms brought against you. My solemn promise. Now be gone with you. Thanking you for your civility." The judge turns, enters his house and slowly closes the door. The minute it shuts, he slides the heavy bolt.

Cooper mingles with the crowd moving slowly toward the tavern. "Do ya believe him, man?" asks a bearded man to his right.

"He's misspoken before, he has," replies Cooper. "But he's lots of witnesses to his promise this time round."

The Tavern keeper, a staunch Whig, passes around containers of rum. "We'll be there to see he upholds that promise," the keep speaks to each small groups as he fills their mugs. "We'll see the bastard keeps his bloody word!"

"Enough, Willem. We don't want to start up any violence either. You keep to that blitherin', you'll get us all roused up."

"Still, I say, we'll go wi' a stout stick, each of us." Willem is not to be silenced.

Cooper downs his rum and takes leave of his comrades. It is a long, dark ride back to Westminster.

The morning, two days before court is to convene, Cooper hurries into the main house from the barn. "Mistress Margaret. Trouble's coming; coming soon. Best you get ready to leave."

"Leave? I should say not! This is my house." Margaret stamps her foot to emphasize the edict. "What's happening?" she adds almost as an afterthought.

"The judge fails to keep his word. He's sending the High Sheriff to take control of the Courthouse. There's upwards of a hundred of our men coming from the countryside to prevent the takeover."

Margaret's face pales and she reels with dizziness. Cooper reaches out to steady his mistress. "Damned Whigs!" breathes Margaret.

Cooper lets go of his mistress' arm and steps back. "Mistress, I am surely loyal to the Articles and I am a Whig. Do not damn me or you'll find yourself alone, and unprotected. You must do as I say if I am to uphold my promises to Master Brush."

"You're loyalty is much appreciated. I, too, must stand my ground." Margaret's swoon has evaporated and her indignance is intact. "I make the decisions in this house."

Later that night, Cooper sneaks down through the snow-crested meadow to have a better view of the Courthouse. He stops as he sees a shadow dart between trees. "Who goes?" he whispers.

Suddenly, his knees buckle as he's hit from behind. He's shoved forward, his face pushed into the frozen snow. A large, rough hand grabs his hair and yanks his face upward, twisting his neck 'til surely it would snap.

"Bloody! It's Cooper." Willem drops is hold and runs his fists across his beard. "Sorry, bloke. But your calling out like that 'most ruined us. We've got to get inside 'fore sun up. You join'n us?"

Cooper shakes his head gasping at the pain in his neck. "I'm for the cause, but I've pledged a duty to protect those Brush women."

"Too damned honorable, y'are. Be off with y'now." Willem touches his finger to his tricorn, turns and gives a night bird whistle. Shadows shuffle quietly toward the King's Highway and the Courthouse.

Cooper lingers long enough to see the last dark figure slip in the court's front door. He walks slowly up the meadow, enters the carriage house, and falls into his straw mattress. His eyes close but he cannot sleep.

When first light makes the world take on a faint, pinkish outline, Cooper rises. He stops in the kitchen, makes a cup of tea and takes one of yesterday's scones. Onncie walks in tidily tying her bleached and heavily starched house-bonnet strings.

"You're lookin' bleary eyed there, Master Cooper. Out courtin' last night were ya?"

"Onncie, you must listen to me. Pack a precious few things and load the shay. There's real trouble brewing and you all must be ready to leave."

"Y'know what Mistress said. "'We're stayin'.'" But there was a fearful look in Onncie's eyes as she spoke.

"Won't do no harm to load the shay. Mistress need not know." Cooper opens the outer door, rounds the corner of the house, and sprints down the hillside. As he nears the King's Highway, he can see the Sheriff's posse assembling by the tavern. He walks boldly through the uniformed group and into John Norton's tavern. A few posse regulars are finishing a rum. Cooper walks to the tavern keep busy behind the bar and orders a pint. Staring idly at the wall just above and to the right of the keep's shoulder, Cooper whispers barely moving his lips. "They're in, all of 'em." He raises the mug to his lips but doesn't swallow.

The keep looks down, just barely nodding that he under-stands. He walks towards the other men and asks, "One more round 'fore y'go?"

The High Sheriff shouts the posse to attention and the men in the tavern dash outside to get in formation.

"March!" The Sheriff gives the order and leads the group down the ice-packed, dirt road toward the courthouse. The Court's beribboned and unctuous officer follows behind. The judge is nowhere in sight.

The Sheriff halts near the courthouse door and signals the officer to come forward. Facing the troops, the officer nervously unrolls the official paper and begins with a faltering voice which grows steadier as he speaks.

"It is the King's proclamation that all persons unlawfully assembled shall disperse. Hear ye the order." Turning toward the courthouse, the emboldened officer shouts, "And, ye damned scoundrels, y'have fifteen minutes to get out or we'll blow a lane through ya!"

Silence. Only the sound of the posse cocking its muskets can be heard. Two minutes pass, then five more. Muffled shuffling sounds come from just inside the entryway.

Willem speaks, his mouth against the inside of the stout door. "We cannot disperse. We will admit the Sheriff and the others if they lay down their arms."

The officer looks toward the Sheriff who remains silent. Another three minutes pass before Willem speaks again. "Have you come for war? We ourselves have come in peace and we are willing to parley with ya."

The Court's officer, growing increasingly impatient, pulls his pistol from his belt and swears, "Only by this weapon shall we parley with such damned rascals."

With perfect timing, Judges Chandler steps from behind the north wall and mounts the threshold of the Courthouse. "This will not do. Sheriff, take your men to the tavern for some refreshment. I will speak with the dissidents."

The disappointed posse release their arms and grumbling, move back down the highway toward the tavern. The judge knocks on the Courthouse door. "Gentlemen. It is only me now. Open the door so we can talk."

Willem opens the heavy door, and allows the judge to enter. "You cheat us again, Judge."

"The posse assembled without my permission. I forbade any arms to enter the town during this Court session." The judge looks around the room as he speaks. "Stay the night quietly here. No one will harm you. Tomorrow, the posse will enter without arms and I will hear what you to say." Chandler's eyes move through the crowd, holding each stare. "Gentlemen, until tomorrow morning." The judge turns his back on the men and leaves as he had come. Willem stares through the small window and watches Chandler stride up the street to the tavern.

At nightfall, the Whigs feeling safe, post a single sentry by the doorway. They talk among themselves of this year's crops, of plans for expanding their small farms, of politics in general. Some doze on courtroom benches. Still others sit apart, brooding about what they feel certain is impending doom. The hours pass. Suddenly, the sentry shouts, "The Sheriff and his men are coming. They're armed!"

The Sheriff leads men close to the Courthouse. He raises his right arm and yells, "Fire!" Three men feebly obey. The shots pound the wooden door. Inside, the men scramble to grab their only weapons, firewood clubs.

Angry that his men have not completed his order, the Sheriff shouts again. "Fire, damn you, fire!" The rum-laden men fire in all directions, some shots actually hit the windows.

"Storm the door!" commands the Sheriff. Quickly the men obey, pounding their musket butts on the wooden door. Someone brings a ramrod and the door shatters, opening a gaping hole. More shots and two Whigs are dead.

The first to fall is young William French, a local lad. Right beside him, arm twisted across his comrade's chest, lies Daniel Houghton. Several more patriots shudder and gasp with wounds inflicted by bullet, bayonet or rifle butt.

The Sheriff's men grab prisoners, any they can get their hands on, and drag them off to jail. Clubs swing; the Whigs charge, many making their way through the door or squeezing through windows into the enveloping night.

Cooper, when he saw the first shots fired, ran up the hill to the house. Bursting through the door, he yells, "Mistress, it is time to go." The women, wakened by the village noise, had finally taken heed of Cooper's warning and were dressed and ready to go.

"Mistress, can you handle the shay? I should stay and guard the house. The Whigs will not stand for this outrage and there is more to come after tonight."

Margaret nods and turns to the two other women. "Cover yourself with the fur. Keep your heads down. 'T will be a wild ride." Small droplets of sweat accumulate on Margaret's brow and she grabs the whip from Cooper's outstretched hand.

"One moment, Mama," pleads Fanny. She jumps from the laden shay and leans over to Cooper who's holding fast to the terrified horses. "'Til we meet again," whispers Fanny and presses her lips to Cooper's cheek. Before he can react, Fanny is back in shay.

"Blood has been shed. It has begun." Cooper murmurs to himself as he walks slowly toward the carriage house, fingers resting unconsciously on his blest cheek.

Margaret frantically cracks the whip across the backs of the horses and the carriage speeds through the darkness. "Where am I going?" Fear explodes in Margaret. "I *must* think this through." Sweat drenches her clothing. "Closest safety is Brattleboro. Can I make it that far?" she wonders as she gasps for air.

Chapter 7

"**No!**" Fanny slams the looking glass across the room. "I will not!"

Margaret bends over to pick up the shattered mirror, taking the moment to calm herself before she speaks. "This is for your own protection. The Buchanans can take care of you."

"You can take care of me," retorts Fanny stomping to the window. "You and Papa have always taken good care of me." Fanny turns toward her mother, tears welling between her lids.

Margaret moves toward her daughter, folding her into an embrace. She strokes the young woman's rigid back, trying to soothe her. "Crean is uncertain, dearest, what his future might be. Ever since the skirmishes in Lexington and Concord, Papa has been unable to get to Boston. Come. Sit on the bed."

Tears dry on Fanny's face, creating little crusty streaks on her fair skin. Margaret, taking hold of Fanny's hand, continues her persuasion. "Fanny, surely you know that at 15 you're marriageable, that you're due to leave us and run your own house." Margaret hopes perhaps Fanny will respond to logic.

"But not to him! Not to that hideous bumbling John Buchanan." Fanny's tears start anew and she jerks away from her mother to pace the floor. "He smells." Fanny shouts at her mother. "His teeth are rotten. Why him?"

Fanny attempts some of her own logic. Standing in front of her mother, the young woman softens her voice and adopts a conciliatory tone. "Mama, if I'm as beautiful and desirable as you say, should I not have my choice of many young suitors? There's Hosiah Johnston, and George Thorpe. They've asked permission to court me."

Margaret smiles at her daughter's tactics. "They cannot care for you well enough, dearest. They have not the Buchanan resources. You are accustomed to the finest. Could you really be happy in a small house with only one servant? Think honestly, Fanny."

Fanny silently concedes the point, but quickly shifts to another approach. "Mama," Fanny takes a deep breath before continuing, "I could go to England. . .or to Ireland. I'd be safe there." Fanny's mind races with plans. "You'd come. We'd be together and Papa could come when his business is done here in the colonies. When England has suppressed these rebels, we'll return to our house in the north country. There'll be plenty of time for me to get a husband." Fanny drops to the rumpled bed next to her mother, giving her a quick hug before continuing. "See, Mama. Not only is it a good plan, it's an adventure."

Margaret sighs. "Dearest, it is, indeed, a plan, but one that will not work. First, passage to England is impossible now. Secondly, Papa has signed the nuptial agreement with Walter Buchanan. You must accept this, Fanny. You will see, years from now, that it was a wise and kind decision that Papa has made."

Fanny throws herself back into the comforters, stuffing her face into the pillows. "No. No," she screams into the feathers. "I hate him. I will always hate him!"

Margaret departs defeated, hoping that Fanny's invectives were directed at young Buchanan and not at Crean. She closes the door gently behind her and goes in search of Crean.

✝   ✝   ✝

It's begun, Crean, and we must make decisions quickly." Walter Buchanan drains his goblet of the last drop of rum. He moves his cuff to his mouth and wipes away minute residue of the now precious liquor. "It'll be awhile before we see such as this again, I'm afraid." Buchanan raises his goblet again and tilts it above his open mouth as if to squeeze just one more droplet from the cup's smooth interior.

"Now that the illegal congress. . . ," Crean turns his head as Buchanan touches his shoulder and interrupts.

"Careful, Crean! Don't call the Continental Congress illegal. You'll be doomed for sure. Caution." The older man pauses and keeps his eyes fast onto his friend's. "Caution is the byword now, my friend. You must act like every wall is your enemy spying on you."

"You're too cautious, but I shall heed your words. Still, now that the Congress has elected that George Washington as commander-in-chief, there are organized plans afoot. War will begin in earnest."

"True. Now, as never before, it is imperative that we—you and I—have a plan to survive. I've built my business here in this new world and I don't intend to see my efforts doomed...or taken from me." Buchanan slams his empty goblet on the tabletop and slumps back in the chair.

Crean stares at his friend and forms his next words carefully. "Walter, like you, I've been extremely successful here. His Majesty has been good to me, but I've also made my own way. I do think, though, that British forces will prevail over these disorganized, rag tag Whigs. Our troops are well trained and ready for battle. Their army runs home at night to feed their pigs and chickens. Many are no more than mere boys. We can't help but succeed."

"These men you call rag tag are zealots to their cause. That makes them hungry and there's no better fuel for success than raw hunger." Buchanan sits forward in his seat and continues. "What we need is a neutral stance, one that lets us win no matter the battlefield victor."

"What it does tell me, dear friend, is that the wedding must be held with great haste. Your son will soon be called to battle and it might be months before he is again here in the city." Crean rises and walks to the window overlooking the bustling avenue. The matter of loyalties is closed; the more pressing need is on the table.

Buchanan stares at Crean's silhouette against the sunlit glass. Silently he thinks, "That Crean is a sly one. There's more than loyalty to the Crown on his mind. With the marriage done he'll dare not turn on me." Aloud, he speaks, "I agree."

Buchanan joins Crean by the window and both stare through the panes, neither seeing beyond the glass. Buchanan turns to his friend and says softly, "I propose June 28th for the nuptials. Does that suit, Crean?"

Crean hesitates just barely before answering. "Margaret will pale for it gives us but a short three weeks to prepare. However, I agree." The two men shake hands. The deal is consummated.

Margaret has lost her patience. She stomps her foot and holding Fanny by her bare shoulders turns the young woman around to face her. "Enough! Stop this weeping and wailing."

"NO!" Fanny screams and jerks to free herself from her mother's grasp. "No-o-o," Fanny draw out the word loudly.

The commotion brings Crean to the bedroom door and he bursts through without knocking. He strides to the middle of the room, abruptly stops, and takes a deep breath to calm himself. This action reduces the noise level and gains the attention of both women. "Fanny. This display of poor manners will stop immediately. You will continue to dress. The carriage is waiting as is your bridegroom."

Fanny takes quick stock of the situation and decides to proceed in a soft voice though the tears still run quietly down her cheeks. "Papa," she pleads. "Papa, why must we hurry? This rebellion will soon be over. There's plenty of time then."

"We've been over this same logic time and time again, child. Did I not maneuver with every power I hold to keep John away from the battlefield in Charlestown? I cannot call in those debts again. There will be many more such…"

Fanny quickly interrupts. "But we won at Bunker Hill. This…"

Crean raises his hand to silence Fanny. "I said enough!" He pulls his watch from the tiny waistcoat pocket and looks at its hands. "Young lady, you and your mother will be dressed and downstairs in precisely 30 minutes. At that time, we will leave for the Buchanan's." Crean pivots on his highly polished heel and struts out of the room.

Neither woman speaks as Margaret helps her daughter finish donning the pale green peau de soi gown the seamstress had hurriedly created these past weeks. She hands Fanny a velvet box containing the heirloom jewels John had presented as the Buchanan's wedding gift. Four generations in his family, he'd said. Fanny lifts the necklace slowly to her neck for Margaret to hook the clasp. Tears christen the emeralds.

Fanny remains silent during the short drive through the city streets. She cannot stop her tears from flowing to the agitation of both parents. She tries; she simply cannot.

The carriage pulls up in the Buchanan's short, fashionable drive and halts at the oversized entrance. Crean steps from the vehicle and helps Margaret descend the two steps, careful to keep her gown from the ground. He leans into the carriage and offers his hand to Fanny. Sighing, she reaches out listlessly with her right hand, and allows her father to guide her down the steps. Crean catches a quick glimpse of color in Fanny's left hand she's kept behind her back. He reaches out grabs the bedraggled Maggy from his daughter's grasp and slams the doll into the carriage.

"Damnation, girl. You shame us."

Meekly, Fanny drops her eyes toward the steps, places her left hand on Crean's linen cuff and enters through the doorway to what she whispers as she crosses the threshold, "my doom!"

Fanny moves, as in a trance, through the rest of the day. The tears continue unbidden and unrestrained. Margaret explains to guests, "Tears of simple joy, just pure joy!" John Buchanan, though puzzled by his bride's aloofness, effuses his pride as he escorts her through the meal and into the evening's dancing. He has claimed New York's fairest jewel. He has won the trophy. What does it matter he's off to battle in three days' time.

Chapter 8

The War Years
1775 – 1783

Fanny places her embroidery in her lap and reaches for the teapot. She carefully lifts the cozy and speaks to Margaret. "More tea, Mama?"

The two sit comfortably in the Buchanan parlor. Margaret is invited several times a week to tea and seldom refuses. These 'social' occasions are her only opportunity to see Fanny. Politics, formerly one of the main reasons for gathering, is now a warrant for an almost nonexistent social season. Many of New York's elite, loyal to the king, have left either to return to England or to move south where Tories or Loyalists, as they now prefer to be called, are in greater number. Those who have remained are circumspect in proclaiming their loyalties either to crown or to liberty.

"You are brave, my dear, to continue serving tea." Margaret offers her cup to Fanny. "Papa has banned all purchase of tea."

"Actually, we've not bought tea," Fanny explains. "There is much in Father Walter's warehouse that he does not openly admit. He slips a box or two home under cover and we serve it only to family and servants."

"You're sure, then, of your servants' loyalty?" Margaret takes the proffered cup.

"Father Walter swears their faithfulness comes from being treated well in the many years they've been with the family. I suppose I must trust his judgment though I do admit to being prudent in my conversations." Fanny picks up her embroidery and prods her needle through a coil of thread, making a French knot.

The two women sit quietly, Margaret watching Fanny's sewing "Your embroidery is quite nice. I do remember how you hated the chore but a year ago, my love."

Fanny looks up and a giggle escapes her throat. "A married woman has certain responsibilities; compliance seems to be one such in this household."

Now that her daughter has opened the subject of marriage, Margaret decides to widen the opportunity. "Has there been word of John?"

Fanny's fingers push the needle in an out several times before she replies. "Father Walter continues to inquire discreetly of the battalion commander, who claims no news is usually good news."

"You've had no letters?" Margaret keeps her gaze fixed on her daughter's face while she takes another sip from the fine, translucent, porcelain cup.

"None." The needle continues its repetitive motion. After a moment, Fanny continues, "But then, I've not written either." Her mind silently finishes the sentence with "and surely don't intend to!" She refuses to meet her mother's eyes and blatantly shifts the subject. "Has Papa left for Boston yet?"

"He plans to leave next week. Since he refuses to request a safety pass, it may be a long journey this time. He speaks of closing out his business in Boston and focusing on what remains here in New York." Margaret places her teacup on the table before continuing. "I'll be glad for him to stay put. I'll feel safer."

Fanny places her embroidery next to her mother's cup and leans toward Margaret as if to straighten the tucker on her mother's dress. "Father Walter is thinking of taking the Patriot's Pledge," she whispers.

Margaret gasps and with great effort keeps her hands from flying to her mouth. Buchanans may trust their servants; she, however does not. "But John serves in the King's Army," she whispers. "And, what about his importation privileges?"

Fanny's eyes scan the room. She rises, walks toward the parlor door, closes it, and returns to her chair. "He feels the King will be evicted from the colonies and better promise may lie eventually with the Patriots. His warehouses are full and there are two ships on their way from England with supplies at this very moment. 'Enough to last through any political turmoil,' he says." Fanny again picks up her embroidery before continuing. "Father Walter is an opportunist, Mama. He will move in whichever direction will bring him profit—or safety."

"Crean will never desert the king." Margaret's voice is firm but whispered. "Yours will be a house divided when John returns. You must stand by your husband."

"I'll stand for me, Mama; only for me!" Fanny rises, offers her mother a hand up. Tea is over for the day.

Chapter 9

Crean rattles the *Royal Gazette* against his knees as he folds it into a less cumbersome mode. "Damnation, Margaret," he snaps. "That supercilious fool, Thomas Paine. His *Common Sense* piece screams sedition."

"Fanny claims it's quite well written."

"She's read it?" Crean's face reddens alarmingly. "Where in God's creation did she get that sordid piece of trash?"

Margaret keeps her eyes on her embroidery, pushing the needle down, then up with annoyingly steady rhythm. These days she fears for her beloved's health far beyond any concern for their wealth. The fire heightens the shadows on Crean's face and Margaret thinks how sallow and drawn he's become these past cold months. His temper flares easily over minutiae he'd heretofore ignored. His mind wanders at odd moments in their times together. Seldom does he come to bed before she sleeps. Margaret misses both the personal intimacy and the intrigue of political meandering.

Aloud, Margaret's calm voice belies her inner anxieties. "Walter brought home a copy in order to assess its impact, or so Fanny says. She found it on the parlor commode and breathed no compunction in studying its contents."

"Pollyrot! Pure pollyrot, that's all it is. Do you know that Paine ends his diatribe with 'the free and independent states of America'? That kind of blathering leads only to outright conflict. Hang the author, dammit, hang him!"

"Sit down, Crean. Here, let me pour you a snifter of brandy. You'll bring on an apoplexy if you continue to let these things plague you so."

"Plague me? Plague me, you say? Can you forget so easily I sit in this chair through the King's good graces?" Crean wipes a dribble from his chin with the cuff of his sleeve. "That dress of yours, my sweet, would be but linen instead of silk and fancy lace."

"You exaggerate, Crean. You've many holdings of which the King knows nothing nor does he give a twit. You've done quite well for yourself. No matter the turn of events here you'll still prosper. Steven Bradley and Walter Buchanan are wise to watch the tide. Perhaps it's time you modify your politics. If only to ease your stress."

Crean stares immobile at the dying flickers on the grate. He finally upends his glass, draining the drink. Ponderously, he rises to stoke the fire and then paces slowly back and forth across the elaborately woven carpet. His shoulders droop, his hands fuss restlessly with his cuff linens. Minutes pass before he speaks.

"Margaret," Crean pulls a velvet tuffet close to his wife's skirts and watches intently as her needle pierces the cloth first up, then down. "Margaret," Crean gently stops her hands from their determined motion. "I must go to Boston. Their General Washington, though how he earned that status, I'll not understand. Washington is rallying troops just south and west of Boston. There will be much trouble and I must be there to represent King George. He deserves that of me."

Margaret dares not speak her fears. The changes she has dreaded are now inevitable. She puts her embroidery on the candle stand and snuffs the taper before rising. Gently, she pulls Crean to his feet beside her and wraps her arms snugly about his middle. "We shall survive this, m'love."

Crean is not so sure.

Margaret fans herself agitatedly though the room is fairly cool with only smoldering coals on the grate next to her chair. "This filthy man came to the door. Onncie was terrified, I tell you…"

"Hush. How can I read with you babbling on so?" Fanny gently strokes her mother's knee, trying to quiet her.

"Thank you, thank you, dearest, for coming. It's so danger-ous these days to travel about the city but I had no strength, no strength at all to come to you. This awful man told Onncie he wouldn't give the letter to anyone but me. Master Crean's orders, he said. Then, soon as he'd handed me the note he was off and gone."

Fanny adjusts the single sheet of paper in order to gain more light on the words her father had written. No wax seal at the torn edge, she notes. The characters are quivery and jagged, not his usual fine hand. Obviously written in haste and with a poor quill. With effort she deciphers the message.

King' troops retreating north from Boston city. All is chaos. Dare not tell you my transient sanctuary. Am on the coast for duration. Lock box under fire grate contains key. Use as necessary. Remember, no matter, you are my true love. Keep our daughter safe. 19 March 1776

Fanny sobs softly, tears shaping little rivulets on her lightly powdered cheeks. The note rests precariously in her trembling fingers. The fan having dropped to the floor; Margaret busies her hands twisting her embroidered handkerchief. Minutes pass before either can speak.

"I must go to him." Margaret manages a trembling whisper.

"You cannot." Fanny takes both her mother's hands firmly in her own. Sheer willpower draws Margaret's eyes up to meet hers. "You don't know where he is. He wants you here. He wants you safe." Fanny releases her grip and gently pulls her mother toward her. "Hush now. We must think this through."

The two women sit embracing, rocking slightly to and fro. Silk skirts mingle and rustle in the movement. An ember shifts on the grate popping little sparks in a short radius gaining the attention of neither woman. Their anguish is almost audible.

Fanny speaks first, as she releases Margaret from her arms. "The letter must be burned."

"No!" Margaret grabs the note, clutching it to her breast. "It is written in his own hand. It is all I have of him."

The act jolts Fanny to reality and she quickly assumes charge in her mother's house. "You have much of him. Look around you. This very room speaks of him. The scent of him lingers. That, however precious, must be the least of our thoughts if we are to manage our way through this crisis."

Fanny loosens Margaret's fingers, retrieves the letter and lays it on the grate. Both women watch as heat chars an edge and intensifies to red. A tiny flame licks into the script and, finally, bursts full blown to devour Crean's message of love.

Few civilians can be seen on New York's streets. The intense, pulsing heat of late July reverberates off the buildings and crude sidewalks. A miasma of fear engulfs the city. Windows are closed and shuttered. The stench overpowers even the strongest of stomachs. Only the greatest necessity sucks the brave from their homes. The market bell does not toll for there are no vendors in the square.

Margaret looks out her open rear window surveying the kitchen garden. "There's enough to feed us for weeks. Thank Jehovah you thought to stock the larder, Onncie. We'll be short on eggs and milk. Those three scraggly hens you bought won't produce much and those hooligan farmers can keep their sour milk!" Margaret slaps the jamb for emphasis. She turns from the window and moves across the cluttered kitchen. "Where's Fanny?"

Onncie tilts her lifted chin toward the back staircase, drops of sweat arcing with the effort. "Up there pacing, I 'magine. She's been at it for hours. Can't sit still since you brought her home."

"I do hope I've done the right thing. The Buchanan's think she'd be far safer with them. Walter said he sees my point that if there's fighting, I need to be here. I know he thinks I'm nothing but a frightened mouse."

"Well, if you ain't, I am!" interrupts Onncie. "It's only weeks since they signed that Declaration but it's like a hainted graveyard in this city. You just expects gobblies and spooks to grab you. I can hardly sleep nights. Never mind the dreadful heat. It's the shootin' that shivers m'bones."

"That's friendly fire, for sure. Most of the so-called patriots—traitors I call 'em—have left to join the militia. They're a far piece from this house, I'd say." Margaret flicks her fan in a futile effort to stir the stagnant air.

Both women turn as they hear rustling on the stairs. They're rewarded with first the lace hemmed petticoat, then the gathered blue silk, the tiny, sashed waist, and finally Fanny's frowning face. She begins talking before her blue slippered foot lands on the scoured plank floor. "I'm taking the carriage to Father Walter's office."

Simultaneous gasps and melded mutterings do not deter Fanny's prepared speech. "I've a strong hand with the horse and I know my way. It's certain he goes to the wharf each day—he must. It is equally certain he'll have news of every coming and going hereabouts, information we need to know. Now—Onncie, have Josiah ready the carriage—now! Go."

Onncie moves quickly towards the door, too stunned to do other than Fanny's bidding. Margaret sinks to a sturdy wooden seat by the hearth emotionally unable to protest. The last of Fanny's skirts swish through the hall doorway before a word of contradiction can be uttered. Moments later she returns pulling on her lace gloves, her bonnet already neatly tied under her determined chin.

"I'll be back before the tower chimes half after three. Refreshment will be ready, I presume." Leaving not a second for reproach or interdiction, Fanny sweeps out into dooryard and strides toward the carriage house.

Onncie, returning toward the house, reaches out to slow her mistress but her fingertips are gruffly rebuffed. "Mistress Fanny, please," pleads Onncie. Noting she is being stoutly ignored, Onncie picks up her skirts and races to the kitchen door. Plunging into the scullery, she bumps headlong into Margaret clinging to the table's edge.

"Willful child!" snorts Onncie.

The two women nervously busy themselves while awaiting Fanny's return. When the tower finally strikes a quarter past three, Margaret bades Onncie to un-shutter and open the front parlor window. Sunlight and stench burst into the room, settling far beyond the sill. Margaret instantly raises a handkerchief to cover her nostrils and lips and determinedly draws a chair up to the windowsill. She wills herself to sit and wait.

† † †

The tower has already chimed the fourth hour before Margaret spies the carriage round the corner and turn in the alleyway to the carriage house. Her face is pale and damp; wet spots stain her dress beneath the arms and down the back. Margaret pushed against the sill trying to rise and follow Onncie's disappearing figure through the doorway. Strength fails her and she drops again onto her sentinel's seat.

Fanny unties her bonnet strings as she strides through the parlor door. Flushed with adventure, she pulls a chair next to mother and begins to speak.

"General Washington's troops are spread outside city perimeters. Father Walter's sources say attacks will begin within a fortnight; no sooner, as ammunition is low and they're awaiting arrival of new supplies. Father Walter is certain there are Patriot's hidden throughout the city ready to show themselves as soon as the main troops start firing." Fanny pauses only long enough to take a deep breath. Handkerchief in hand, she dabs at her brow and neck as she eagerly continues her report.

Royalist troops are ready, practicing in secret areas away from the barracks. Only a token few are visible. The strategy, claims Father Walter, is to fool Washington into thinking we are poorly protected."

Onncie, who has closed the shutters and shut the sash, interrupts. "Whose guns do we hear in the dark of night? Are we safe?"

"Most assuredly we are safe. Washington's troops will meet resistance as soon as they advance."

Margaret finally gains calm enough to speak. "Will the Buchanan's stay or will Walter send his family south?"

"He will never leave his ships and docks. His warehouses are stocked to bursting." Fanny ceases speaking; her eyes move to mother's face, to Onncie's. Both women, intently expectant, wait for her to continue. Very softly, Fanny iterates the secret she discovered during her visit. "No harm will befall Father Walter. Tucked under the edge of his big desk blotter I saw…" Fanny's pause was less for effect than out of exhilaration at her father-in-law's cunning. She leaned closer and whispered, "I saw a Patriot's Pass."

Chapter 10

Onncie heard it first. Rather, she smelled the acrid smoke. Her room in the back on the third floor had a sizeable window which she had opened hoping for a few wisps of air during the night hours. Fully awake the moment her lungs accepted faint traces of gunpowder residue, Onncie rises from her linened bed and dashes to the sill. A red haze brightens the eastern sky not unlike an August sunrise. Smoke wafting on artificial breezes created by intense blazes offers up to Onncie the mixture of burning wood ash and that of dusky musket residue. Her nostrils flare exaggeratedly. Protesting, her lungs lurch to expunge the foulness. Then, and only then, Onncie hears the cacophony of battle.

Onncie turns from the window, races past her shawl, flings open the door and dashes down the short hallway to the back stairs clad only in her tucked chemise. Her clenched fist bangs on each servant's door as she flies by. Down the stairs she dashes, taking every other step like an over excited child. On the landing to the second floor, she pivots and shoves open the heavy door. Strong hands grab her shoulders and Onncie stifles her scream in mid breath.

"Quiet! Quiet at once," Fanny commands. "You sound like a terrified cat."

Onncie's knees give way and she sinks to the floor, Fanny still holding fast to her arms. The dark hallway reels around her and Onncie focuses her eyes on the single flame she can see. Someone is talking to her, but who? She concentrates and slowly her senses return. Margaret holds a burning taper just above her head. Fanny squats on the floor beside her. Cook peers over the head of the scullery maid and Josiah stands staring at her, nightcap set awry on his unkempt head. Onncie turns her attention to Fanny who's speaking to her, repeating the words again and again.

"Onncie, talk to me. What is it? What happened?"

Inhaling deeply, Onncie tries to talk. Her breath gets in the way of words and it's a moment before she can coordinate the two. "The shooting, it's begun!" More gulping for air then, "I saw it from my window." As she spoke a cannon rumbled, the aftershock making its way to the floor beneath them.

Fanny speaks quickly and firmly to assuage their immediate panic. "Josiah, check all the gates and shutters. Bolt any not already locked." She turns to the cook and maid, her stare defying them to challenge her. "Fill kettles with water. Gather all the linens on the first floor and bring them to the kitchen. We'll need to soak them in case of fire. Find all the buckets you can and have them filled and ready." Fanny turns to Onncie, the gesture dismissing the others. "Onncie gather your wits and get dressed. We must not be caught sleeping—or even looking like it."

Margaret shakes her head as if to clear her brain of the realities around her. She speaks her first words of the night's events. "I'm so afraid. What will become of us without Crean?"

"We must be strong. It is you and me now, Mother, who will hold forth against whatever enemy comes knocking." Fanny puts her arm around her mother's waist and guides the trembling woman to her bedroom. "Get dressed now for I suspect we've much to do today." Fanny squeezes Margaret comfortingly.

Fanny climbs the back stairs and walks to Onncie's room. Not bothering to knock, she enters and strides to the window. Fanny stares toward the hazy rose horizon mesmerized by the sight. She cannot see the streets below but the clatter of rushing boots rises to her ears. Friend or foe, she wonders.

They have not changed clothes in eight days. Sweat and hard labor have taken toll on once elegant garments. Fanny's left sleeve has partially pulled from her bodice while she jammed wrapped silver up the chimney. Soot settled on her scalp adding to other accumulated grime. Margaret's hands were scratched and scarred from ripping floorboards beneath the cupboards that she and Josiah and shoved aside and then replaced. Much of their

54

treasures had been securely hidden. Margaret had wisely asserted they leave enough of their possessions in full view that any looters would gain a fair enough haul so they would not go smashing, poking about the house but merely think them unprepared.

There has been little time for eating but Fanny insisted they nourish themselves twice each day. Once when they all rose from their sleeping spots on the kitchen floor and again before they collapsed again at sundown. Not once had anyone in the household had contact with an outsider. No one had come knocking. Sometimes, it seemed, there was no one about on the streets. Other times, the shouts and clamoring seemed to penetrate the stout walls. Still, this family (indeed they were a family even if no blood linked them) of five women and one man were an island unto themselves in the midst of a battle torn city. All light has disappeared from shutter cracks; streets are deafeningly silent. Night has fallen on the outside world. Inside, they dare to light a single candle.

Fanny sighs as she drops her weary and thinning frame onto the scullery stool. "I'm so tired I doubt I can climb the stairs to watch from Onncie's window tonight."

"Then rest, my dearest." Margaret puts one arm around her daughter's shoulders, with the other strokes Fanny's dirty locks. "I'll stand guard tonight. I feel a need for a bit of air, no matter how putrid it blows."

After restlessly pacing the house, checking bolts and locks, touching furniture for meager reassurance, Fanny finally settles on the kitchen floor. Instantly, she sleeps. Vivid, blaring dreams keep her tossing on the makeshift pallet. Into this phantasm creeps an eerie sound. The scratching does not fit the dream. Fanny stirs, runs her hand across her eyes, unable to rouse to consciousness. The scratching continues. Slowly, Fanny sorts between her fitful, sleep induced miasma and the persistent, intrusive scraping. Her mind having arrived on the brink of reality, grasps the impact of the extrinsic sound and as instantly as she slept, she wakes.

Heart pulsating in staccato percussion, Fanny crawls through the dark kitchen toward the sound. Reaching out to the scratching, her hand touches the door and she quickly orients herself in the darkness. Is that breathing she hears? "Who's there?" Her whisper is barely audible. More scraping though it seems muted now. No trickster would be so persistent, Fanny thinks.

Fanny reaches for the bolt without rising. Slowly and silently she moves the bar back along its shaft. She must move her body sideways to allow the door to open just slightly. Fetid, human breath pants into her face. Willing outward calm, Fanny eases the door wider until she can see a figure propped against the jamb. The odor of blood curls into her nostrils. A groan escapes the dark form. "My God!" Fanny exclaims.

The words wake those near her. Fanny hears Cook whimper. "Josiah, come here quickly. Onncie, bring the candle. Do be quiet, all of you."

Together Josiah and Fanny pull the body into the kitchen. Josiah shuts the door and shifts the bolt back into secured position. Onncie lights the candle and lowers it toward the hulk silent on the floor. Blood covers his face and has soaked the tattered, blue coat. His breeches are filthy and torn, his feet rapped in rags. Everything is stained with aging layers of sweat. Onncie gasps, "Good God a' mighty. It's Cooper."

The remaining hours before dawn are spent cleaning and treating the wounded man. The commotion, slight though it is, draws Margaret from her watch and she joins the nursing.

"Should we shelter a Patriot?" poses Josiah.

Margaret and Fanny respond almost as one, "Such a question!"

Margaret vehemently continues, "Who cares the color of his coat. This is Cooper. He has served us well and we'll not turn him out."

Fanny wonders softly, "How do you suppose he found us?" She touches his brow, careful not to rouse him from his fretful sleep.

Light has begun to seep in through the shutters. Soon the sun will heat the stagnant air. Still, it is quiet outside on the street. No one seems about his business. Inside the house, the boring, constrained routine continues. Everyone moves carefully, avoiding the restless form in the far corner of the kitchen.

Margaret and Fanny are making the rounds of the first floor when the knocking begins. Both women start, their eyes meeting, eyebrows arched. "Who can it be?" whispers Margaret, her voice shaking. "Could they know Cooper is here?"

Fanny raises her forefinger to her lips and moves into the hallway towards the front door. Margaret follows, tears on the brink of dripping down her cheeks, she is so frightened. Fanny motions Margaret to move behind her and then places her hand against the door latch. "Who knocks, please?" Fanny manages somehow to make her voice steady. No answer but another knock assaults the door.

Louder this time, Fanny repeats her query. A tired, masculine voice responds, "Lieutenant Briggs, ma'am, His Majesty's troops."

Fanny opens the door just enough for the lieutenant to see her full face. "How may I help you?" She could see the man's exhaustion in his sagging shoulders, his strained eyes and days' growth of blond stubble along his cheeks and chin. No other soldiers were within her range of vision, just this one tired man.

"Ma'am, I'm to tell those who still reside along this street that the battle is ended and the King's troops are victorious."

Fanny opens the door a little wider, enough that she can look up and down the street. All the houses are intact. None look occupied, probably shut up like their own against the skirmishes.

Noting her surveillance, the lieutenant volunteers, "Your street escaped the fires and most of the fighting. Though, not two blocks away, not a house stands. Burned to the ground, they were. Best I be continuing my rounds, ma'am."

"Thank you, lieutenant, I appreciate the news."

The soldier starts to turn but hesitates. "Ma'am, best you be careful. There may be a few stray enemy still lurking about these streets. It'll be your duty to turn any such straggler into the King's commandant."

"Thank you. We'll be most cautious. Is it safe to go out, sir?"

"I'd wait a day or two. Our captain'll be about rounding up strays and bringing life back to normal as soon as possible." He raises his right hand to his brow and finishes his duty with, "Good day, ma'am."

Chapter 11

Weeks have passed since George Washington and his troops were beaten back from the city. The stifling summer heat has abated somewhat. Autumn smells have nearly replaced the stench of fire and gunpowder. Houses and businesses have been rebuilt with amazing rapidity given the scarcity of supplies and manpower. The city has resumed its routines confident the King's Army will not again be challenged on these streets.

The pace of Cooper's healing cannot compete with the city's recuperation. Fanny had immediately cleared a small space in the larder, just enough room for a pallet back behind the flour barrels and now almost empty molasses keg. Cooper had groaned loudly as Fanny and Josiah dragged his semiconscious body through the narrow opening. Once cooper was situated, Fanny added a short, wooden stool, and candlestick. From this stool, Margaret, Onncie, and Fanny took turns watching over him. They wiped his brow as his intermittent fevers soared. They sang softly to quiet his nervous spasms and bring on coma like slumbers. Josiah had notched two quite inconspicuous holes in the outer wall near Cooper's pallet. This allowed some small amount of outside air to circulate and later in his recuperation offered Cooper a mouse's eye view of the decaying dooryard garden.

In late October, more than two months after his surreptitious arrival, Cooper was well enough to move about the kitchen during the dark, night hours. Immersed in the blackness of the deserted scullery, he and Fanny would talk of the mountains in the New Hampshire Grants, remarking on memories of meadow flowers, or the river sparkling in the sunlight. They never spoke of the war or its causes, only of happier times. These late night trysts brought the two young people exigent emotional relief. Cooper was glad to be free from his daytime larder prison. Fanny needed respite from Margaret's growing terrors. Crean had sent no further messages. By mid-November, Cooper knew it was time to leave. He could endanger this household no longer.

"Go safely," whispers Fanny as she hands Cooper a neatly wrapped package of cheese, bread, and three apples. The tower clock begins to strike: one...two...three. Fanny moves quickly forward placing her hands gently on Cooper's chest. She tiptoes in order to reach his face and presses her lips precisely where the still crimson scar bisects his right cheek. The chime continues six... seven... "Hurry, you must reach the wharf before 10 o'clock or you'll miss the row boat I've arranged for you. Go. Now."

Wanting desperately to grab Fanny, Cooper knows he must not and he simply places his forefinger over her trembling lips. The young man, clad in dark wool cloak taken from Crean's chifferobe, turns, lifts the door latch and slips through the small opening. Before shutting the door, he pivots to face Fanny one last time. "I'll send word as soon as I learn anything," he promises. The clock strikes its ninth and final peal as Cooper evaporates into the dooryard's black void.

Fanny hears the muffled click of the carriage house gate and slowly pulls the kitchen door into its jamb. Her cheeks are damp with tears but she makes no sound. Lifting her woolen skirts a few inches off the floor, Fanny climbs the back stairs to the second floor. She stops briefly at Mother Margaret's door. Hearing nothing, she moves on to her own room, enters quietly, and drops onto her bed free at last to sob aloud.

Mother Margaret lifts the ornate, broad silver serving knife ready to slice into the annual Twelfth Night minced meat pie. "I cannot bear to think where Crean might be this night."

Fanny quickly interjects into her mother's words, "We must believe him safe. We've not heard otherwise. Shall we sing as we serve?" Fanny looks around the table where all the household has gathered for the traditional celebration. No guests are present; an early curfew remains following the past summer's deadly skirmishes. Josiah and cook keep their eyes downward, seeming to stare unseeingly into their plates. Onncie manages a small smile but shakes her head almost imperceptibly and silently mouths the words, "not today." Fanny takes the knife from her mother, speaking gently, "Mother let me. You deserve the first slice, the piece of honor."

Margaret sighs and sinks into her chair. She takes the proffered slice of minced meat pie and places it half-heartedly in front of her. Fanny hands each person a piece in turn, saving the last small serving for herself. Cook has done the house proud concocting this sweet from what she could scavenge at the marketplace. The last of Crean's rum has soaked the meat and fruits to a fine ripeness and the meager cups of treasured sugar complete the fermentation. Cook skimped on the lard, there was so little left, and the pastry was a bit bland. Still it was minced meat pie and this was Twelfth Night in the new year, 1777 anno domini.

Fanny rubs the sleep from her eyes before folding the comforter back from her head. The room is damp and cold. Onncie has not yet come to light a fire in the grate. Fanny pulls the down comforter around her shoulders as she rises and moves to pull back the dense, winter draperies designed to keep the night bitterness at bay. She lifts the shutter latch, opens the right panel and steps to the window. Frost coats the panels and Fanny manipulates the comforter with her elbow in order to erase one glass panel. Movement catches her eye and she leans closer to better see the young lad scuttling down the front pathway. Even at this distance Fanny can see holes in the shabby scarf knotted round his head. His hands are jammed into his pants pockets but his ragged sleeves, too short or too worn, fall short of protecting his wrists and his skin appears red and cracked. His oversized and well-worn boots seem to be someone's discards and filthy cloth strips wrap around each instep attempting to hold some makeshift sole in place. "What is such a boy doing at our door?" Fanny wonders.

Even as Fanny ponders the lad's presence, a soft knock comes at her door and she moves quickly across the carpeted floor, her feet twitching in rejection of the cold against her bare skin. The comforter drags behind her, sliding from her shoulder as she reaches to open the door. Onncie enters quickly, breathing hard from her run up the front staircase.

"Best you read this 'fore I give it to Mistress Margaret," wheezes Onncie. "It bodes poorly, but that's m'Irish darkness thinkin', I suspect."

Fanny moves to the bed as she begins to unfold the dirty square of much handled paper. She motions Onncie to sit beside her but the maid moves to the grate to light a fire. Fanny notes the grimy creases and she inspects both sides of the small parchment before beginning to decipher the message.

He in jail, Boston
Ask SB due Yale
4 Feb. C

Fanny reads the cryptic words three times before letting her hands drop to her lap. Onncie moves to the bed and takes the paper from Fanny. "Lawd!" she gasps, quickly crossing herself in a long neglected habit. "Mistress Margaret goin' to swoon daid when she see this one."

Still barefoot and wrapped in the comforter, Fanny leads Onncie to Margaret's bedroom. Not bothering to knock, Fanny pushes open the door and strides across to her mother's bed. She flings herself atop the mound of covers and begins to sob. Startled into consciousness, Margaret, in one motion, bolts upright and grabs her trembling daughter. Onncie moves to comfort them both.

Mother and daughter sit opposite each other at the small round table draped in damask, the heat from the bedroom grate warming only their closest sides. The tea in their cups cools as the two discuss possibilities for gaining more information. Onncie rests on the small velvet slipper chair she's pulled close to the fire and silently listens to the conversation.

"No. You must stay here," commands Margaret. "I am the one who will go."

"You cannot do this alone," protests Fanny, reaching to caress her mother's cold hand. The weeping is done and a plan of action unfolds. "At least take Onncie."

Margaret controls the moment. "Onncie will stay here to care for the house. You, Missy, will return to the Buchanan's. You'll be safe there and will be needed if word comes about John."

When Fanny inhales as if to protest, Margaret swiftly continues. "We must make arrangements quickly if I'm to be at Yale in time to meet Master Bradley. I'll need to leave within the week. Traveling will be slow and I must move cautiously,"

Recognizing defeat, Fanny's mind rapidly lays out her own tasks. "Father Buchanan may be able to provide a Patriot's pass. I'll visit his office this afternoon. He's sure to be prudent, I'm confident of that much."

Turning to Onncie, Margaret continues, "You and I will pack. Not too many things just enough to get me safely to Boston. An extra carriage rug…"

Fanny interjects, "Boston! You're only going to New Haven!"

"By then I'll be half way to Boston. If Crean's in Boston, then that's where I'll be."

Chapter 12

Fanny smoothes the folds of her skirt unconsciously as she listens to Mother Buchanan's idle prattling. She is excruciatingly aware of the letter tucked into her tatted pouch; the letter delivered by Onncie not more than an hour ago. The maid had arrived in the Brush's carriage ostensibly to inquire over some domestic decisions that must be made in Margaret's absence. Mother Buchanan, always ready for new gossip, had invited Onncie into the parlor for tea. This total breach of etiquette could only be excused by Mistress Buchanan's insatiable desire to be in the midst of clandestine proceedings. Fanny trusts her mother-in-law's love and loyalty but knows only too well her propensity to tittle-tattle. Margaret's safety could well depend on keeping Mistress Buchanan's store of information to a minimum. The news of Crean's imprisonment for alleged embezzlement has become common knowledge following the return to New York of the King's solicitor. Such gossip spread quickly over the teacups and brandy snifters of New York's elite. Margaret's departure was equally known. It was in the details that danger lay.

Onncie's tea time chattering contained only homely bits on squabbles among the staff and the trials of obtaining horse fodder in these trying times. Mistress Buchanan's overt attempts to bring Margaret into the conversation were simply ignored; either Fanny or Onncie led the talk off onto some new path. When Mistress Buchanan finally realized the futility of her efforts, she rang for the downstairs maid, politely signaling an end to this sociability. Fanny walked beside Onncie as she makes her way to the kitchen exit and the waiting carriage. At the door, Onncie leaned forward to hug Fanny (a boldness that caused some whispering among the kitchen staff). Fanny felt a slight pressure at her hip as Onncie released the hug and Fanny realized that her maid has surreptitiously slid something into her lace pouch.

"My dear. Are you listening to anything I say? Anything at all? Mistress Buchanan's impatience fills the air.

"Oh! I'm so sorry Mother Buchanan." Fanny offers an answer she knows will soothe her mother-in-law, "I was just thinking about John. It's been so long since there's been any word. I worry about his safety." Fanny stops short of any hypocritical mutterings about missing her husband. Such words leaving her lips she knows would sound hollow and false. "I'm feeling the need for a short rest. If you'll excuse me, I'll lie down for a bit." Not waiting for any assent, Fanny rises, leans to brush her lips against the older woman's forehead, and walks purposefully out the parlor door.

Safely in her own bedroom, Fanny pulls the folded paper from her pouch. Before breaking the blue wax seal, she plops onto her bed, tucks her beloved doll Maggy against her chest, and tugs at the coverlet, partially draping it over her feet and legs. The parchment shakes in her trembling fingers and she pulls the covers higher before opening the letter. The familiar handwriting in sepia ink scrawls firmly across the page.

Dearest One,

Following some initial confusion, I met up with 'our friend.' In his kindness he offered details of the Boston predicament. There is some misunderstanding, I am sure, about funds that our beloved took to be his own but are being disputed in their ownership. I go to Boston in the morning (8 Feb.) to seek the truth. I shall find temporary lodging near to our beloved's location and then decide how to proceed.

You are well and content, I pray. This note I will send by personal courier and trust that it reaches you by the time I have visited our beloved. Most lovingly, Your Mother.

Fanny paces back and forth across the parlor rug, her silk slippers scuffing the fibers as she walks. She has just arrived for her weekly appearance at the Brush house, an agreed upon necessity in the days before Margaret's departure last winter. During these visits Onncie and she share news and arrange domestic necessities. Fanny welcomes he respite from the hectic Buchanan household. Indeed, she finds a certain peace in the near vacant house. Often Fanny wanders room to room reviving memories of not so many months ago when guests reveled in Brush hospitality. How dearly she misses her parents. Tears well up as she listens to Onncie's voice repeat the phrases she's heard on so many previous visits.

"Nary a word! Not a single word. No letter, no messengers. Eleven weeks and not a single bi' a news. What ha' become of your mother and father?" Onncie's voice begins to keen, "What will 'come of us?"

"Calm yourself," soothes Fanny, her own voice issuing a slight tremor. "Father Buchanan says the battles between here and Boston hinder the post rider's routes. Letters can end up in bonfires at best, in enemy hands at worst. I choose to believe that no news bodes well."

It is an oft repeated conversation. Words and phrases may vary slightly; the thoughts and fears remain the same. One time, Fanny may speak her fears and Onncie offers comfort; another, the roles reverse. In this manner, the two manage to cope with their fears and to find just enough hope to keep them going

Fanny drops onto a footstool before switching the conversation's focus. "Father Buchanan has received word there are many skirmishes in the New Hampshire Grants, especially near Westminster. He also told us at dinner last night that scoundrel Ethan Allen and his band of renegades have been talking about forming their own republic. What foolishness that man instigates. Surely, the King's army will hang him!"

When Onncie offers no reply, the conversation moves on to domestic issues that need resolution before she returns to the Buchanan's. The two women adjourn to the kitchen where they check the larder and then sit at the long, wooden table joined by the other servants for a tipple of chilled berry wine.

Fanny rises to make her departure. As she embraces Onncie, Fanny searches for words to allay their shared fears. None surface. Neither woman has even an inkling another eight weeks will pass before the news they so eagerly await arrives on their doorstep.

Shortly past two o'clock on a sweltering August afternoon a carriage pulls to a stop in front of the Brush house. Dust settles around the horse's feet as the door slowly opens and a rather plain footman emerges. He strides up the walk, stopping on the step to pull a handkerchief from his sleeve and mop his sweating brow before raising the brass knocker. Several moments pass without response and he knocks again. The door opens to reveal an old man in silk livery.

"Sir?" asks Josiah, eyes squinting into the afternoon glare.

"I bring a message for Mistress Fanny Buchanan from General Stephen Bradley. May I enter?"

Josiah steps aside motioning the footman into the dark, somewhat cooler hallway. "Wait here while I see if Mistress is receiving today." Josiah's moves quickly down the hallway, through the large and silent dining room, into the pantry, finally emerging into the kitchen where Fanny chats with the servants. Face flushed with excitement, Josiah interrupts without waiting. "Mistress, someone is here. Someone with news from Mister Bradley. He called him General, the man did." Before Josiah can say more, Fanny jumps up, knocking a mug across the table in her haste. Onncie moves just as quickly. "Is he a Patriot? How did he get through the sentries? General? Master Bradley, Uncle Stephen a general? Since when?" Fanny quells her urge to race to the foyer to pose this burst of questions. Instead, breathing deeply several times, she speaks to Josiah. "Tell the messenger I shall receive him in the parlor momentarily."

Turning to Onncie, she continues, "Join me, please. I cannot bear this news alone, no matter it be good or bad."

There is just time for Fanny to arrange her skirts before Josiah knocks on the heavy parlor door. "Enter."

Josiah steps aside and motions the footman through the doorway. The messenger bows briefly and proffers a neatly folded and sealed missile. He stands erect and moves toward the door in deference to Fanny's privacy. He waits quietly with his back to the door as if expecting some response to the message; a response he is to deliver.

Fanny, with Onncie peering over her shoulder, reads the letter silently.

Stephen R. Bradley, esq. requests an audience with Mistress Fanny Buchanan on Friday, 6 August, at 3 o'clock. Kindly reply by my messenger. Gen'S. R. B., Continental Army

Fanny rises and walks to Margaret's elegant writing desk. Onncie follows and watches closely as Fanny removes a sheet of paper, dips a quill into the ink and compose her reply. Onncie nods in silent agreement. Fanny carefully folds the paper three times, removes Margaret's seal from a little drawer and impresses it into the hot wax Onncie has just dropped onto the note. Fanny hands the reply to Onncie who in turn carries it across the room, handing it to the waiting footman. He bows silently and departs without further communication.

† † †

"You are most gracious to see me on such short notice." General Bradley swirls his snifter with Crean's precious brandy inside. Fanny waits nervously; Onncie doing needlework in a far chair by the drawn draperies. "You are also a wise young woman to plan a quiet dinner for us at the Buchanan's. It would have been unwise to spend the evening alone together in this house. I am watched closely here in this city.

"How is it that you are here at all?" Fanny shifts the warm air with her fan.

"There are parley between Loyalists and Patriots each side trying to protect its business interests even in the midst of war. I am part of these meetings and must remain discreet. Walter Buchanan is respected by both sides and as his daughter-in-law you are acceptable company."

"I am my father's daughter! I still serve the King."

"That is why our meeting in this house must be short. I have much to tell you before we depart for the Buchanan's." Bradley turns to Onncie and speaks softly, "Best you pour your mistress a snifter of this brandy. You might find need of one yourself."

Bradley returns his attention to Fanny and waits for Onncie to join them with the drink. "You must be strong, Fanny, for what

I'm about to tell you will bring much sorrow. I regret the necessity to be blunt but there is a great deal to tell and little time in which to tell it."

Fanny clutches the snifter stem; an almost inaudible gasp escapes her lips. Onncie squeezes her shoulder, letting her hand remain for reassurance. "Get on with it, Uncle Stephen. . . er, General Bradley. After all this time, I'm prepared for most anything."

Taking a long sip from his own goblet, Bradley begins. "Your mother is a courageous and bold woman. She made her way to Boston and visited Crean—you'll excuse me if I refer to your father by his Christian name. She met with Crean in prison. By the time she first arrived, his trial was over and he'd been found guilty of embezzlement from the King's coffers. Stolen from those he was appointed to protect, the notice said. His prison term was to be ten years but because of the current conflicts between the King and the colonists, he was to be executed by hanging on 15 August." Bradley reaches out to take Fanny's hand as sobs rack her small body.

"Margaret was devastated but determined to find some relief from such a punishment. She visited first one judge, then another. She called on powerful friends, though the few Loyalists still in Boston felt her a pariah. No one was willing to take a stand for Crean. I'm sorry, Fanny, but I give the truth."

Tears run silently down Fanny's cheeks. She lets them fall from her chin onto her dress without interruption. "Continue, please. I must hear it all."

"Your mother devised a plan. How it worked, I'll never know, but work it did. She went on assigned visiting day, dressed in two layers of clothing and an extra shawl. No one searched her—she's such a gracious and convincing woman. While the guard took a break, Margaret shed her outer layer of clothes and Crean donned them. He left the prison room without a single question while Margaret remained behind. Perhaps it was the overcrowded prison or too few guards but your mother's scheme was successful. He left the grounds without confrontation and made his way west to Connecticut. This part I'll tell you in a moment. But let me continue with Margaret's fate. When the guard returned and found Margaret alone, he locked her in the room and ran for reinforcements. When Crean could not be found, they kept Margaret in his stead. To what purpose I'll never understand, but in that jail she remains. She is being treated well. I have corresponded with her—to give her news of Crean and to be certain she is in no immediate danger."

Bradley pauses for another sip of brandy, reaches out to pat Fanny's hand and then continues. "News of Crean is less happy."

"Less happy? What could be less happy?" Fanny whimpers into Onncie's chest. The maid holds her close as Bradley goes on with his story.

"Your father made it safely to New Haven with plans to travel on to Westminster. It just so happened I was also in New Haven meeting with John Adams. Crean learned of my presence and asked for a meeting. I met him in a waterfront tavern run by fierce Patriots; he was brave to come. He told me of his conviction, his guilt, and his sorrow at leaving Margaret helpless in prison. He so loved her, you know.

"I told Crean there was little I could do for him. I'm ashamed to say my anger at his desertion of your mother closed my thoughts to his predicament. He seemed to understand and left the tavern. The next morning, a lad came to my boarding room with a note. Your father requested, and I still have the paper in my Westminster office, he requested that I care for his properties in the New Hampshire Grants. He asked that I look after you and Margaret and try to gain her release. He ended with a plea for forgiveness."

"Where is he? Where is my father?" Fanny's sobs almost obliterate Bradley's words.

"Fanny, this is hard to say. Crean hanged himself that night. Your father is dead."

"Where is mother? Where is she?" Fanny is near swooning; Onncie holds her close.

"I'm sorry, Fanny, she is still in prison. I've not been able to gain her release."

Chapter 13

Contrary to the Buchanan's vehement opposition, Fanny has moved back into her childhood home. Word of Crean's death and Margaret's imprisonment has spread plague-like through the city's various social strata and Fanny fears an unoccupied house a ready target. Fanny has become a social oddity, daughter of scandal (guilty herself by association, it seems) and wife of an unaccounted for Loyalist soldier. Were it not for her boldness and beauty, and the Buchanan's unimpeachable, absolute reign of the social realm, Fanny could have been ostracized completely. Fanny accepted few invitations and only when the older Buchanans would be present. Her pride was sorely beaten and the energy it took to attend even the smallest function drained her emotional reserves to the silt. Those who attended her select "at home" afternoons came more out of curiosity than loyalty. She refused to wear mourning though her heart grieved beyond imagining. Around it all, the war continues.

All Hallows Eve passes without the expected Patriots attack. Political gossipmongers finally abandon the summer's popular topic of those New Hampshire upstarts founding their own Republic of Vermont, claiming as their own all the disputed lands between the Connecticut River and Lake Champlain. Those with vested land grants gnash and gnarl invectives. Loyalist, General Burgoyne's surprise surrender at Saratoga earlier in the month has supplanted the Loyalist's jubilation at Howe's August victories over General Washington at Brandywine Creek and Germantown. Their strategies for separating the northern Patriots from those south of New York City have collapsed. The city is becoming a Loyalist island in the midst of enemy territory.

Fanny has taken to spending much of her at home time in the kitchen with the three remaining servants. The four are family, as close and trusting as if the same blood coursed their veins. Sitting around the sturdy, provincial table, they share news garnered in

71

the marketplace, barren as it is these days, or from Fanny's brief sojourns into society. They have reached unspoken agreement to avoid conjecturing on Margaret's status or Cooper's safety. These topics inevitably bring sighs, tears, and then unsettled silence. Instead, they focus on war news, tips on where meat or fresh produce might be gotten, or just remark endlessly on the weather's current idiosyncrasies. Walter Buchanan provisions the household with goods and gossip but his supply of both is dwindling as winter approaches. Today, the conversation is more animated than usual, centered as it is on fresh information—new to their ears if not to the Loyalist strongholds at large. The infamous Ethan Allen has been captured and imprisoned.

"Papa always said when that trouble monger was caught, the uprisings would fade." Fanny fairly bouncing on her seat with long pent up energy, "We'll see a change now, for certain." She continues chattering unaware the others' attention has shifted until Onncie touches her finger to her lips.

"What is it?" whispers Fanny, listening intently.

"Something...someone's at the carriage gate," Josiah whispers back.

"They don't sound too secretive makin' all that rattlin'," Onncie offers aloud, rising to go to the kitchen door. She opens the door and moves into the dooryard, Fanny right on her swishing hem tail.

Onncie stops short. Fanny collides from behind managing to peer around Onncie's shoulder. Both women gasp simultaneously. "Mama!" "Mistress Margaret!"

Margaret rushing toward them, catches her toe in her pelisse, stumbles but regains her balance just as Fanny and Onncie reach her. The three embrace in a gyrating huddle. Sobs, tears, laughter, all emerge from the conflux. A tall, neatly attired gentleman stands in the background, the hint of a smile teasing his lips. He neither moves nor speaks, waiting for the three women to finish their exuberant greetings.

Josiah and Cook have joined the group; voices and laughter cavort in the late autumn sunlight, no one caring how far the sounds travel. Like a swarm of insects, the clan moves toward the house stopping momentarily to ask a question, then restarting as a unit, only to stop again for some momentary exclamation. The man follows slowly, a few feet distant, free of the magnet that attracts the others.

The chattering continues into the kitchen. Cook stirs the coals and fills the kettle. Josiah pulls out fresh mugs, setting them on the table, all the while straining to hear each and every word his mistress offers. No one notices the gentleman waiting patiently by the door.

"Oh, my!" exclaims Margaret. "How could I have forgotten." She moves quickly to the stranger, takes his arm and pulls him into the gathering. "This is Patrick. Patrick Wall, my husband."

Pandemonium evaporates. Silence is instantaneous. Only the kettle's gentle hissing fills the void. No one moves for an eternity frozen into a few seconds of time.

At last, the gentleman steps toward Fanny, right hand extended. He bows just slightly, waits for the aghast young woman to offer her fingertips, then raises her hand almost to his lips. "You are even lovelier that Margaret described you, Mistress Fanny."

Fanny jerks her hand free, clutching both fists to her chest. Her lips extend tautly, forming a thin, straight, horizontal slash between chin and nose. She says nothing, just stares first at the interloper and then at her mother.

Patrick again bows briefly and moves on to greet Onncie, then Josiah and Cook. They remain mute, each responding with a slight bow or curtsy. Margaret steps toward her daughter, her voice tremulous as she speaks. "There is so much to tell dearest one. I'll not remember each and every detail at first telling, but we'll sort it all out as you hear it all. Come, let's sit in the parlor. Patrick, do join us. Onncie, will you serve us please." Margaret is again in control of her household.

The three sit in front of the fire lit by Onncie. Fanny holds her steaming cup in both hands, glaring at Patrick who has unwittingly selected Crean's chair and made himself quite comfortable. Margaret talks softly, steadily, occasionally sipping from her mug. Fanny has hardly listened through the telling of Crean's escape. She's relived those scenes repeatedly over the past months. She wants no new information to alter the script she's developed in her mind. Fanny has finally accepted her own version of Crean's sins; any other would thrust her soul into turmoil again.

"They told me if the Crown couldn't hang Crean, they'd hang me in his stead. The Crown needs retribution, they claimed." Margaret at last jots Fanny's attention. Noting Fanny's awakened interest, Margaret continues her saga.

"We were free to move about within the compound walls. Indeed, we were not much guarded. We cooked for ourselves did our own washing whenever they gave us enough water. We even developed our own little social groups. That's how I met Patrick." Margaret reaches out to touch Patrick's knee. He smiles in return. Fanny grimaces impolitely.

There were those of us who, shall we say, had experienced a little more culture than some of the others. We gravitated toward each other, sharing stories, compiling strategies for our constrained existence. We became a cadre of sorts." Margaret pauses for another sip. "Master Bradley wrote me about Crean's death. He was kind enough to have the letter delivered personally by Mistress Wellington. She was most comforting in my initial shock and sorrow. They would not let her visit again. "Twas Patrick who took up the role of comforter. For days I could not stop weeping. I thought I myself would die from the grief of it. There would be no need for the King's hanging. But Patrick, Patrick bless his soul, encouraged me. He reminded me I had a duty to return to you and to care for what Crean had left behind. He built hope into my fragile spirit."

Tears emerge unbidden as rekindled memories remind Margaret of those devastating months in Boston. Patrick rises, offering his linen handkerchief to her. He places his hand on her shoulder, squeezing momentarily in reassurance. He says nothing, however, and returns to his chair.

Patrick wrote a petition for my release. He was ignored but never gave up. He managed to get another plea, this time from outside. Again, no response."

Fanny interrupts, "Master Wall, why were you imprisoned?"

This unexpected interjection startles both Margaret and Patrick. He turns his attention to Fanny and quickly replies, "I was the Governor's tailor but my political sympathies leaned more toward Patriot thinking. I wrote a small, but volatile treatise suggesting the King rethink his stance on the colonies. Within days I found myself gaoled."

"You're a Patriot!" Fanny jumps to her feet, crossed the rug, and places her face within inches of her mother's. "You married a Patriot?" she screams.

Margaret remains quite still as she speaks, "In prison, dearest Fanny, political lines blur. It is survival that matters. It is the day to day kindnesses that overshadow differences. Locked up, unable to talk with those I love, separated from all I cherish. Fanny, such isolation…"

"You turned against all Papa stood for! How could you denounce him so quickly?"

"Fanny, your father was dead. Dead by his own hand. What could it possibly matter to me then whether the King is right or whether these new Patriots are justified in claiming freedom?"

Patrick rises and very gently takes Fanny's arm, leading her back to her seat. Sobs wrack her slight frame. She doesn't resist. Seating himself, Patrick continues the story.

"My confinement term was nearly up. Why I did not receive a death sentence remains a mystery to me and to many others. However, I was about to be released and I pleaded with the commandant for your mother's freedom also. He laughed and said only if she were my wife could such a thing be granted."

"A minor detail like that didn't slow Patrick," chuckles Margaret. "He arranged for a cleric to post the bans. After the prescribed time had elapsed, the cleric came to the gaol and with all the other prisoners as witnesses, performed the ceremony."

"We were released on schedule just a fortnight ago," Patrick concludes.

"I had written Master Bradley of these events and asked he send money that we might make our way to New York City. He was most generous and prompt." Margaret relaxes back into her chair and finishes the remaining, now cold, contents of her cup.

The story is told. No one feels moved to add to the tale. All stare into the prancing flames that seem to consume their separate emotions. Minutes pass before Fanny is the first to speak.

"Master Wall, I cannot accept you as my father. I will try, sir, to accept you as my mother's husband."

"Fair enough." Patrick nods acceptance.

"This has been a Loyal house," continues Fanny. Obviously, it is now my mother's house. It is she who makes the decisions here and I will abide by her preferences. However, I am not yet ready to disabuse His Royal Highness. You both must know that."

Fanny rises, drops a slight curtsy, and turns to leave the parlor. At the heavy wooden door, she stops and faces her mother. One single remaining tear drops silently down her cheek. She opens the door to find Onncie sitting on a small, straight backed chair, doing her needlework. Onncie smiles at Fanny who ignores the proffered comfort and walks regally up the stairs. In her own room, she flings herself across the bed. Emotional exhaustion chases her into sleep.

Fanny hears the knocking as if in a fog. Someone is calling her to supper. She cannot reach through the haze to respond. Too much effort. It all takes too much effort. She drifts back into oblivion. When she wakes, she opens her eyes to darkness. No one has pulled the drapes. Cold air presses aggressively around her body. Fanny doesn't bother to undress but crawls under the comforter pulling it over her head. Thus she tries to obliterate the sounds of love making coming from the adjoining room.

Chapter 14

Heat has returned to the city. Cannon smoke from across the Hudson River mingles with the mephitic air. Fanny sits with Margaret and Patrick in the kitchen dooryard eating a meager supper. She barely listens as her mother chatters incessantly. These weekly dinners together ae gradually becoming more bearable. Fanny, in a fit of extreme pique, had moved back with the Buchanans shortly after the new year. She had found it oppressive and depressing to share the house with Patrick and Margaret as they developed their newfound intimacies. Fanny desperately missed her beloved Papa and she detested the interloper who was usurping his place in Margaret's heart and home. Even more, she hated the talk of Patriot ideologies so contrary to Crean's political philosophies.

The faint rumble of distant cannon fire and Margaret's gasp bring Fanny from her reverie to the conversation at hand. Patrick's words calm Margaret. "A decisive victory for either side is doubtful. Both armies are well prepared but their hearts are not in this battle across the river. Now that we've…er. The Patriot's (Patrick switches venue in deference to Fanny's staunch loyalties) have brought in the French, the British are beginning to focus their energies further south in the Carolinas and Georgia."

"You know a lot for a tailor!" Fanny snaps. "Where have you been spying this week?"

"Enough, Fanny!" Margaret reaches out firmly grasping her daughter's arm. More calmly, she continues, "Times are changing. No matter who wins these battles, we need to be knowledgeable and wise to survive. Our future—your future—depends on Crean's holdings which now sit on both sides of the fence. Best you remember that."

Fanny drops her eyes to her plate in silent recognition of her mother's authority. She does not apologize.

"Patrick has been meeting with our solicitor about Crean's estate."

"Wise of you," responds Walter Buchanan, lifting his meat filled fork to his mouth. His eyes move around the dinner table seeking signs of subtle agreement from the other diners. These weekly dinners between the two families have become political and social strategy sessions for the Walls and Buchanans. Walter's gaze pauses almost imperceptibly on Fanny's face. He's pleased to see her attentiveness and silently praises his own role in converting his daughter-in-law's hostilities over the past three years.

"He says there should be no problem with the properties here in New York," offers Patrick. "The deeds will be transferred to me; the process is already in place. There is money in Crean's still unsettled accounts that can be authorized for Fanny. The problem lies in just what currency will be in effect at the time of settlement."

"I think that issue will be settled within the next few months." Walter takes a sip from his wine goblet before continuing. "A courier arrived just this morning with news from the south. Cornwallis has reached Yorktown in Virginia with those Carolina troops snapping at his heels like hounds at the fox. The French armada is gathered at the mouth of the Chesapeake. The northern militia moves swiftly southward along the Susquehanna River. Unless Cornwallis acts quickly, he'll find himself trapped. A victory here for the Patriots will just about bring this whole mess to a close."

"What of the Grant properties?" Fanny raises the question, looking straight at Margaret. She still finds it difficult to consult with Patrick.

Patrick's answer forces Fanny's gaze from Margaret's face to his. "The Republic of Vermont. We must remember to acknowledge these legalities."

"They've taken Papa's land. Those renegades had no right..."

Always the mediator, Margaret interjects herself between the two. "Master Bradley has managed to save some of the properties for us. You know that, Fanny. His generosity goes far beyond his legal duties to Papa."

78

"Let us move through one challenge at a time." Patrick wipes his lips with the napkin tucked into his weskit. Fanny winces at this plebian habit.

Mother Buchanan tactfully switches the conversation to her favorite and ever hopeful topic. "Walter has been in touch with the commandant again. John does not appear on any of the casualty lists."

"Nor does he appear on any battalion roster," adds Walter. He has long given up hope of locating his son. He now believes him a deserter but refuses to publicly acknowledge this disgrace. Better John simply evaporates into anonymity.

Fanny stops listening. Like conversations are repeated incessantly. Mother Buchanan eases the loss of her son by fawning over her daughter-in-law on every possible occasion during the day. Fanny drifts into visions of flower filled meadows, and trickling brooks. The world is much safer and happier inside her daydreams. Fanny allows no one to intrude into that sacred space.

Before closing the lid to her trunk, Fanny cuddles her doll, Maggy, to her chest. The old linen of the doll's fading dress scratches against the fine silk of Fanny's bodice. "Maggy, Maggy," croons Fanny. "We're off on a new adventure. What will we find? Whom shall we meet?" Fanny places the beloved doll on top of the fine new clothes just recently finished by Margaret's seamstress. She gently smoothes the doll's skirt, stands a moment staring into the trunk and finally drops the lid into place and snaps the lock. The key, on its silken string, she places around her neck. Moving to the bed, she picks up her emerald wedding necklace and returns it to its original velvet box. Fanny turns to the Buchanan's upstairs maid waiting silently by the door. "You may have Johann take the trunk now. The Walls will be along shortly to retrieve it."

Fanny hears for the final time the swish of her skirt echo down the stairs into the Buchanan's elaborately tiled foyer. Waiting at the bottom, Mother and Father Buchanan look up, forced smiles on their lips. It is a sad moment, this parting. Fanny steps toward the two dear people who have loved and protected her these past eight years. She reaches out her hand to touch Father Buchanan's bearded cheek, the lace of her glove scratching across the stubbly ends of his greying facial hair. She stands on tiptoe and places a light kiss on his lips. She can feel him trembling, striving to keep control. Before either he or she can weep, Fanny turns to embrace Mother Buchanan. Here tears cannot be stemmed.

"Mother, I wish to return this necklace to you."

"No, dearest it was John's gift to you. He would want you to have it, I'm sure." Mistress Buchanan pushes the box away toward Fanny.

"John may come home some day and want this memory. Besides, it has been in your family for a very long time, it belongs with you." Fanny places the box in Mother Buchanan's hands and gently curls the woman's fingers around the velvet softness. In her heart, Fanny knows she wants nothing to remind her of this man she so hated and with whom she had the briefest of unwanted intimacies.

Finally managing to regain his voice, Walter Buchanan speaks, "Fanny dearest, you know, of course, that you are welcome in this house forever. You are truly our daughter and nothing shall ever change that."

"I'll not plead again for you to stay," weeps Mother Buchanan. "I've exhausted every logic and emotion to keep you here. You need to find a new life, I know, but I shall miss you terribly."

As if on cue, the large knocker at the front door sounds the arrival of the Wall's carriage. Johann silently appears and answers the knock. Josiah stands on the threshold. "It is time, Mistress Fanny."

Fanny hugs and kisses the Buchanans one more time then follows Josiah out the door and to the waiting carriage. The valet opens the highly varnished and decorated door, offers his arm to Fanny in assistance, then shuts the door and climbs into the forward seat. Inside the carriage, Margaret hugs her daughter across the floor space between seats. Patrick smiles without speaking while Onncie gently pats Fanny's shaking hand. The horses snort into the city heat and step out across the cobblestones.

"I am 23 years old, beginning a fresh new life. My childhood home now belongs to another. Only my love for the Buchanans and my memories remain from the past. This adventure can bring me nothing worse than what I have endured these past years. So be it." Fanny's silent words are meant for none but herself. She closes her eyes and listens to the clop, clop of horse hooves taking her northward to Westminster in the Republic of Vermont.

Chapter 15
The Allen Era
1783 – 1790

"Master Stephen, your wife, Merab, is a delightful young woman. Why did you not tell us of your marriage?" Margaret raises a spoonful of steaming, sweetened porridge to her mouth in anticipation of his answer.

You jilted me for another," laughs Stephen. "A man can wait just so long."

"Marriage has not changed your flirting habits, sir." Margaret teases in return.

Margaret, Patrick, and Fanny are enjoying breakfast following last night's arrival in Westminster. Stephen Bradley had graciously offered his hospitality upon learning of their move to Vermont. Almost, but not all of Crean's Westminster holdings had been confiscated during the war and had been sold to highest bidders. Bradley had managed to purchase two parcels, neither of which held the homestead.

"Little Stephen is so adorable, and almost 18 months old. How could you have kept such a secret from us?" adds Fanny.

Patrick remains silent on such domesticity. His experiences bring nothing to the conversation and he is not overly fond of young children. Instead he rhythmically spoons his porridge into his mouth.

Stephen answers blandly, "Such meager messages were difficult during the war and since then I've gained more business than I can manage on any given day. Personal issues seem to fall amongst the sheaves of papers on my desk. Now that you're back in Westminster you'll have great chance to get acquainted. Merab is as delighted as I to have you stay with us. Even with little Stephen running about there is more room than we can occupy." Turning to include Patrick into the conversation, he adds, "Still, can you believe, she wants to add another wing to the south end."

Patrick smiles and offers no comment.

Fanny daintily wipes her lips, noticing the finely turned linen. "Merab is doing well by Stephen," she thinks silently. Aloud, she cleverly moves the conversation along, "Today, I think I'll stroll the avenue. Mama and Master Wall will be busy with you on business, I gather."

"You are quite generous to call our little street an 'avenue,' my dear," chuckles Stephen. "But you will notice the new merchants along the way. You no longer have to drive to Brattleboro for supplies. We now have our very own mercantile establishment. Not up to your standards, I'm sure, but quite sufficient for us up here in the wilderness." Stephen laughs to assure Fanny he's still teasing and then turns to Patrick. "Shall we say 11 o'clock, then? I shall have the papers arranged by then for your perusal."

Patrick looks to Margaret, sees her slight nod and responds, "Agreed."

The morning meal finished, each rises to go their own way until the midday repast which will be meager in this heat and humidity along the Connecticut River valley. Fanny gathers her bonnet and parasol before beginning her determined stroll. She picks up her sketch pad as an afterthought.

Fanny moves past the courthouse as she continues her walk for a second turn around the village. Her mind focuses on her childhood when life seemed so simple and she knew the meaning of contentedness. She does not speak to those few persons she passes for she quite literally does not see them, so intent is she upon her memories. The little beads of perspiration forming at the edge of her bonnet go untended; her silk stocking cling damply to her thighs. Fanny remains deep in her reverie as she stops before her beloved homestead. She turns to stare at the familiar meadow stretching toward the river. She dares to trespass and at last sinks into the deep grasses and wildflowers halfway down the gentle slope. Only then does she return from her daze. Her eyes search her surroundings and note the dry, crisping edges on leaves starved for water in the searing August heat, the flower petals so much paler than she remembered. Fanny unfolds her sketch pad and halts the forming tears by putting charcoal point to paper, intricately forming on the page what she sees close before her. Thus she sits and works unmindful of the bothersome gnats and the rivulets of sweat that attract them, 'til the sun peaks in the cloudless sky.

Merab has offered luncheon on the lawn under the ancient, spreading maple tree and instructed cook's helper to keep the large, paper fan rigged to a limb moving at a steady but slow pace. Thus the heat is bearable.

Margaret takes a long, deep breath before delivering the information she knows will upset Fanny. She looks across the table at her daughter holding the Bradley's little boy who contentedly licks cream from his fingers while Fanny tries to feed him a succulent raspberry. Why Stephen burdened his son with such a bizarre title for a middle name proves a puzzlement, ponders Margaret silently in a vain attempt to put off the necessary. She raises her goblet to her lips and lets the cool spring water ooze over her tongue. Another deep breath and she begins, "Fanny, we've gained some interesting information this morning." She nods toward Stephen Bradley as she continues. "As you know, many of Papa's holdings have been taken but much still remains, enough to keep us well if we remain in Vermont. The prime parcels are gone. What's left is mainly farming land."

Fanny looks up from Czar's antics, knowing instinctively there is a harsher truth coming. She lifts the little boy to the ground and relinquishes custody to the cook's assistant. She folds her hands onto her rumpled linen skirt, forcing them to relax. She has learned this neutral gesture over the past year and is somewhat comforted to know her body will not betray her inner turmoil. The hint of a smile touches her lips. Fanny appears the perfect portrait of a gracious, composed young woman.

This gesticulation is not wasted on Margaret as she continues. "There are no lawful monies included in Papa's estate, just land. Taxes are due on most of it. This will require withdrawals from funds gained in the New York sales." Margaret pauses for another soothing drink of water. Fanny does not move.

Stephen interrupts to ease Margarete's burden. "Fanny, Crean's last written instructions to me were to divide his holding three ways: one-third to your mother, one-third to you, the remaining third to his daughter in Ireland."

Fanny's right thumb twitches spasmodically. Nothing else betrays her surprise.

Margaret continues, "You've known all along Crean left his daughter in the old country. We seldom spoke of her because it pained him so. Papa felt he'd failed her terribly. Besides, you'd come to fill his life with such joy."

"What is her name?" Fanny's posture is motionless, nothing changes except her lips as they enunciate the question.

"Elizabeth Martha." Margaret reaches out to touch Fanny's bare arm.

"Crean believed her to be married. His last correspondence to her never received a response and that was years ago." Stephen speaks in a professional manner hoping to keep the situation from deteriorating. "Now that a claim will be put to his holdings, all heirs must be duly notified. Due diligence must be made to find Elizabeth. I will file the papers in the Courthouse this week and then begin an earnest search for the woman." Stephen reaches to straighten the collar of his linen shirt which is getting damper by the moment. "It might take years."

"What if you never find her?" Fanny's eyes turn toward Stephen, her right eyebrow rising to emphasize the question.

"We have five years to locate her. If, in that period she cannot be found, the estate will be divided among the remaining two heirs. As I'm sure you're aware, Fanny, your portion will be assigned to John Buchanan."

"I think not!" Fanny bolts to her feet and faces Stephen Bradley, her back turned to Margaret. "That man will get not one bloody shilling from me!"

"Should Master Buchanan be proclaimed among the war dead, Patrick will become executor of your share. I speak only the law, Fanny."

Fanny turns abruptly, stomping a few steps from the table before she turns. "And, if I marry again before the inheritance is distributed, what then?"

† † †

Leaves on the mountainside west of town reflect the early October sun in brilliant colors from crimson to amber. Breezes rising briskly from the river valley pull the early faders from their stems and toss them about in primal autumn dance. John Norton, the local innkeeper is busy preparing rooms and tavern for the Assembly about to gather at the courthouse.

Merab and Cook have enlisted Fanny and Onncie's help in preparing the tarts, breads, sweetmeats, and wines for the upcoming parties. Stephen loves to entertain and during the next few weeks the house will be filled with delegates from across Vermont. Hosting evening parties allows Stephen a certain control over the direction issues flow. At the very least, he will be privy to early trends toward final decisions.

All of Westminster is astir. Delegates will begin arriving the very next day, gathering lodging as they can find it, at the inn and in nearby homes.

Stephen's excitement radiates from his face as he glances around the supper table. He lifts his wine goblet, almost rising from his chair. "To the Assembly, may we conduct ourselves and our business with honor and integrity."

Margaret and Patrick respond enthusiastically with, "hear, hear!" Merab smiles and takes a sip of fruity wine brewed in their cellar last year. Fanny raises her goblet but neither sips nor comments.

"It's so nice to have you tonight, Margaret, Patrick." Merab plays the consummate hostess. "We've missed having you here since you've moved to the farm. I know Fanny finds your absence disheartening, but we keep her too busy to overly fret." She turns to Fanny with a conspiratorial smile before continuing. "Stephen, I heard today at the store that the governor has insisted Ethan Allen participate. Is this true?"

"True enough and the Council urged him to accept the appointment. He's still smarting under the sting of his near impeachment. One has to acknowledge Allen's integrity in refusing to take the oath. If he does not believe in an omnipotent God, how can he possibly swear by one? The governor has promised he can participate without having to swear the oath."

Fanny's interest is piqued. "If he does not believe in God, what does he believe in—himself, I gather."

Stephen laughs. "Well, yes, Ethan certainly believes in himself, far more than most men. But he is not without religion. He proclaims himself a deist, believing that nature is what constructs and rules the universe. And, he's willing to debate that issue far beyond anyone's endurance."

"Sounds like a pompous ass to me," mutters Fanny staring at her half empty plate.

Merab titters softly as Margaret admonishes her daughter's obscenity then composes herself. "Well, Fanny, you shall meet him soon enough. He's on Stephen's guest list for the night of opening session. I suspect you'll find him quite dashing."

"I suspect I'll find him quite the dolt," snaps Fanny. "From Papa's descriptions, he's sure to be crude and overbearing!"

"Unless your manners improve, missy, he'll find you the crude and overbearing one!" Margaret's vexation brings closure to the topic.

Fanny begs her hostess' pardon and rises from the table. "I'm feeling slightly faint and shall retire for the evening." Fanny moves through the doorway, starts up the stairs, and thinks better of it. She slips through the kitchen and out into the dooryard. The crisp, evening air grabs at her flesh; Fanny regrets she did not stop for her shawl. Aiming to cool her frustration, she strides across the dried lawn, crunching the leaves beneath her feet. Reaching the roadway, she turns south toward her meadow.

Fanny stares out the lightly frosted bedroom window, barely seeing the delegates arrive below, alone or in groups of two or three. Her thoughts tumble about unable to settle on a single focus. She feels her heart throbbing—in her chest, in her neck, her temple, even her finger tips. Molars clench together, her hands fidget with the lace on her silk bodice. She'd chosen the burgundy, a color as deep as the fall asters she cherished. A glance at the looking glass had proven Merab's statement that the richness of the hue surely heightened the color of her cheeks. The neckline was cut quite low; fashionable in New York, Merab had commented then adding that those in Vermont would surely take notice of Fanny's modishness.

That comment had worried Fanny a little, wondering whether she might tone down her wardrobe rather than alienate possible new friends. However, her concern was fleeting and she'd opted for the power her beauty and panache would give her when she must first encounter that awful scoundrel, Ethan Allen. Her father's enemy was her enemy. She owed Crean that much.

A light tap on the door brings Fanny from her reverie and she moves across the room unaware of the lilting swish of the elegant silk. She steels herself for the message the maid brings. "Mistress Bradley awaits your presence." The young woman drops a quick curtsy and trots down the hall to the back stairs.

"Papa, we'll fell that arrogant ass!" Fanny arches her neck a bare inch then straightens her shoulders, fingers teasing her bodice neckline a scoche lower. She begins her slow, graceful walk down the richly polished hallway.

Pausing on the first step of the grand staircase she places her fingers on the shiny, curved rail, brings a slight but aloof smile to her lips and begins her descent to the party already at noticeable decibels below. Inside this perfect portrait, Fanny's nerves quiver in anticipation of her dreaded confrontation.

Fanny is just three steps from the bottom before she slowly turns her head to study the gathered guests. Most of the people she does not know by sight but perhaps by reputation. How to connect the two? "Will I recognize him?" she wonders. A short, round, bewigged man smiles openly at her, signs of his sweat heightening the flush in his face. Knowing that Allen is tall and most likely quite physically fit, Fanny nods ever so slightly and quickly lets her gaze move past the admirer. The room is filled with men talking and gesturing intently. Men crowd the doorways and into the rooms beyond. The smell of ale and rum mix with the body odors created of too many spirited men in too small a space—more like a tavern than Uncle Stephen's fine home. Fanny resists a momentary urge to flee and then takes the final step in the closest group of several men.

Almost as one, the men pause briefly in their conversation, nod absently at Fanny and return to their heated debate. Fanny, unused to having her beauty so ignored, feels the beginnings of a snit curl within her taut ribcage. Quickly she changes her tactics. "Do excuse me," she murmurs sweetly as she places her fingertips gently on the cuff of the nearest delegate and shuffles her voluminous skirts sideways to squeeze through the group. She looks directly into the eyes of each as she passes through. "oh, don't let me interrupt…Excuse me…thank you, gentlemen." Her perfume lingers, leaving a sensory memory for the beguiled men as she moves into the next cluster of guests.

Fanny moves deliberately but charmingly from group to group. Here she stops to make an astute comment on a bit of conversation she has overheard. In another, she remarks appreciatively on the dedication of those gathered. To still another, Fanny offers to have their goblets refilled. Nowhere does she linger long enough to require introductions yet by the time she has moved on to the next room every man present knows she is Mistress Fanny Buchanan, treasured guest of Stephen Bradley, and heiress to notorious Yorker Crean Brush's contested estate.

Having circulated through all four public rooms, Fanny approaches the bountiful sideboard and pours herself a goblet of red wine. She lifts the vessel to her nose and sniffs the fruity aroma, satisfied, she sips at the refreshment before turning to survey the room. The prey has been elusive.

Discouraged, Fanny feels the need for a jolt of brisk night air and makes her way smiling but silent to the side door. Finding the door ajar, she slips unnoticed into the darkness. The leaf covered lawn is lit here and there through the windows. Shadows far outnumber illuminations and Fanny moves slowly toward a parlor window. From this location she can watch the delegates without having to extend herself. The cauldron of conversation is discernable only as chaotic din out here on the lawn. Fanny amuses herself trying to guess at what's being said by interpreting gestures and expressions. At the same time, she remains attentive to her search. So intent is she that her shivers go unnoticed.

"For such an accomplished *eminence grise*, you have certainly chosen a strange place to observe our political strategists."

The deep, taunting voice came from the blackest darkness behind her. Fanny whirls catching her skirt on the shrubbery, wine sloshing over the rim of her cup, just missing her silks as it splashed to the dew dampened earth. "Damnation!" The curse bursts from her lips even as she turns.

A tall hulk of a being partially emerges from the shadows. "Quite spirited too, I see."

"You startled me, sir! Not the best of manners on your part either I must say." Fanny rakes a deep breath to steady her shivering now turned to vigorous shaking. "Show yourself, sir, or be off from pestering me."

"Pester? I do not intend to pester but to come meet the loveliest vision yet seen in our Vermont republic." As he speaks, the figure moves into the paler shadows next to Fanny. His smile is full and the sparkle in his eyes defies the semi-darkness. He bows slightly never taking his eyes from Fanny's face.

Fanny tilts her face upward. This apparition, this man stands two full heads taller than she. Fanny instinctively steps backward to ease the immediate strain on her neck and perhaps to protect herself. The countenance she studies in the dimness is pleasing but not overly handsome. Creases around his mouth define good humor, intensity, and a few decades of living. Her gaze wanders to his linens and waistcoat. A sensible man, not taken to finery, she decides. Fingers holding easily to his lapel display no jewelry. His hands are quite large, squarish, showing signs of physical labor.

"Your tongue will soon wag if you don't stop staring," the smile broadens as he speaks. "You do not seem one whose beauty disguises the lack of thinking power."

"Indeed, sir, your rudeness exceeds your ability to skulk about in the night, preying on the unsuspecting." Fascinated by this masculine creature, Fanny continues the verbal encounter. "Your name, sir? You've not taken the time for introductions."

"My, my, you are one for proper manners, even if you yourself skulk, as you say, outside windows. Do forgive me my improprieties. I shall forgive you yours."

Not to be distracted, Fanny responds in a syrupy tone, "How kind you are, sir, but still you remain nameless."

The figure bends slightly at the waist, makes a full, wide sweep with his left hand, "General Ethan Allen at your service, ma'am."

"Damnation!" Fanny's response is more of a squeak than a shout pronounced as she turns and runs toward the door.

"Your vocabulary appears somewhat limited," Ethan speaks to her back as Fanny disappears through the doorway.

Chapter 16

Stephen returns from the Assembly both exhilarated and exhausted. Debates have been lively with some delegates being overly fond of their own rhetoric. All in all, the process is moving well.

At dinner Stephen regales Merab and Fanny with stories of the day's arguments. "Our Ethan's passion for the cause deafens him to others' ideas. Chittenden had twice to demand him 'sit down.' If he weren't such a genius…and, of course our most stalwart patriot, he'd probably have been tarred and feathered long ago."

"Sticky feathers are no stranger to Ethan," laughs Merab. "But it's usually him and his Greens that do the tarring. Remember that Tory over near Bennington…"

"Is there no one to discuss other than the arrogant general himself?" blurts Fanny who heretofore has contributed nothing to the conversation.

"Your face reddens, my dear," Merab smiles. "Do you really find Ethan that repugnant? He can be most charming."

"Ah, charming. Speaking of charming, you must have used your wiles quite satisfactorily on our good general." Stephen reaches into his vest pocket as he speaks. "He sends a message to you."

"I need no message from him!" Fanny pushes aside the offered paper watching as Stephen places it on the linen halfway between the two of them.

"Ethan thought you might be resistant so he sent a verbal message as well." Stephen, smiling broadly, pauses waiting for Fanny's response.

Fanny stares fixedly at Stephen, fork halfway to her mouth. Seconds pass without a single movement around the table. Finally, Fanny nods almost imperceptibly.

"Ethan will come to call tomorrow after the assembly adjourns for the evening. He wishes to discuss with you the contents of his missive." Stephen, with great difficulty, stifles a laugh.

"Oh, damnation!" Fanny shoves her chair backward, slams her napkin to the table and stands defiantly. She stalks past Stephen, stops, turns to pick up the folded paper on the table, then strides from the room.

Merab rolls her eyes ceilingward, "Our little Fanny is struggling with a demon."

"That demon will win. Mind you, Ethan is a persistent one." Stephen seals his prophecy with a large gulp from his goblet.

Upstairs in her room, Fanny looks out the window, staring into the clear, crisp night. She focuses on the brightest star, and whispers aloud, "Oh, Papa. Why isn't life neat and consistent like petals around their pistil?" A sob escapes, caught up in her breath. "Oh rot it's more like dandelion fluff in a chaotic wind, carrying you about to who knows where." Brushing absently at the damp rivulets on her cheeks, Fanny slowly moves across the room and drops heavily onto her bed. She hitches herself up to a semi-sitting position and pulls her tattered doll close to her neck. Several minutes pass before she leans to the candle stand and draws the glowing taper closer. Deliberately, she breaks the seal on Ethan's note.

Where do you stand on the status of God?

Fanny laughs out loud, hugging Maggy to her chest. "God?" He asks about God?" she giggles to her doll. "What a strange creature he is!"

The following day drags by like a humid hot August afternoon. Dusk cannot arrive quickly enough. Fanny busies herself through the morning helping Mareb. In the afternoon, she strolls through the town ostensibly to visit the general emporium, unwilling to admit even to herself she is hoping for a glance of Ethan. As the late October sun crests Hickory Ridge, Fanny studies the dresses in her wardrobe. "mmmm, the red's too fancy" Fanny speaks softly to Maggy lying on the bed, button eyes staring at her mistress. "Perhaps the dark blue is more aloof, 'twill put a distance between us—a good thing, Maggy." Fanny continues pulling out her skirts, fingering the fabric, pondering. Finally, she selects a gown of soft, fine, umber wool. She holds the dress to her and swirls in circles to the bed. "What do you think, Maggy? Mmmm?

Sedate but not prudish. Understated but definitely elegant. D'you agree Maggy dearest?" Maggy remains unblinkingly loyal to all decisions.

During dinner, Stephen and Ethan talk animatedly about the day's politics. Merab joins in occasionally with a question. Fanny toys silently with the food on her plate periodically putting a morsel into her mouth. She is ignorant of what she's eating though she had helped prepare the sumptuous fare. She hears almost nothing of the conversation so intent is she on the turmoil rumbling inside her soul. Fanny feels Merab's gentle touch on her arm and hears Stephen saying to Ethan, "The fire is blazing nicely in the library. Why don't you and Fanny take your brandy in there. I have much work to do before tomorrow's session and Merab feels called to supervise in the kitchen." Stephen and Merab, both smiling, stand and leave by separate doors.

"This seems well plotted, does it not?" asks Ethan and offers his arm to Fanny.

Settled into chairs, both stare fixedly in the orange and red flickers above the logs. Without preamble, Ethan speaks, "What is your answer? I await your thoughts."

"About God, you mean?" replies Fanny turning to look at her adversary. "Why do you ask about God?"

"Fanny…may I call you Fanny, Mistress Buchanan?" Ethan continues after a brief nod from Fanny. "Fanny, I am 45 years on this earth. I've been a soldier, exiled and imprisoned across the ocean for three years. I've fought the Yorkers—never mortally harmed a one of them, mind you," he adds at Fanny's flinch. "I helped found this magnificent Republic of Vermont and was almost ostracized for my stance on God." Ethan pauses for a long sip of brandy. He exhales a sigh and continues, "Yet it is my daughter who caused me pause on this God thing."

"Your daughter?"

"Yes, Lorraine; she died a few months back, of the consumption. She was young, perhaps your age. Ethan looks directly into Fanny's eyes. "Just 20."

"Close." Fanny drops her eyes to her brandy but decides against a swallow.

"It's been a year of great loss for me, Fanny. First, my wife Mary died—also of consumption. She was a pious woman, mighty pious. Enough to drive a man to drink." As if in remembrance of Mary's harshness, Ethan takes another deep swig of liquor. "I've never been one to hover by my own hearthside, but after Mary died, I took off up north to the wilderness where Ira and I are buying up land."

"Ira?" Fanny looks at Ethan.

"Sorry, I forget you're from the other side of the mountains—politically, I mean." Ethan smiles and continues. "My brother, at least he's one of them. Anyway, I'm up on the Onion River and I get word that Lorraine is dying. I feel obliged to return quickly to Sunderland." He stops as Fanny's eyebrows form two perfect arches above her widened eyes. "I do love my children, truly, but it was to Mary that Lorraine was attached. When I got there, she was almost gone; could hardly speak. She motioned me to pull my chair close and to bend so I could hear. 'Whose faith shall I embrace, Papa? Yours as atheist or that of mother, a good faithful Christian?' I did not want to answer her, Fanny. Mary and I were so different in our ideas. But my daughter was dying and this was a question of great importance to her. I paced beside her bed torn between my understanding of God's creation and Lorraine's need for comfort. I am not an atheist, Fanny. I believe as the deists, but Mary could not see the difference."

"What did you tell Lorraine?" Fanny cannot keep from reaching out to touch Ethan's sleeve.

"'That of your mother,' was all I could manage." Ethan sits very still for what seems minutes. Neither says anything, each staring into the fire. At last, Ethan turns his gaze toward Fanny and asks, "Now, Mistress Fanny, what is your stance on God?"

No impertinence rises in Fanny, no sharp and witty retort. Compassion fills her chest and she cautiously responds. "God was not a common topic in our household. Oh, we went to church as was only proper. Mother Margaret was raised devoutly and Papa had a hint of Rome in his heart, I think. But, somehow the intellect of it was never part of our conversations."

"So, what have you deduced?" Ethan takes another long drink keeping his eyes on Fanny's face.

"Goodness is the important ingredient, I think, no matter what stance you take—Greek, Roman, Calvin. Goodness and caring. Oh, I don't abide with all this sin, hell, and damnation doctrine that sets the preachers on fire in their high and mighty pulpits. They're just trying to scare you into righteousness—and that just won't work with me." Fanny looks straight at Ethan. "I don't scare easily."

"And here I thought you a shivery, little violet," laughs Ethan.

"Violets are quite brave and resilient, sir." A hint of flirtatiousness enters Fanny's voice. "After all they can withstand a late spring frost and have you seen how quickly they rebound if you accidentally step on one?"

"I shall be more careful and observant in the future." Ethan reaches out and takes Fanny's small hand in his. She does not withdraw but turns her eyes to study the embers of the dying fire.

"Perhaps it is time for me to go. May I call again tomorrow evening?" Ethan releases Fanny's hand and stands facing her.

"You must ask Stephen that question, sir." Fanny laughs softly. "It is their welcome you need to court."

"I shall do just that. And, now, I shall show myself the door. Good evening, Mistress Fanny. A good evening, indeed."

The crisp, night air has brought a dampness to the fallen leaves and the sound under their slowly strolling feet is muffled. Fanny pulls her cloak more tightly about her shoulders as a swish of wind catches her bonnet brim. Ethan talks softly, an effort that takes much control for this man who likes nothing better than to hold forth in oratory tones. He has left the tavern in the midst of the evening's political pontificating to stroll with Fanny. They have known each other but four days, yet yearning for these late evening together stalks their daylight hours.

Fanny smiles to herself, only half listening to Ethan's words, remembering how foolishly she'd answered Merab's questions that morning. Preparing apples for drying in the kitchen, Merab had asked, "Will Patrick be buying up that acreage on the Woodell farm?" Fanny had answered, "Oh, I think the brown woolen will do just fine." Merab had stared at her, knife in hand, stopped in its peeling. Then they had both broken into giggles that brought tears. "My, you are a distracted waif," Merab had finally managed.

Fanny's toe catches a root and she grabs at Ethan's arm to steady herself. He stops his walking but not his talking and Fanny is brought back into his conversation. "I'm oldest of the eight," he continues. Ethan looks down at Fanny's upturned face, hesitates a moment before asking, "The way is strewn with obstacles, may I take your arm?" Fanny leans into his side in response. Ethan takes her arm gently squeezing it to his waist. "She's such a wee one but very strong it seems," he thinks to himself as they begin strolling again.

Picking up his familial oratory where he left off, Ethan speaks, "Six boys and two girls. Only, Lydia, may she rest in peace, had any decorum. I've always said, 'only two women were delivered of seven devils, Mary Magdalene and my mother.'"

Fanny quickly interjects, "This is my favorite spot, down in the meadow. This was our homestead you know." She looks toward his face wondering if, in the darkness, he can sense her impishness. "C'mon, let's sneak down to the river. Don't let your big feet make too much noise." She darts to the side of the familiar house, pulling Ethan behind her.

Once down to the last rise in the meadow, Fanny finds herself slightly embarrassed at her boldness and quite at loss for words. Ethan, sensing the tension, removes his own mantle and spreads it with a gallant sweep onto the ground. Without speaking, Fanny sits quickly, surprised at the warmth she feels from his garment, even through her own clothes. Ethan drops beside her and they sit quietly neither touching nor speaking. Feeling a need to lighten the silence, Fanny offers, "Are all the rest of your siblings still living?"

As though he'd never broken the rhythm of his story, Ethan continues the iteration. "Only Levi, Lucy, an Ira remain. Ira's the youngest and the brains, well except for me," he chuckles. His tone harshens, "Currently, we're not associating with Levi. He's a thorn we cannot tolerate."

Fanny's attention, having just begun to wander again, is piqued. "What has Levi done that so angers you?"

"He's a traitor to all the Allens stand for!" Ethan spits the words unable to keep the animosity from his voice.

Fanny, irresistibly, draws close to his body, now warm from his volatile passion. The intensity of his anger is like a magnet. She remains silent, knowing the rest of the tale will unfold.

"Ever an opportunist, Levi, is earning his fortune off the Tories! Damn his soul, if he has one. He and that wife of his, Nancy; they're down in the Carolina swamps, selling supplies to the enemy.

Fanny feels the heat of her own ire rising from her stomach as she moves away from Ethan. "Don't forget for one moment, General Allen, that like my father whom you so hate, I am a Loyalist. That means, as I'm sure your logic extends that I am your enemy as well. While speaking, Fanny has risen and is looking down though only slightly, in her companion's puzzled face. She turns to leave, but Ethan grabs her wrist. He is incredibly strong and her efforts to free herself are meek and ineffective.

"Ethan pulls her back beside him. "Your spirit excites me, Mistress Loyalist." He reaches around Fanny, drawing her close and kisses her full on the mouth.

Fanny twists, trying to resist. Another intense, previously unknown passion invades her body and she folds into Ethan's embrace. He holds her tightly, his breath coming hard. In order to curb his own prurience, Ethan speaks.

"Ira and I fixed his bursting breeches, however. Ira, when he was secretary of the Council of Safety, passed a ruling against the enemies of America—Loyalists, in deference to your sensitivities, my dear." He bends to kiss her again. Caught in the intellect of what Ethan was telling Fanny stiffens slightly, "Go on, General. I've become interested in your politics."

"Following right up on Ira's pronouncement I raised a complaint against brother Levi." Ethan's pride in his own acumen was evident. "Ten thousand of Levi's precious acres up near Burlington were legally confiscated and sold."

"Let me understand this quite clearly sir." Fanny has pulled away from Ethan so she can look him in the face. "Your, no, I mean Ira's law, allowed this upstart of a republic to confiscate land from those who legally purchased and worked it?"

"Tis only fair. We had to fund the militia some way." Retorts Ethan rising to his feet. He is hopeful his full stature will stem the direction this revelation seems to be taking.

"Fair, my bonnet! That same piece of legislation robbed me of my inheritance. How many acres do you think Papa lost to your pseudo legal scarfing?' Fanny jerks her skirts above her ankles and stomps up the hill. Midway, she turns and screams shrilly, "I've had enough of you Allens. What did Papa ever do to your precious cause?"

Staring after her, Ethan shouts back. "He did ill to liberty and to the king, as I hear it told."

Chapter 17

Fanny sits near the kitchen window watching the first real snow of the season decorate the maple branches. Thin white birches sway as the November wind whips up from the river. She breathes in the steam from the chamomile tea Merab has prescribed for her erratic moods. Fanny's slim fingers drum impatiently around the mug giving evidence of the herb's failure. She reaches with her right hand, letting her forefinger etch tiny letters in the frost at the corner of the pane. "papa," she writes then obliterates with her fingertip. She shivers, pulls her shawl more closely about her and takes another sip of the steaming brew.

Neither Stephen nor Merab have dared ask what is foremost in their minds. Ethan had been noticeable absent from their home during the final days of Assembly and Fanny abruptly leaves the room at any mention of his name. The Assembly has long since adjourned, dispersing delegates in all directions. Ethan's departing words to Stephen at the final session had not been comforting. "You board a tempest in your home, friend. Do not get caught in Fury's gale for there lies the hell of which sermons are born."

Fanny's mind has been a torment; logic raging against emotion, her loyalty to Crean shoving hard against this strange sensation that pervades her body when she thinks of Ethan. Margaret and Patrick's frustration in making little headway with the estate simply fuels Fanny's anger. Lack of any communication from Ethan brings sighs of depression and withdrawal from the Bradley family hubbub around her. What little energy Fanny can muster allows her to follow Merab about, mutely obeying household instructions without really being present to the task.

Merab's patience thins. Seeing Fanny huddled by the window she pulls up a stool beside her. "My dear, you do yourself little good moping about like this. You must accept these changes whether they be in the law of the land or in your personal circumstances. The war is over and you'll not be going back to

100

the glories of society you once enjoyed. I don't know what words you and Ethan had. I don't care. You're here, here in Westminster now and your life will be what you make of it. I'll help you where I can, but you must choose your own direction."

Fanny turns to look at her friend. She stares blindly into Merab's eyes as if she's heard nothing. Neither moves for what seems an eternity. A tear releases from Fanny's eye, then another and another. Without warning, sobs burst from her throat and she gasps to gain her breath. Merab reaches and pulls Fanny to her, comforting her with strokes and sounds more like kitten purrs than words. Minutes pass before Fanny can calm herself.

"I don't know what to do." Fanny hiccups before she can continue. "This country, as it calls itself, has no resemblance to anything I've known. I know so few people here. Mother Margaret focuses her time around Patrick and land claims, she no time for me."

"Tut, shhh" interjects Merab. "Your mother adores you and Patrick truly thinks of your wellbeing. So, let's take a stab at fixing what's fixable. We'll plan a special tea in your honor. We'll find an exceptional reason for the event."

"When there's nothing special about me, we can't just invent a reason."

"And, why not!" Merab stands and begins to pace. "You've been here too long for a welcome."

Beginning to be drawn into Merab's enthusiasm, Fanny offers shyly, "Would they be interested in my paintings?"

"A perfect idea. Of course. We'll set them up around the library an offer tea in the parlor." Before Fanny can lose interest, Merab continues, "Let's go look at what you have. I don't believe I've seen them all." She takes Fanny by the hand and gently guides her toward the stairs.

The tea had been a great success. Fourteen ladies had accepted, arrived in their finery and honestly admired Fanny's talent with charcoal and paint brush. Fanny's ability to produce the Latin names for her floral subjects impressed most and caused but a few women to think her haughty. Merab's tea board was bountiful, as always, leaving no opportunity for snide complaint. Reciprocal invitations were received and Fanny dutifully accepted. Fanny's mood had heartily improved and the Bradley household fell back into its peaceful routine.

Fanny steps carefully over the ice on the Bradley's front steps. Laden with purchases from the dry goods store, Fanny thinks about the gifts she'll make for the Bradleys, her mother, Patrick, Onncie, and even the servants. Merab has said they wouldn't practice the English custom of boxing but would host a Christmas feast. "I've a lot to accomplish in the next two weeks." Fanny thinks to herself.

Her hands full, Fanny is unable to manage the latch and thumps on the door with her elbow. After a moment the door opens and Fanny sidles into the welcome warmth. Even though the walk took only minutes, her fingers and toes feel quite frozen. She smiles a thank you at Cook and rushes up the stairs to hide her bounty. Fanny turns at the top and shouts back, "Tell Mistress Bradley, I'm quite ready for tea. I'll be down shortly."

Fanny dumps her parcels on the bed and laughs at her old doll, Maggy. "you could use a new dress as well, my dearest." She pics up the doll and cuddles her. "Where would I be without you? Will they think me odd if I make a gift for you too?" She lays the doll back on the pillow, straightening her faded apron. "What will they know, eh."

Fanny removes her bonnet, throws her cloak on the chair for the maid to hang later. She straightens her curls and almost skips out of the room in anticipation of a sumptuous tea.

Merab, having heard Fanny on the stairs is pouring tea when the young woman enters the parlor. Vapor curls from the porcelain cup as Fanny takes the offering and seats herself next to Merab. She selects a small, currant scone from under the linen and relaxes back into the comfortably upholstered chair. Merab raises her own cup to her lips and sips carefully to avoid scalding her tongue. A quiet peace sits between the two.

Merab pulls a letter from her apron pocket and proffers it to Fanny. She says nothing but eyes Fanny steadily.

102

"For me? Wasn't it just last week I had a letter from Mother Buchanan? Who else would write?" Fanny holds the sealed parchment closer to the taper for a better view. Her face pales as she sees the waxen seal embossed with EA. As suddenly as she paled, the color flushes back to her cheeks, her body pulsing with the intensity of the heat. She places the letter in her lap and stares at it.

"Would you like me to leave while you read it?" Merab's voice interrupts Fanny's panic.

"No. No, stay please." Fanny's eyes continue to focus on the missive. She lifts her cup to her lips but does not drink. Perhaps, if she keeps her hands thus, she won't have to open the letter. After a moment, Fanny takes a small swallow, then another; places her cup on its elaborate saucer, and finishes the scone. Carefully, she places the china on the tea tray and sits back. Unable to stem the tremor in her hands she picks at the seal and finally opens the single page. She reads the bold and curling script aloud to Merab.

My dear Mistress Loyalist,

Brother Levi and wife have returned to the fold, acknowledging the error of their ways (more or less, perhaps mostly less). Ira and I have made amends as loving families are dutifully bound to do. All is forgiven and we move forward in our mutual pursuits. Can you find your way to the same amnesty?

I shall journey from Sunderland to Westminster on the 20th of this month. Will you be so kind as to receive me that we might discuss our differences and our compatibilities?

> *Ever hopefully yours,*
> *(Gen'l) Ethan Allen, Patriot*

Fanny did not read the post script to Merab: *the memory of your kiss lingers long on my lips.*

Fanny sucks the droplet of blood from her thumb. Her fingertips bear the brunt of her distraction as she stitches the new apron for Cook. Indeed, Fanny had hoped the number of gifts waiting to be assembled would keep her mind and heart occupied.

Yet fantasies of Ethan lure her mind in one direction only. What little light manages to penetrate the frosted panes casts shadows on Fanny's handwork and she moves the candle closer. She pulls her fine shawl tighter and manages to stitch the fringe into the apron hem. "Damnation!" she mutters in her frustration. "I'll never get finished before he gets here."

Throwing her sewing onto the bed, Fanny rises and paces window to door and back, then to the bed. She grabs Maggy to her chests and continues her frantic pacing. "Maggy, m'love, what shall I do? We're so different he and I. Perhaps I can grow to understand his politics. His perspective on religion is of no matter me, but his arrogance is unbearable.

The doll's gaze remains unblinking, a seeming comfort to Fanny. "He's a military general to his very core, a characteristic he expects all to honor. He's no patience for the weak kneed." Fanny stops as a giggle escapes her lips. "Then, of course, neither do I." Fanny resumes her pacing. "There's something I can't define. Logic I can follow but this is a feeling inside me, deep down. The heat of it, when he's near me, dissolves my rational abilities." Fanny stops pacing and flops onto the bed still holding her doll close. A heavy sigh emerges from somewhere within her soul.

Snow falls steadily, accumulating rapidly on the ground and trees. Fanny pulls gowns from her wardrobe, holding each to her body before tossing them in a heap on the bed. The red velvet catches her interest and she pirouettes before her mirror. "Mmmm, too bold!" She tosses the dress on top of the pile. The brown wool: "too sedate." Fanny paces, eyeing the mounded gowns, yanking one from near the bottom. "I wore this last time." Back into the heap it goes. Fanny throws herself, distraught, onto the bed. "This is ridiculous. Why I'm in such a dither I can't imagine. Surely I can gather my wits for such a simple task." She stares at the rumpled mess, rises and removes the red velvet. "This will have to do. If he thinks me brazen, so be it."

Still holding the gown, Fanny walks to the window and studies the small white flakes, so thick she can barely see the huge maple. "Small flakes, large snow; large flakes, small snow' the natives say. I do hope he won't get stranded coming through the mountains."

Fanny has already determined she wants to be out of the house when he arrives and since she's not sure of his timing, this appears difficult to arrange. The snow further complicates her coy plan. She'd planned a walk to her favorite meadow so she could come in after Ethan had settled into the parlor. She'd be all red cheeked and winded from her walk, a look she imagined flattering. Besides, her nonchalance at his arrival might prick his arrogance. Too cold for that now. Surely he couldn't arrive until just before supper. Perhaps a last minute dash to the dry goods for some necessary item would suit her strategy. She could linger at the shop watching for his arrival. "Shall I dress now or wait for supper?" she wonders in a whisper. So nervous she can't sit still, Fanny opts for dressing and sewing with Merab until such time as she can exclaim the need for more ribbon, grab her cloak and carry out her plan.

"Calm yourself, Fanny," Merab looks up from her quilting frame. "You're worse than a skitterish fawn. Look here, your thread's in a twist. Get up, walk around, ease your nerves."

Though it's far too soon, Fanny decides to enact her strategy. "Goodness, I'm almost out of this ribbon. I'll just run get some more before Master Glidden closes the shop." Merab smiles and returns to her work.

Fanny wanders the shop, touching the sugar barrel, smelling the exotic cloves just arrived from some import ship in New York. "Perhaps Father Buchanan's vessel brought these," she muses. Mistress Glidden, a runny nosed toddler clinging to her skirt, asks again if Fanny would like some assistance. "Just passing a boring afternoon. Everything is so peaceful and pleasant here." Fanny doubts neither the shopkeeper nor his wife believe her prattle.

Finally, she can no longer put off her return to the house and asks for two meters of the grey grosgrain. She strolls as slowly as the frigid air and swirling snow allows. Too soon, Fanny finds herself at the Bradley' door.

Supper is a strained affair. Stephen and Merab chatter a bit too loudly exchanging glances when Fanny fails to rise to their conversational inquiries. The parlor clock chimes seven times, jarring Fanny beyond her limits of civility. "Please excuse me. I must have caught a chill. Be so kind as to send Cook with a hot brick for my bed."

"Certainly, my dear," answers Merab looking only at the winter squash on her plate. As soon as Fanny has left the room both burst into laughter.

Night brings more snow and little sleep for Fanny. She drifts into a dreamless stupor sometime after the village tower clock strikes two. A gentle tapping at the bedroom door brings her to consciousness and she realizes the snow has stopped and sunlight filters through the frosted window onto her voluminous comforter. "Yes?" she murmurs, running her tongue across a night's accumulation of fuzz on her teeth.

"Mistress wants you downstairs. You're to hurry, she says." Cook shuffles, her house slippers making swishing noises on the waxed floor. Fanny hears the sound recede and climbs, stretching from her toasty bed. The shock of the frigid floor hard against her warm feet completes her waking.

Fanny shortens her toilette routine to a minimum. Glancing in the mirror, she opts to merely tie her hair back with a ribbon rather than brush a full 100 strokes and plait it with a touch of color. Fanny's curiosity at Merab's bidding overcomes her usual attentiveness to perfection. Could there be a note apologizing for his delay? She throws her shawl, cast aside last evening, over her rumpled nightdress and moves through the door. Deciding that Merab must still be in the kitchen, Fanny heads for the back stairs and skips down, hardly grasping the rail.

Cook looks up and nods toward the dining room. "She's in there."

Fanny grabs a plate of hot muffins held out by Cook and shoulders through the unlatched door. "What's the big…"

All are looking at her, even little Czar who has managed a place at table this morning. No one utters a word while she stares at Ethan, sitting next to Stephen, calmly chewing a morsel of breakfast.

"Umm, I, uh, well…"

Merab rises to take the plate before it falls from Fanny's shaking hands. She takes the younger woman's elbow and guides her to the table.

Ethan smiles, "You're seldom without appropriate words, Mistress Loyalist. Good morning. Have I ridden all this way to see you in your nightdress?"

Merab and Stephen wait for a verbal outburst. None comes. Fanny slides into her chair, unfolds the serviette into lap and inhales deeply. Looking around the table, she turns to Merab, "Might I have some porridge, please? I find myself famished this morning."

Having downed the first spoonful, noticing but not enjoying the warmth against the soft tissues of her mouth, Fanny wills calm into her voice. Looking straight at Ethan, she speaks. "Your trip, I trust, was without major incident." The words were not a question but a statement. Her eyes did not waver. Instinctively, Fanny knew that whatever their relationship might become, it would always be a battle of wills. She had just made the decision she was up to the challenge.

✝ ✝ ✝

Fanny only slightly recognizes the clatter and laughter around her. The whole household, servants included, are eating and drinking the Christmas feast. Little Czar, unable to claim his usual attention, crawls under the table tugging at various skirts and leggings to no notice whatsoever. Fanny, lost in reverie of her last couple of days with Ethan, jumps at Czar's unexpected touch. She peers under the linen cloth to see the little boy's impish smile and whispers, "You want to be someplace else too, eh monkey. Come on, let's go into the parlor and I'll tell you a story." Only Merab notices their departure and offers a slight nod in their direction.

Seated in front of the fire, Fanny pulls the lad onto her lap. "What story shall we have, Czar? You've already heard about the baby Jesus enough times, hmm? Let's see here." He snuggles close and waits.

'There was once a young maid and a handsome officer. They can't meet in public because she believes in the king and he believes..."

"No! That story's about Uncle Et'an and you." Czar sits up and looks into Fanny's face. "Ebryone tell th't story. I want diff'ent story." He sticks his thumb between cherubic lips and begins to suck.

"Who's everyone?" Fanny struggles to keep her voice from rising.

Bored with this direction, Czar hops own from Fanny's lap; she grabs his chubby arm. "Monkey, who tells that story?"

With the pure honesty of childhood innocence, Czar looks up, pulls his arm away, and giggles. "Funny story. Mamma laugh. Cook laugh. Ebryone laugh. Papa too."

Fanny watches the flames darting between the logs, lost again in her thoughts of Ethan. "If only he hadn't gone home to his daughters for Christmas," she thinks. "Just three more days; I only have to wait three more days. Given the apparent gossip, we'll have to find new ways to be together." She feels the warmth of his lips on her neck, a memory that brings a flush to her whole being.

Ethan stands by the river, his cloak covered by an extra blanket, his head warm inside the fur hat. Occasionally, he glances up the hill, hoping to see Fanny's brightly painted pung appear on the snow covered road. She's already late and the cold is now an annoyance. He paces to keep his blood pumping heat. At last he hears the rapid jingle of sleigh bells and looks up to see her horse at full gallop, Fanny standing tall at the reins. Ethan moves to rescue her until realizing she's in full control of the beast, simply enjoying the thrill of the ride. He watches as she slows the horse to a trot, turns him around and walks the sweating animal down the hill.

Fanny laughs as she hops off the sled. "I'm so late, I thought you might have given up on me."

"Not wait for the fairest maid in all the land? Never." Ethan bows mockingly. "I'm damn near frozen, woman." He pulls Fanny to him, bends and kisses her eager face. "Best we wipe down this creature before he takes a chill." Ethan removes he blanket from his shoulders and rubs the lather from the horse. Fanny wonders at Ethan's concern whether for the horse or for her honor.Ethan drops the now damp blanket onto the pung and pulls Fanny down beside him. The pungent odor of wet horse surrounds them as they embrace passionately. Fanny's fur bonnet falls from her head as Ethan yanks at the strings. Their rambunctious tussling startles the horse into a quick side step upsetting the pung and tossing the lovers into the snow. Amid laughter and gasps, the two manage to right the sled and quiet the horse. They fall exhausted onto the pung. Ethan, still breathing heavily, reaches up and pulls the pins from Fanny's hair. He caresses her cheek, then bends close, pulling her body tight to his. Her response is so lustful, so wanting, Ethan pulls back. "This is too much for even me, wench."

Fanny holds her breath to gain control. When she can speak it is barely a whisper. "The great general is afraid, eh?" She taunts. "Of a tiny, weak Loyalist, is it?"

"You do bring out the beast in me." He kisses her lightly then pushes her gently to arm's length. "This will not do. There's too much at stake here for you as well as me."

"Since when are you worried about what people think?" Fanny looks fiercely into his eyes, her passion shifting from lust to anger.

"You're living in Stephen's home and we must not bring him dishonor. I carry enough ill repute on my shoulders now— however poorly placed that may be—and you, dear one, court controversy in your very walk and talk. Perhaps it is what I most admire about you. We two are more alike than you might wish to think."

Fanny sighs, snuggling into Ethan's chest, anger gone as quickly as it had risen. Tilting her chin up, she flicks her eyelashes in overstated, mock coquetry. "Whatever shall we do, sir? Whatever shall we do?" The two collapse in laughter. The horse turns his head, offers a snort, and stomps his hoof. It's going to be a long wait.

    January has been exceptionally cold and snowy. Ethan's visits from Sunderland to Westminster have been kept to a minimum by the puckish weather. As discreet as they've tried to be, their liaisons have not gone unnoticed.

    On one occasion, Fanny meets confrontation head on in Master Glidden's shop. Browsing leisurely to while away her boredom, the shopkeeper engages Fanny in lighthearted political postulation.

    "Statehood for Vermont cannot be far in the future, mistress." Master Glidden wraps a package for a customer as he speaks.

    "New York will never let that happen, sir. Much must be settled; all those back taxes due, land disputes still raging. Yorkers have long memories and are quite as stubborn as Vermonters."

    "Oh, surely as you're standing here, Mistress, Vermont will gain statehood. And if you marry General Allen, you will become queen of the new state."

    Fanny turns on her toe to come full face with the shopkeeper. "Yes," she hisses, "and, if I should marry the devil, I would be queen of hell!" Her rapid departure leaves everyone gaping. Repetition of the incident keeps the townsfolk a-twitter for the better part of the month.

† † †

    Fanny looks lethargically out the window as she wipes a pitcher. Her lithe figure is clothed in a simple house dress covered with an apron whose long strings are drawn under her hem and between her knees forming leggings of sorts. She balances herself atop the short, three-legged stool by leaning against the shelving. Aloud she muses, "only February can look so cold and dreary." Inwardly, she remembers the hectic city social season do doubt created to while away winter doldrums. Life in the mountain frontier offers fewer distractions, unless of course, one counts Ethan. The General, she smiles to herself, requires total attention.

As if on cue, the door flies open. Ethan strides with great motive into the room.

"Well, good morning, sir!" Fanny gasps and giggles in one breath. "An unexpected pleasure indeed."

"'Tis always a delight when my eyes feast upon you, Fanny. Here, let me help you down before you tumble and drop that artifact."

"Not to worry, the pitcher is already cracked and mended. Merab's sentimentality urges her to keep such treasures."

"Not much for sentimentality, myself," smiles Ethan. Fanny nods her agreement. "Now hear my offer." Ethan leads Fanny toward the table and tosses his cloak over the back of the nearest chair. "If we're to be married at all, now is the time.'

Fanny's knees shiver and little bumps race up her spine but her voice is strong as she asks, "And, just what do you mean by now?"

"This moment. The judges are breakfasting with Stephen. I'll ask Moses to do the formal words—though you know I take little worth with such tom foolery."

Fanny's mind races. Where is Margaret? I can't get married looking like a frau. This man means "now!" Merab, she's gone for the morning. Aloud, her voice is strong and calm. "I'll just change my gown.

"We'll be off to Sunderland as soon as the words are said woman. Have the maid pack only a few items. We'll send for the rest."

Fanny drops a curtsy in mock obeisance and escapes through the door. Twenty minutes later, flushed but well adorned, Fanny returns to find Ethan pacing impatiently, hands clasped behind his back.

"Woman, you dally. If we're to reach comfort before nightfall, we need to push on."

"You're getting me as I am, Ethan. Be sure you're able to cope with the power of a whirlwind. This is your last chance to renege on your offer." Fanny walks to Ethan and slips her tiny hand into the crook of his arm. "Shall we proceed?"

Ethan knocks on the door but does not wait for an answer. He and Fanny walk into the library where pipe smoke curls above each head. Conversation ceases. Stephen looks toward the two with expectation. Before he can speak, Ethan moves directly in front of Moses Robinson, Chief Justice for Vermont.

"Judge Robinson, this young woman and myself have concluded to marry each other, and to have you perform the ceremony"

"When?" asks the judge, somewhat surprised.

"Now!" replies Ethan. "For myself," he continued, "I have no great opinion of such formality and from what I can discover, she thinks as little of it as I do. But as a decent respect for the opinions of mankind seems to require it, you will proceed."

"General," says the judge, "this is an important matter, and have you given it serious consideration?"

"Certainly," replies Ethan. Glancing at Fanny, he adds, "I do not think it requires much consideration."

"Well then, we shall begin. Gentlemen, you shall be witnesses." Judge Robinson gestures around the room.

Finally, able to get in a word, Stephen Bradley says, "Shall we not wait for Margaret and Merab. Surely, Fanny, you will want them present."

Her voice strong and determined, Fanny replies, "You gentlemen will make fine witnesses. I need no other. Please, begin." She nods to the chief justice.

Fanny hardly hears the words, lost in excitement as she is. She tries valiantly to concentrate. "...Ethan Allen, do you promise to live with Frances Buchanan agreeable to the laws of God"

"Stop!" Ethan drops Fanny's hand and stalks to the window. He stands silently for what seems minutes. No one speaks. Fanny stares at his back. Finally, Ethan turns and says, "God? If you mean God as written in the great book of Nature, yes. Go on."

Following a collective sigh, the ceremony continues without further interruption. When Judge Robinson declares the ceremony complete, Ethan salutes those gathered, looks at Fanny and says, "Come Mistress Allen it is time to depart for home."

Once outside the library door Ethan swoops Fanny into his arms and nearly smothers her with passionate kisses. Thus, exactly one month short of ten years after her father, Crean Brush, had placed £100 bounty on Ethan's head, Fanny unites the warring factors. She believes, somehow, Crean would approve.

Chapter 18

Fanny lies relaxed under the huge, fluffy comforter, staring at her sleeping husband. "How different from my first wedding night," she thinks. Ethan's passion had not over powered his consideration of her. Together they had searched and fondled, finding their shared pleasures. Fanny was glad they had found an inn with a private room, for their love making had been active and often raucously loud. Their innkeep was one of Vermont's Green Mountain Boys and had given Ethan a mighty slap on the back as they ascended to their room. He had even been bold enough to wink right at Fanny.

She stirs slightly, then leans over the edge of the bed searching for the chamber pot. Finding it tucked just under the nightstand, she climbs from the warm bed and moves to empty her bladder. Either her movement or the sound of her release wakens Ethan. Ethan smiles sleepily. "So, the grand princess actually pisses."

"You hush your mouth, General, or I'll dump the contents on your burly head."

"Come here, wench, I have need of you." Ethan reaches over, grabs Fanny's naked arm and pulls her back onto the bed. "You are a lovely creature indeed," he manages to whisper before he buries his face between her breasts. His next sounds are not words but leave no doubt as to his passion.

Sated, the two lie close together. Fanny smiles and runs her forefinger along Ethan's stubbly cheek. "You're thinking something devilish, you are," growls Ethan.

"Not devilish, really—besides, you don't believe in the devil."

"True, but there is a natural tendency among some humans—you uppermost among them—to tempt the laws of nature in a very twisted way."

"My thoughts are quite simple, really. In my innermost heart, I know. I know that today we have made a baby." Fanny

114

smiles and moves to cuddle even closer to her still sweaty, sticky husband.

"Damnation! I hope not." Ethan heaves aside the comforter and sits upright, staring down at Fanny. Even his vehement tone does not wipe the smile from Fanny's lips. "I've sired five children already. Three are still at home waiting to greet you."

"Ethan, you speak often of Nature's Law. Bearing children is the grandest nature has to offer. You can't cite one without the other. If you choose not to create babies then, perhaps, you should forego pleasures of the flesh."

Ethan chuckles. "I'm not ready for that sacrifice just yet, wife. Come here, if you're already pregnant, once more won't add to the cradle. Besides, creating the first five was nowhere near as exhilarating as is number six."

"And here I thought you an old, old man at 49." Fanny giggles as she rolls on top of him.

Fanny adjusts the fur lap robe to cover her feet which have become quite frozen during the sleigh ride toward Sunderland. Fresh snow had fallen during the night and the horse was stepping carefully through the virgin drifts. Ethan was careful not to rush the beast. A misstep by the steed could toss the sleigh at the very least or, at worst, break his leg. Such a calamity meant certain death to the animal and grave danger to the humans. Homesteads were scarce in this section of the mountains and any village at least another four hours' distance with the horse doing all the work.

Fanny listens quietly to sounds of the forest. Loudest are the swish of the horse hooves through the snow, each step tossing a cluster of snow puffs to the rear. Sleigh bells seem muted by the cold. Invisible chickadees chatter "danger" to each other as the sleigh moves through their territory. Every now and again the brush rustles and Fanny can only imagine the small critter darting away or, perhaps, peering inquisitively at the passing strangers. Fanny is experiencing a contentment very foreign to her being. "I'm totally safe with this man," she thinks silently. "He is a man to take command of any situation; and I am willing to let him do so." Almost dozing, she softly wonders aloud, "What did you tell the girls about me?"

Ethan rises from his own reverie, waiting a moment before answering. His left arm pulls Fanny closer, his right manages the reins. "Mmm. Tell them about you? Well, nothing. I told them nothing."

Though surprised by his answer, Fanny stays huddled close. "They do know I'm coming; that we're married?"

"No." Ethan does not elaborate.

"Ethan! Surely you didn't neglect to tell your own children you were bringing another woman into their home."

A minute passes before Ethan speaks. Fanny determines not to interrupt the silence.

"Truthfully, my love, I only decided to marry you on the trip over to Westminster. I withheld no information from them; there was no information."

"You've not spoken of me in all these weeks? They don't know you've been courting me? Ethan, what will they think!"

"Think? They're girls. Who knows what they'll think. I've no understanding of the silly ideas that flit about in young girls' brains. I suspect they'll be glad to have a burden lifted with you to take charge of the house."

Fanny's serenity evaporates. "Surely, General, you did not hire a housekeeper as your bride! There are cheaper ways to run a household I assure you."

Ethan roars with laughter. "Woman, you satisfy my lust in more ways than one. I am, indeed, a lucky lout to have a woman of such passion in both body and rhetoric. Now sit still before you upset the sleigh. Sit, knowing you are the treasure of my life. A housekeeper I can hire. You are a value to me far beyond what money can buy."

"Ethan! Please. Be serious. You're about to toss a cannon shot into the middle of your family. Surely, you don't want to wound those young beings." Fanny searches frantically for a strategy to guide her husband's thinking. "You're a genius at political planning, Ethan. How would you plan a surprise attack?"

Relieved his bride has settled down even a bit, Ethan ponders her question, all the while admiring her cunning. "Well, first I'd discuss the lay of the land analyze the artillery and manpower, then find the point of greatest surprise."

"The point of surprise we already have. Let's think about the territory we're about to take on. Tell me about your daughters. I'm recognizing I know as little about them as they about me."

"Well, Lorraine was the oldest. I told you about her death; it's still so fresh and painful. Joseph, my only son, died when he was but twelve, also of consumption. I was away when he died. Mary never forgave me my absence during that sadness."

"Surely that was a difficult time for her." Fanny raises her face and kisses Ethan lightly on his chin.

"Times were difficult for all of us. I was imprisoned and not free to tend to domestic issues. She could hardly blame me for those circumstances."

"Tell me about the girls, the ones I'm about to mother."

"They're a rowdy bunch, at least since Mary died. Ira's been supervising them mostly. They give me no quarter when it comes to discipline. I'm an inconvenience to them, I dare say." Ethan ponders his own words.

"How does their care fall to Ira? Isn't he as busy as you?"

"Fanny, my love, you have a great deal to learn about your new family. The very first thing you need to know is that Ira is the 'Great Caretaker' of us all. While I am the oldest and he is the baby, Ira brings the order out of chaos in our diverse clan. It will serve you well to understand this little anomaly."

"Heeded, my love. Now who is the oldest of your little beauties?"

"Lucy, a child of great spirit much like you. Certainly, those proclivities don't derive from her mother's dourness so I suspect I must lay claim to siring such behavior. She's 16 and ready to run me out covered with tar and feathers."

"Learned that from her father too, I surmise." Fanny nestles closer and adjusts the robe.

"Most say she's a beauty, and I've a father's prejudice. Lucy is clever and this I admire. She's taught herself to read and write, with help from Ira, of course. Mary never learned. Thought book learning to be of little use on the raw frontier. Favored laying everything in her God's lap." Ethan speaks to the horse, giving encouragement up a rocky rise. He turns to Fanny, "Climb down. Better we walk through here. It'll give the horse a rest."

Walking and talking at the same time was difficult in the cold. Ethan and Fanny took separate sides of the sleigh to help the runners over the rough spots. Progress was difficult, taking a full thirty minutes to crest the slope. As they reached the top, the valley below came into view.

"Spectacular!" gasps Fanny. "I've never seen such a sight." She walks gingerly to the snow covered edge and stares at the valley below.

"Careful, Love, you don't want to start a slide." Ethan walks to Fanny's side and wraps the robe around her shoulders." He surveys the panorama before him, taking in a deep breath and exhaling into the tendrils of hair escaping from Fanny's fur hat.

"I've been many places on this earth but these mountains are surely the most spectacular of all creation. I'm not sure what I believe about life after death. However, if Nature recycles the air and water and plants, then logic tell us there is a next step for us humans. Should I have the opportunity to return, I'll come back as a mighty white stallion. I'd roam these majestic mountains and valleys, coming each night to this very spot. I'd stand on my hind legs and bellow out my pride at this great beauty."

Fanny snuggles even further into Ethan's chest, scratching her cheek on his cloak closing. She says nothing. She senses words would only interrupt his spiritual communion.

Ethan lets go of Fanny and moves cautiously closer to the edge. "Fanny, I swear on all that I believe, these mountains are me, and I am the mountains. We cannot be separated."

Back in the sleigh, enjoying the steady, rocking motion down the mountain, Fanny rekindles the conversation. "Lucy and I will find something in common, I'm sure. Now who's next?"

Ethan sighs, knowing he can't escape his wife's persistence. Yet he knows so little of his daughters. "Mary Ann is 12, at least I think she's 12. She's the quiet one; always looking at things without speaking. I constantly feel she's judging my every move. Ira tells me her health is not the best, but I've seen no signs of illness."

"Twelve, mmm," Fanny murmurs. "Not the most pleasant of times in a young girl's life. Soon to be a woman but not understanding all those changes."

Taking to the subject at last, Ethan continues: "The last of the lot is Pamelia. Mary's choice of names, not mine. I don't think the girl likes the name either. She has some burr under her blanket anyway. She's only five."

"Poor dear, she must be missing her mother terribly." Fanny rests against Ethan as she thinks about her new stepdaughters. "I've exactly no experience as a mother," she thinks silently. "Lucy will be a challenge. Certainly I was. Gracious, I was married at her age. Perhaps the place to start is with Pamelia. If we can become friends, then the burden will ease."

Ethan, having helped Fanny from the sleigh, strides to the main door of the large house he and Ira share. Fanny walks behind him, seeming to use Ethan as a shield for what is about occur. He thrusts open the doors and bellows, "Ira, girls I've returned. Come quickly."

Silence. Fanny thinks she hears some rustling coming from what must be the rear of the house. Ethan turns to the left and shoves open a heavy, paneled door. "There you are. Nothing interrupts your record keeping. I'm home and I've brought a surprise." Ethan leans over the desk neatly stacked with sheaves of paper and cuffs his younger brother on the chin.

Ira finishes his jotting and carefully places his quill in its stand. At last he looks up, calmly surveying his brother. "You're always surprise enough, Ethan." Seeing a bit of fur behind Ethan and noting the girls peering silently through the door jamb, Ira stands and walks around the desk.

Seizing the moment, Fanny steps from behind Ethan and offers her still gloved hand to her new brother-in-law. "Good day, Ira. I am Fanny."

Interjecting quickly, Ethan adds, "Brother, this is my new wife. You will soon learn what a treasure she is."

"If beauty is considered treasure, then surely you have chosen wisely, brother." Ira takes Fanny's extended hand, raising it to his lips before addressing her directly. "Welcome to our humble home, my dear. Ethan delights in surprising us; he has outdone himself this time." Ira turns to the girls and beckons, "Do come in. You must meet Mistress Fanny."

The girls surreptitiously observe Fanny's elaborate fur cloak and lined boots, the likes of which they've never seen. At the same time, Fanny is studying the girls' plain woolen dresses and untidy hair. "This is where I'll start," thinks Fanny. "Every girl likes to look pretty."

Fanny moves closer to the girls, reaching out to touch the older girl's shoulder. "You must be Lucy. Your father has spoken well of you."

The younger girls look anxiously up at Lucy, anticipating a saucy response. "I'm surprised he's spoken of me at all. Certainly, he's never spoken of you, at least in this house."

Fanny chuckles and drops her hand from Lucy's shoulder. "You have your father's boldness indeed. I'm delighted to meet you." Turning to the middle girl, she adds, "And, you are Mary Ann, I presume."

Eyes to the floor, the girl drops a curtsy but says nothing. Undaunted, Fanny, moves to the youngest and squats so their faces are level. "Pamelia, you are the sprite your father described. Your eyes are the color of a forest doe. How blessed you are."

"Are you our new mother?" squeaks Pamelia.

"You have but one true mother in life, little one. A mother is a special gift. I'm not a replacement. As your father's wife, I would like to be your friend. I trust we will come to respect and love each other over time."

Ethan and Ira glance at one another. Ira nods his approval before moving to offer Fanny his arm to help her rise. All three adults ignore Lucy's barely audible snort.

The girls seize this opportunity to scuttle off to the kitchen to discuss this new intervention into their lives. None utters a word until they're safely past sight and sound of the adults.

Lucy stamps her foot. "Mother not dead a year, and sister Lorraine still warm in her grave! How dare he take another woman."

MaryAnn buries her face in Lucy's shoulder and begins to cry. Pamelia smiles up at her two sisters. "She seems like a lovely lady; don't you think?"

After the long and chilling ride, Ethan needs to stretch and exercise his stiff body. To Ira he says, "Would you be kind enough to show Fanny to our room? I'll go wipe down the horse and put the sleigh to rest." Without waiting for an answer, Ethan strides from the room. Fanny and Ira hear the front door latch settle into its slot before they speak.

"This house has had no woman's touch since Mary's death almost a year ago. I have to admit, Mary's presence was quite plain and often, well, shall we say, shrewish." Quickly assessing Fanny's downward glance, Ira continues, "Speaking ill of the dead is presumptuous or at least inconsiderate of the still living, but you'll rapidly realize I'm a forthright man. Toddling behind the woodshed takes up time better spent elsewhere. This is my house. Well, mostly; Ethan owns a portion but he's shown no interest in managing any of it. Mary respected my wishes. I'm not a man taken to frill and fancy but Mary was less even than I. You will bring a change to our surroundings, I'm quite sure. Good cheer will be a welcome addition to a household drenched in dourness, and threat of the devil at every turn."

"Do you, like Ethan, call yourself a Deist?" Fanny looks up, holding her gaze steady with Ira's.

"Deist? I don't rightly know. Mostly I do know that Mary's angry and avenging God has no place in my life. Beyond that, I've not decided, nor put much energy into considering the issue. Come, let me show you the house." Ira offers his arm; the subject is dismissed and the tour begins.

Fanny looks around the room as she tosses her fur cloak onto the bed. The space is not small but exudes a darkness that draws the walls inward. "Oppressive" strikes Fanny as she moves about examining the furnishings. A dull brown, coarse coverlet rests under her cloak, making a jarring comparison. The walls have been plastered, dun colored linen panels cover the windows. Fanny yanks them to the side and peers at the view. "Quite pleasant," she thinks already considering the colors she will bring to the space. The cold draft from the panes causes her to reclose the ugly curtains. Next to the north window sits a simple desk covered with stacks of parchment. Fanny picks up the top sheet from the closest pile and reads the sprawling script. Ethan's she presumes. She runs her hand along the desk's surface, pushing aside dust as she moves. The chair, large and comfortable, smells of Ethan. The new and delightful sensation rushes between her legs as she bends to sniff the leather. Fanny continues her study of the room. There is a large armoire ("Shrunk" as Grandfather would say, thinks Fanny.) and she pulls open the doors. Only two, dark homespun dresses hang on pegs. Ethan has claims most of the hooks for his own, carefully arranged garments. The narrow shelves hold mostly male garments and accessories. A much mended petticoat occupies one slot. The contents smell musty.

Aloud, to no one, Fanny says, "Mary, the smell of you must go. Thank goodness I packed crushed lavender among my clothes in the trunk." She begins tearing Mary's no longer needed gowns from their pegs. The petticoat she dumps on the floor with the dresses, pushing them to the side with her foot. "We'll need another room for my things. I'm sure Ira can spare us more space." Fanny continues her perusal. There are two straight, wooden, slatted back chairs; one either side of the small grate in front of the fireplace. Candle stands are placed next to the chairs and one by the bed. A rug, braided from old rags, covers the flooring between bed and fireplace. There are no sconces, no decoration. This room offers no frivolity, no comfort, and certainly, no beauty. "Things must change and change quickly," mutters Fanny.

Ethan burst through the door. "Change what, my love?" He grabs Fanny around her waist, swings her around once then drops her on the bed. The underlying bed ropes groan.

"First of all, we'll need to retie the bed," laughs Fanny. "We'll keep the whole family awake satisfying your natural needs."

Ethan plops beside his wife. "Dreary, would you say?" as he looks about the room.

"You're usually a man of gross overstatement. This time you're totally under stating the condition. Whose pleasure do I need to gain to begin my overhaul, yours or Ira's?"

"This is my space, so come please me, you little tart!" Ethan grabs Fanny and rolls on top of her.

"Whoa there, stallion," she laughs, struggling to extricate herself. "I'm a woman on a mission, not to be deterred from her task." Pulling herself away from Ethan, Fanny stands and strides to the north window. She yanks the curtains, pulling rod and all to the floor. Ethan moves to the west window and follows suit. They both roar with laughter.

"One caveat, love," Ethan warns. "My desk is not to be touched. "This is where I work, and I am accustomed to no intrusions."

"No intrusions?" Fanny asks coquettishly, as she rubs her body against his.

During the weeks that follow Fanny's arrival in Sunderland, she spends her days assessing and planning what will evolve into almost a total interior renovation of the sleeping quarters, the kitchen and the main parlor. She has decided not to risk riling Ira by making too many public changes. Fanny coyly requested an empty room be outfitted to handle her wardrobe and her painting easels and supplies. Rather taken aback by Fanny's excesses, Ira ponders her petitions and finally grants her wishes. He is really quite grateful for the mood change that seems to have blossomed almost immediately in Fanny's presence.

Fanny has written Patrick to authorize some of her monies be posted to Boston to buy silks, fine linens, and furnishings for her redecorating. Included in her purchases are fabrics and accessories for the girls. She would have preferred having her goods come from New York where Mother Buchanan could have supervised the purchases but as an Allen that would be the ultimate abomination. Already, Margaret, now over her miff at missing the nuptials, has sent barrels of fine china and other necessities that had been carefully stored since the move from New York.

Fanny has faced only one refusal since becoming mistress of Sunderland. Quite quickly, she realized the need for servants. Since Mary's death, the girls have cooked, cleaned, and supervised the garden. There has been little time for pleasure or personal pursuits. Fanny wrote Onncie inquiring if she'd be willing to fill the role of housekeeper and nanny at Sunderland.

The reply had been quite simple and straight forward: *"I am no longer up to such exuberant challenges. Besides, Mistress Margaret needs me here. Your mother and I have chosen a young woman who should be capable of caring for your new family. Her name is Emma Forrest and she will accompany the next shipment of goods to Sunderland. I offer you good wishes. You will be a fine wife and hostess. Your mother has trained you well. Deepest affection, Onncie"*

Today Emma arrives. Fanny and the girls are atwitter with expectation. Even Ira catches the anticipatory excitement. Lucy seems the most exhilarated, darting to the window every few minutes to stare up the lane. Whether she looks forward to being relieved of many of her duties or she anticipates the companionship of someone her own age, not even Lucy can explain. Fanny, trying to set an example of decorum for the girls, sits by the fire working on her embroidery. She, too, peeks through the curtains when the girls are not in the parlor. Only Ethan, at the printers in Bennington, seems unmoved by Emma's impending arrival.

As her needles goes rhythmically up and down through the linen, Fanny thinks about Ethan's demand for money. His new book is nearly finished and his contract with the printer requires some prepayment. "All my money, and much of Ira's, is tied up in our Onion River land corporation up north," he'd said. "My earlier writings were well received so there is no reason to believe we shall not recuperate this investment.'

Fanny is not quite so sure. She's read some of the chapters and finds them tedious and spiteful. "Even if he is revered by many, he might better stick to politics and avoid belittling religion," she thinks. As blustery and egotistical as Ethan seems, he has his vulnerable spots and Fanny finds she must expend a great deal of energy soothing his emotional wounds. Fanny experiences only infrequent chagrin that the simple act of marriage has transferred her inheritance from Patrick's charge to Ethan's. Stephen Bradley's wisdom has slowed the legal practicalities and Patrick must still endorse her expenditures.

The clock in Ira's study chimes four times. Fanny rises to note that winter's early darkness begins to descend on the snowy scene outside. Suddenly, she feels queasy and steadies herself on the sill. She gags and covers her mouth with her hand. At the same moment she notices a dark spot in the distance, moving toward the house. Her momentary uneasiness vanishes.

"Girls. Come quickly. She's here!"

Lucy, Mary Ann, and Pamelia bump into each other trying to get through the door. Lucy pushes through first and rushes to the window. The other girls squeeze between their sister and Fanny. Their breath coats the frigid panes and they use their sleeves to clear the steam. Fanny runs her hands through Lucy's hair trying to bring order to escaping locks. Lucy impatiently brushes her hand away. Undaunted, Fanny turns her attentions to the younger girls and straightens bows made from newly purchased ribbon. All the commotion draws Ira from his office and he joins them at the window.

The heavily laden sleigh does not stop at the front door but turns into the drive and proceeds to the back entrance. This is a delivery, not a visitor.

"Girls!" admonishes Fanny. "Walk slowly; rest your right fingers in your left palm. We don't want to appear rude."

Ira chuckles but neither he nor Fanny misses the quick twist of Lucy's head and the tip of her tongue stuck out derisively. Unable to resist, Fanny sticks out her own tongue at Lucy's retreating back. Ira lovingly joshes Fanny, saying, "It's hard to figure which of you is more impertinent."

The young woman stands quietly just outside the kitchen door awaiting an invitation to enter. Her wool bonnet is not new but clean and secured with a tidy ribbon. Wisps of pale curls stick to the frost collected on the brim. Her cloak has been neatly patched; a twist of wool fabric wraps around her hands, scant protection against the bitter cold. The three girls stare at the newcomer neither moving nor speaking. Fanny swishes into the kitchen motioning the woman to enter. "Do come in, Emma. You must be frozen through to the very marrow of your bones. Pamelia, dear, close the door before we all freeze. Mary Ann, stoke up the fire. Lucy, twist the kettle over the flame. Tea will do us all a world of good."

Fanny moves quickly and efficiently around the room, setting cups, measuring tea. She politely urges Emma to remove her cloak, showing her a convenient peg just inside the pantry where she can hang it. Fanny chatters as she works trying to set the new servant and her stepdaughters at ease. Ira flees the scene after a brief, if pompous welcoming. "I'll take my tea in the office," he exclaims as he vanishes through the kitchen door. "A little rum wouldn't hurt in the pot," he adds as if an afterthought.

"The Allen men do love their rum," Fanny offers to Emma.

"The same demon claims most men in these parts." Lucy speaks her first words since Emma's arrival. "You can't set Uncle Ira and Father apart from other sinners."

"Lucy, dear," Fanny admonishes, "We've agreed that devils, demons, and sinners are a thing of the past in this house. We'll weigh our errors based on good manners and refined taste. Come, dear, please fill the teapot." Turning to Pamelia, Fanny continues uninterrupted, "Little one, you can show Emma where to carry the tea for Uncle Ira. Here, let's put fresh scones on the tray."

Fanny, at last, plops onto the kitchen bench. To no one in particular, she says, "We'll take tea here with Emma this time. We'll get to know each other that way." Fanny feels she has set a comfortable tone for this new relationship. Fanny controls the domestic role in the house, no doubt about it, but she wants an amiable respect between all the females. Margaret has trained her daughter well. If only Fanny can teach Ethan's daughter with the same skill.

When Emma and Pamelia return, Fanny smiles and invites them all to sit around the table. Fanny continues to be the main conversationalist but Emma holds her own, offering just enough information about herself to satisfy Allen curiosity. Fanny encourages each daughter to speak of their own interests to help Emma learn the family ethos.

Tea over, Fanny assigns Lucy the task of helping Emma prepare dinner, a simple meal tonight with Ethan expected quite late. Ira makes few demands on culinary prowess and Fanny's appetite suffers these days. Indeed, Fanny now succumbs to a weariness she didn't feel a few minute before. "If you'll excuse me, I think I'll lie down for a while." She slowly climbs the narrow, steep, back stairs, leaving the young girls to their own devices.

Chapter 19

Spring comes late in the mountains. The first wild flowers are just appearing at the edge of the woods and the late May sun at last feels warm to the skin. Fanny lies on the daybed she has put in her own room, a damp towel across her brow. Her slightly rounded stomach rises and falls with each breath. Her body indicates relaxation, but Fanny's mind races from one issue to the next.

"How Ethan can write when he drinks so much, I cannot fathom!" Fanny remembers the row they had just last night when Ethan spilled his tankard of rum onto the dinner linen. Lucy had stomped out and Pamelia had giggled and slid under the table anticipating Fanny's tongue lashing. Emma's arrival to clean up the resultant mess stemmed Fanny's outburst but her anger had lingered unleashed. Thank goodness Ira was up in Onion River on business. The two men seemed often at battle these days. Ira, like Fanny, had read much of Ethan's work and declared it "polly rot." While Fanny worried about social implications Ira focused on the business damages Ethan's publication might wreak.

Fanny feels a twitch deep inside her womb. "Oh!" she gasps."The first sign of life; surely a good omen." Fanny rolls to her side, placing her hand where a moment before she'd felt motion. The act moves her thoughts from Ethan to the adjustments a new baby will inflict into this already crowded household. Fanny realizes she must soon tell the girls they will have a new sibling by first snow fall. She's been reluctant to share this information with other than Ethan.

Ira has become ever more possessive of their shared homestead these past months. Fanny is sympathetic but feels if they are to maintain their status as community leaders—after all, Ethan and Ira are the backbone of a growing Vermont—they simply must uphold their social responsibilities. Fanny's dinner parties and afternoon teas have become frequent affairs. Ira retreats more and more to his study or to Burlington for business.

Lucy's prickly behavior continues. Fanny remains equally persistent in her efforts to build, at the very least, civility in the household. Mary Ann now speaks her needs but little more. "Pamelia, the dear child," muses Fanny, "at least I've found a modicum of success there. She so loves her pretty dresses and baubles."

A gentle tap on the door rouses Fanny from her reverie. "Come in," she manages drowsily. She rolls over to face the door, the cloths sliding to the floor.

The door opens slowly and a fist filled with brilliant Johnny Jump Ups appears; nothing more. Fanny smiles, unable to resist this peace offering. "Ethan, you may come in." The smile on her lips is transfused into her words. "Did you offer General Washington posies at the treaty?"

Ethan eases his large frame into the room, grinning, and still extending the flowers. "You know I was banned from the proceedings. Besides, you, my love, are the only one on this earth to whom I would relinquish my pride." He moves to the day bed. "May I sit beside you?"

Fanny takes the fragrant offering and pats the small space next to her. "If you can fit, you can sit," she giggles.

Ethan wiggles his buttocks, shifting Fanny to the side and making room. She reaches up her arms and pulls his face to hers. "You smell sweeter than the flowers," he mutters huskily. By pulling her close, Ethan manages to squeeze alongside his wife, an arm beneath her neck and around her shoulders keeps her from falling off the bed. She snuggles her face into his chest taking in the musky smell of this man she loves so deeply yet drives her to frustration at most every turn.

"The Susquehanna Company has offered me a proposal." Ethan speaks softly, running his fingertips in small circles along Fanny's arm. When she doesn't respond, he decides to continue. "They want me to go to their land holdings and find a way for them to become independent from Pennsylvania. They're quite discontent with statehood demands.

"You refused, of course." Fanny lifts her face and kisses the underside of Ethan's chin.

"They're offering a handsome fee; a small portion just to go, the remainder when Susquehanna becomes independent."

"How shrewd!" Fanny fails to hide the sarcasm she feels.

"They're counting on the same success I had here in Vermont."

"But that took years." Fanny's patience dwindles rapidly. "There's so much to do here. We need our own home. Onion River Company demands your attention; Ira and Levi cannot be allowed to run it all. More importantly, I want you here when our baby is born. Ethan, you need to remember I'm not Mary. I married you to be with you, part of your life; not have you off gallivanting around the countryside."

Ethan kisses the top of Fanny's head, inhaling the sweetness of her clean hair. For a moment his thoughts wander. "This is why I welcome her weekly bathing; one of her more pleasurable extravagances," he thinks. Aloud, he speaks softly, "You love to bargain, my sweet. Here's a proposition for you. I'll accept Susquehanna's proposal and when I return I'll build you a new house."

Fanny lies quietly, pondering Ethan's offer. Several moments pass before she responds. "You build me a house, then you flit off to Pennsylvania."

Ethan laughs, hugging her. "The proposal will be withdrawn before I can create a home to meet your desires. Here's my counter offer. I'll talk with Ira about building a house up north and work a contract with him. I'll accept Susquehanna's proposal and we'll both profit."

"Promise to be home for the birthing?"

"Indeed!"

"Then, done. You can talk with Ira the moment he comes home and when you've accomplished that part, you can let Susquehanna know how eager you are to accept."

Ethan rises and smiles at his wife still lying on the day bed. "You are a master at bargaining, Mistress Allen." He neglects to tell her he's already accepted Susquehanna's offer and agreed to head south by mid-June. "Let's hope Ira gets home soon," he mutters mostly to himself as he heads for his desk in the next room.

No longer able to relax, Fanny rises reticently. She pulls her hand mirror from the dressing table, examines her face and hair. She tugs at the tousles around her face; with little energy to comb them out, she sighs and places the looking glass back on the table. She bends to pull her silk slippers from beneath the day bed where Ethan had inadvertently kicked them. Another sigh. "Where has all my energy gone?" She gathers her old doll Maggy into her arms from the chair where the stuffed persona spends her days watching Fanny frantically moving through life. Fanny plops onto the seat, pulling Maggy to her chest. "You are my fulcrum, Maggy. You anchor my past, you guide me through the present, and you'll be there to take me beyond the grave. 'Tis then you'll return to your true owner, my dearest mother." Fanny turns the doll, face to face, smiles at the inert features. "Now, dearest Maggy, if Ethan is correct, we'll simply rot away in the earth and return to dirt itself, nourishing life as it goes on without us." She hugs the doll against her chest again. "Either way it seems, Ethan's hypotheses or prevailing religious doctrine, we'll go lifeless into the ground and, somehow, reunite with our beloved Catherine." Fanny stands and replaces Maggy on the seat; fluffs the doll's skirt, and whispers, "But not yet, dearest, not yet. I'm off to the kitchen to oversee supper. Tonight I really must tell the girls they're to have a brother. At least, I hope it's a boy. Ethan so wants another son. Keep guard, Maggy."

The girls sit around the kitchen table. Emma kneads dough and chatters as she works. Only Pamelia jumps up to greet Fanny. Fanny gives the little girl a quick hug and kiss on the top of her head before moving to watch Emma's energetic thrusting back and forth in the bread bowl. Fanny reaches to replace the lid on the starter crock. "The sour smell makes me queasy."

Lucy glances at Emma and raises her eyebrow but doesn't allow a smile to form on her lips. Emma keeps kneading offering no response. Quick as a darting squirrel, Mary Ann reaches out, grabs a bit of dough and pops it in her mouth.

"Oh, Mary Ann, spit that out!" Fanny grabs for her arm. "You'll get worms. Here, spit it into my hand." Mary Ann stares up at Fanny, her eyes wide but not frightened. She knows Lucy wants her to disobey Fanny, but what if she did get worms? Slowly she rolls out her tongue and lets the bit of dough fall off into Fanny's hand. She forces a little spittle to follow suit.

"Thank you, dear." Fanny drops the bit into the hog slop bucket and returns to the table. "Tonight, we'll have a special supper. Your father and I have news to share."

Lucy rolls her eyes but says nothing. Emma keeps kneading, refusing to look at Lucy for fear her laughter will burst forth. Certainly, the "news" has been kitchen gossip for some time now. Emma hopes Lucy can be gracious rather than offer her usual impertinence for she truly likes her mistress. She finds the oldest Allen daughter angry and resentful but also a welcome companion to help overcome her own loneliness.

As she leaves the kitchen, Fanny turns to speak, "Girls, wear one of your new dresses tonight. Let's make it a special occasion. Emma, set wine goblets at their places. A toast will be in order. Even little Pamelia may have a taste." To Mary Ann and Pamelia, she adds, "Best you finish your lessons so you can recite to your father at supper. He been inquiring on your progress."

Fanny worries how the girls will take all this news. Her anxiety raises the bile in her stomach and she returns to her room to rest again.

Ethan and Fanny banter back and forth as they eat. The girls remain quiet except when asked a direct question. Lucy wonders how long it will take before the "news" is shared. She senses apprehension in both adults.

As Emma collects plates, Ethan reaches for his glass. "Ladies, Fanny and I have some exciting news to share with you all. Emma, you need not leave. This affects you as well."

Fanny interrupts, raising her own glass. "Your father is building us a new house!"

A collective gasp rises from the girls. Emma continues to stack the dishes unobtrusively on the side board. She wants to hear it all.

Almost as surprised as the girls, Ethan responds while looking questioningly at Fanny. "We're crowded here. Besides, we're our own family again and Brother Ira needs his peace. Fanny and I will draw up plans to present to Ira; something suitable up on the Onion River. It's time I got back to farming."

It's Fanny's turn to be surprised. Farming!" Becoming a farmer's wife ranks rather low on the list of Fanny's priorities. Indeed, any conscious list does not include such a role. A general's wife, yes; an author's, perhaps, or certainly a statesman's—but a farmer's wife, no.

Collectively, the girls glance from their father to Fanny. Lucy's mouth forms a circle but no words come forth. Mary Ann focuses on Fanny's face noting her stepmother's confusion. "This certainly isn't what she intended," the 12-year- old thinks to herself. Pamelia jumps up and runs to Fanny. "May I have chickens; my very own chicks? May I?" Fanny puts her arm around the little girl but continues to stare at Ethan. Pamelia persists until Ethan finally says, "We'll see, little one. It'll be yet another spring before we move, I'm sure. There's a great deal to be done in the meanwhile." Turning to Fanny, Ethan continues, "There's more to tell is there not, Fanny?"

Fanny feels like the breath has been knocked from her lungs. She stalls for time by turning to Pamelia. Fanny smiles back at the little girl, all the while demanding her brain and lungs to function. At last she manages to find her breath and words. "I promise you the very first chick hatched at our new home. The very first. Now go back to your seat so your father can continue his news." Fanny looks up at her husband anger filling her eyes. She raises her arm and gestures toward Ethan. "Sir, do continue!"

Ethan accepts his wife's unspoken antagonism and draws deeply from his goblet. With a great sigh, Ethan rises from his seat and walks to his wife, placing his large hands on her dainty shoulders. He bends to kiss his wife's head then looks at each girl before speaking. "Ladies! I am proud to announce there will be a new Allen—a son, I trust—before we embark on our adventure to the north country. You will be entrusted to find excellent dispositions in these coming months, to ardently pursue your studies, and to keep your fingers busy doing whatever it is ladies do to prepare for the arrival of infants. You are Allens. You will rise to the task. In the meantime, I shall be off to the Susquehanna to save that land trust from the evils of statehood." With a flourish, he bends to whisper in Fanny's ear. "We do lovely battle together do we not, my love?"

Lucy jumps from the table and storms through the door into the kitchen. Emma picks up the plates from the sideboard and quietly follows, hoping to forestall any audible outburst. Mary Ann speaks first, "I hope it's a girl. They stay home." Turning to Fanny, she continues, offering her stepmother her first support. "May I help with the birthing? I'm old enough now."

Fanny extends her hand and smiles. "Of course, Mary Ann, but that's a long time away; not until November, at least. We'll work on little garments, and pretty blankets."

Not to be excluded, Pamelia offers, "Me too, Fanny; me too?"

"Certainly. The two of you will be my official readers as well. I do love poetry and you can take turns reading to me as I work. 'Tis said to calm the infant in the womb." Rising, she glares at Ethan. "Will you see me to my room, Ethan? I'm feeling a bit faint."

"I can imagine. Here, take my arm." Ethan offers his hand then encircles Fanny's shoulders with his other arm. He feels her rigidity and a moment of dread rises within him. He doesn't want to cause harmful stress. Mental dueling with a wife is far different than doing strategic battle with his political colleagues. Still, Fanny raises far more enjoyable repartee than stolid, cranky Mary. As they mount the stairs, Ethan speaks. "Have I offended you deeply?"

"Deeply."

"Then, I humbly apologize and beg your forgiveness. What can I do to appease you, my beloved?"

"Rot in that Hell you don't believe in!" Tears drip down Fanny's cheeks. She makes no effort to stem the flow.

Ethan guides Fanny into their room and seats her on the bed. He drops to his knees in front of her. "Fanny, you know I'm impulsive and often brusque but I would never intentionally harm you."

Sobbing uncontrollably now, Fanny manages her reply through gulps and gasps. "You had already accepted their proposal; I know it. How could you?"

Ethan begins unbuttoning Fanny's bodice. "Let me help you get undressed. Then you can sleep." As his fingers work clumsily on the tiny buttons, Ethan speaks softly. "True. I did, Fanny. I've such a worry. My funds are tied up in the Onion River land project. You want a new house and with a baby on the way…" He helps Fanny to her feet and lets her gown drop to the floor. "I need the money, Fanny."

"And the adventure." Her sobs grow further apart. Fanny sits back on the bed and slowly reclines on top of the comforter. Sweat beads cover her forehead and neck. Her face is blotched scarlet from crying. She manages a whisper. "Your book is almost done. You've nothing to look forward to but more domesticity, Ethan. I suspect you're even afraid to have another baby. You're a warrior with sword or with pen. But I'm not your opponent; not ever. Please don't treat me like one."

Ethan lies beside her enfolding her into an embrace before he responds. "Your intelligence is a delightful challenge, Fanny. My life focuses on challenges. Dull witted people bore me, offer no foils. I'm alive when deep into an intellectual encounter. I don't think of you as adversary, but as the greatest love of my life beyond my devotion to these mountains. You're right, these, er, uh, negotiations, shall we call them; I let them set us up against each other. Can you find it in yourself to forgive me?"

"Perhaps," she mutters, burying her face into his chest. "Just don't push me too far, Ethan. My mighty intelligence, as you seem to call it, is always capable of out challenging you." Ethan strokes her hair and she seems to doze. After several minutes, Fanny whispers, "Besides, you are the father of my child." She drifts into sleep.

Fanny sits motionless, her gloved hands resting on her rounded belly, back straight, rigid. She stares unblinkingly at Thomas Follett. The rotund, sweating man stirs about in his papers, one forefinger drumming on the desk. His discomfort arises both from the heat and from the outlandishly resolute woman and her request.

Wiping his brow with an already damp handkerchief, he furthers his position. "Madam, I rent rooms, of course. But in all my years of operating this establishment I have never; I repeat, never, made a contract with a woman."

Fanny's gaze remains on her adversary's face and her voice serenely steady. "I see, Master Follett. Then surely, you'll grow no younger before you learn the technique. At the risk of repeating myself, ad nauseum, my husband is in Massachusetts on business with the Susquehanna Land Company. Thus, I am left to negotiate our transactions here in Bennington. I bring a letter of credit, more than enough to cover any arrangements with you."

Fanny hesitates, adjusting her strategy. A letter of contract written by Ethan sits secure in her purse. She prefers to negotiate herself however, for the sheer audacity of the act. Fanny decides to drop the affrontive antagonism and opts for a more feminine ploy, a tack perhaps more palatable and more easily understood by Follett. "You can see, Master Follett, that I am with child. The sooner our family can make this move to Bennington, the better it will for the unborn babe."

The landlord bites. "Um, when will this addition present itself, Mistress Allen?"

"Tis a child not an 'addition' as you call it; sired by your revered General and my husband, Ethan Allen." Fanny cannot resist the taunt, adding to the man's fluster. "The event appears scheduled for November. That leaves us less than four months to settle and prepare. Will you kindly show me what you have available? We'll need at least five rooms, all together and as private as possible." Fanny rises and starts for the door. When she does not hear Follett do likewise, she turns. "Shall we begin?"

Follett pulls open a desk drawer and removes a ring of keys. Fanny knows she has won. The landlord mops his brow again and walks, eyes on his key ring, to the door. Feeling a little guilty and wanting to pacify her conquest, she says, "May I take your arm? This heat weakens me so." Fanny's proffered smile might melt a glacier.

Follett offers his arm but does not answer. His pride wavers between defeat and being the recipient of this beautiful woman's considerable charm. Besides, having General Allen in his establishment is an honor not to be treated lightly. On a more down to earth rationale, Follett's wife will no doubt be invited to Mistress Allen's famous teas, and his kitchen coffer will benefit from the woman's noted extravagances. Follett no longer feels defeated. He wonders, however, why the move away from Ira and Sunderland and just how he might get this information to share later with his wife—and tavern regulars.

The pair ascend the wide staircase, itself an extravagance in such a building. Follett leads Fanny to the north wing where he currently has available lodging. He unlocks the doors of each room, throwing them wide.

"Please, Mistress. See the mountain view; all but the end room have this magnificence."

Not wanting to appear overly eager, Fanny walks slowly, running her hand along the bureau top, making an obvious show of checking her glove for dust. "You need a new feather duster, Master Follett."

"The rooms have been empty for several weeks, Madam. We dust daily all occupied spaces."

Fanny stands at the window, studying the view. "You're quite correct, the scenery is majestic from this perspective."

The bantering give and take continues as the pair move from room to room. Fanny realizes there are six empty rooms and decides she will negotiate to get them all. They might as well take the whole wing; better for Ethan's writing—and the baby won't disturb other lodgers. Emma can have the small room on the end by the back stairs, the room with only a small window and no view. There's space for a cradle as well should the baby prove fretful.

"I've seen enough, Master Follett. Shall we return to your office to complete our business?"

"Indeed Madam." He offers his arm and, this time, returns Fanny's smile.

Following some minor dickering, Follett has written a two-page contract for all six rooms in the north wing for a price quite below what each room would bring separately. General Allen's presence will bring new excitement to his tavern where added revenues will more than make up the difference in his lodging deficit. Follett expresses surprise as Fanny begins to read his loosely constructed agreement. "Mistress Allen, have you so little trust in my integrity?"

"You will find me a stern task mistress, Mr. Follett. A woman must pay far more attention to detail when conducting business or she will be considered slovenly. This I've learned quickly after only one encounter with my dear sister-in-law, Nancy—a clever, and very rich woman."

"Indeed, but less than careful with whom she transacts her business." Follett mops his brow yet again; an act beginning to irritate Fanny.

Still reading, Fanny lets the comment pass. Looking up at her new landlord, Fanny says, "This seems in order, but you really should pay more attention to your ciphering. You've miscalculated the total by ten dollars." Handing him the sheets, she continues, "Change the figures on page two and then I shall put my signature below yours. We wouldn't want any future misunderstandings, now would we." Fanny offers her sweetest smile.

Having made his corrections Follett watches Fanny place her signature. "Master Ira will surely be missing your company."

"Yes I trust he will; and I, his. With their Onion river company expanding, Ira and the General will be spending additional time in the north, working more closely with Levi. When our new homestead is completed, we'll join them. 'Til then, we shall enjoy the hospitality of your lodgings." Fanny hands the contract over to the innkeeper and rises from her chair.

"Will Master Ira be selling his Sunderland properties?" asks Follett.

"That is surely a question only my brother-in-law can answer. Good day, sir." Fanny walks unescorted to the door. She turns to speak once again, her tone confident and a little arrogant. Fanny recognizes the need to remain a step beyond her landlord's authority. "Our stores and belongings will begin arriving within the week. Can you assure me they will be treated safely?"

Follett half rises, nods slightly before answering. "With the greatest security and caution, Mistress." He struggles to maintain his composure. What a coup! General Allen in his lodgings; he can't wait to tell his wife. The news will spread through Bennington by nightfall.

† † †

Fanny lies quietly in her new bed. Emma sits by her side, fanning slowly. The late July heat is oppressive. Fanny swats at her face. "Emma, we must find a way to prevent these black flies from getting in."

"They're quite late this year, Mistress. Usually gone by the end of June. Surely, the pests will disappear soon. Emma continues her steady back and forth movement with the big feather fan. Trying to divert Fanny's attention, she adds, "When will the General return from the Susquehanas, ma'am?"

"His last letter spoke of being home by mid-September—in time for publication of his new book. The printer has just begun setting type." Fanny swats at her face again. "That reminds me, I must have Patrick authorize Stephen to release funds to cover those costs. Where are the girls, Emma?"

"Out peeking in the seamstress's window, no doubt. Bennington styles have caught their fancy, it seems."

Fanny keeps her thoughts silent on Bennington's fashion status. Aloud, she says, "Perhaps a new gown will erase their moping about leaving Sunderland. I'll write a note to the seamstress, ordering one for each." Smiling at Emma, she continues. "You will have Lucy's old gown Emma. You could use a little cheering up yourself."

Emma nodded slightly, continuing her rhythmic motion back and forth, back and forth. Even a hand-me-down at-home dress was far more elegant than anything Emma had owned before. "I should feel grateful," she thought to herself. "But, will I ever have a new gown made just for me?"

Fanny interrupted Emma's silent musings. "Almost all our invitations to this afternoon's tea have been accepted. Mistress Follett was first to respond. That woman is a twit, however she

139

does oversee her kitchen quite well. Have you inspected the scones and sweets, Emma?"

"Yes'm. And, I measured out your special tea so there'll be no added extravagance nor none left for the inn's larder." Noticing Fanny grab at her stomach, Emma adds, "Are you all right, Mistress?"

"Yes, but suddenly, I've this premonition. This baby, this child yet without a face or name, already has a destiny. I can feel it in the infant's stirring. How strange to know, to truly see, such a thing." Fanny closes her eyes and naps.

Fanny squints as she passes her needle up and down through the fine cloth. Ethan's pen moves quickly across the page. He stops to dip his nib into the ink. "Twill be a fine bonnet, m'lass," he grins.

Fanny seldom joins Ethan in his "office" as they've come to call this particular rented space. Now just into her ninth month of pregnancy, she no longer gives teas or elaborate dinner parties. Her need to be close to her husband grows greater each day, a characteristic she doesn't fully understand. Ethan fulfilled his promise to return from the Wyomings in the Susquehanna district but had agree to a second trip before the snow fell. Fanny had been persistent in her pleadings to prevent this additional trek and just yesterday Ethan had finally written a letter to the Susquehanna Company postponing his visit until the following spring.

"I've made so many of these little sets, I'm becoming quite bored with them," Fanny chuckles. "The girls and Emma have been equally diligent. Surely this infant will be the best dressed in all of Vermont." Fanny sighs deeply and tucks her needle half way through a stitch and places the work in what little lap remains.

"Ethan, will New York persuade Congress to invade Vermont? You've said so little about this insanity the last couple of weeks."

Ethan places his pen in the stand a drop of ink oozes down the glass. He takes his blotter and mops up the errant blob before rising to rub Fanny's shoulders. "You have enough discomfort; why should I bother you with politics?" He massages her right shoulder, deeply, slowly, trying to bring ease to the tenseness he recognizes in her muscles. Fanny rests her head against his strong hands as he works. For moments, neither speaks.

Finally, Fanny responds. "Such politics impact our lives, Ethan. No matter what, I want to know; to be prepared; to plan our strategy."

Switching to Fanny's left shoulder as he talks, Ethan says, "Sometimes I think you're more of a political being than even I, m'love." He bends to kiss her hair. "The latest word is that Congress will refuse to get involved in local pettiness. They've denied yet again, Vermont's petition for statehood. But they won't go so far as to invade these mountains to discipline us for our sins of standing firm as a republic—or for our negotiations to the north with New France. Such an endeavor is too costly. They're still reeling under indebtedness from the fight for liberty. Besides, I think they find New York a quarrelsome lot." Ethan feels Fanny's tension rise at his remarks. "Do I insult you, Mistress Yorker?"

Fanny turns to look up at her husband, a small smile lighting her slightly puffy face. "I'm a daughter of liberty these days; you've convinced me. At least, in bed, you've convinced me. Though during long afternoons, I'm less sure. Just don't go dropping judgment on my old friends."

Ethan decides a switch in topic would be wise. "Ira has begun his new house up north. He finally received funds from the sale of Sunderland. He writes that little will be accomplished through the winter months but he expects both our place and his will be ready by next summer. He's invited brother Heber's widow, Sarah, to keep house for him."

"A kindness, indeed. You've said how she struggles since Heber's death—and long before that with his illness." Fanny reaches up and pats Ethan's hands. "Enough, dearest. Your own kindnesses are much appreciated by this rotund wife. I feel better already. Back to your work and I'll be back to mine."

Ethan returns to his chair but turns to his wife before picking up his pen. "I've also heard from Stephen that Patrick has transferred authority of your inheritance over to me. I should be able to draw on these funds by the new year. I'll be needing the monies for the printing and the construction on our Onion River home."

"Does Stephen speak of progress on locating Crean's Irish daughter?" asks Fanny, avoiding the direct topic of mounting expenses. A slight twinge of fear grabs at her stomach.

"He mentions nothing." Ethan returns to his writing.

Chapter 20

Ethan's pacing stops abruptly as a cry breaks the silence in the hallway. Emma had condemned him to exile when he started giving orders midway through Fanny's labor. He'd attended none of his previous children's arrivals and felt that dismissal was, perhaps, a good thing. Fanny had certainly seemed to approve Emma's command, "Be gone with ya." Ethan pauses by the door, leans his ear to the thick panel and listens. All he can detect are the sounds of bustling activity and low, soothing indecipherable conversation frequently interrupted by bursts of squealing infant complaints.

"What a journey you just had," exclaims Ethan, wiping the light sweat from his forehead, then stuffing the damp linen back up his sleeve. He walks to his office, strolls to the window and stands quiet, enjoying the majestic view. Sighing he moves to his desk, pulls out his journal and enters a notation: "Born this day, November 4th, in the year 1784. . ." Ethan places his pen back in its holder, rises and strides to the birthing room. He yanks on his weskit, straightens his sleeves before offering a confident knock. "May I come in?"

Lucy opens the door, just enough to slide through, bringing with her a bundle of wiggling blanket. She smiles at her father then hands him the baby. "Careful, she's a squirmer."

"She?" than gasps and starts to unfold the cloth. "*It* is a girl?"

Lucy laughs, "Another girl. How will you survive this, Papa?"

Ethan raises the bundle up to his face, chuckling. "Guess we'll just have to try again."

"Papa! Not now; this is not the time to thinking such things."

The door opens and Emma invites Ethan into the room. Fanny is propped on several pillows, her damp hair straggling across the linen. She looks pale but a smile emerges as Ethan enters with the child. Lucy closes the door behind her father but turns down the hall to tell her sisters the news.

Ethan holds the baby in one arm and pulls a chair beside the bed with the other. "She's quite beautiful, this little girl of ours. We'll have to choose a name suitable to such charm."

Fanny smiles back at him. "I've been thinking of 'Margaret' after mother would be nice."

Ethan holds the baby girl up again and stares at her intently. "Truly, Margaret 'tis a lovely name but doesn't quite bring the excitement this little creature demands. I'm thinking 'Fanny' would do her well, after the most beautiful, charming woman I know."

Fanny reaches out and touches Ethan's knee. "You are kind, dearest. At the moment I feel neither; only quite tired."

"In honor of our own patriotic merger, shall we compromise and call her Frances Margaret?" Ethan reaches to stroke Fanny's brow.

"Oh, Ethan. I'm at a current disadvantage in this negotiation," smiles Fanny. She closes her eyes momentarily. Opening them moments later, she sighs, "All right then, Francis Margaret it is but I shall always call her Margaret."

Ethan watches his new daughter intently. As if satisfied that she now has an appropriate name, her eyelids flutter and slowly relax; her pursed lips intuitively begin to suck. Ethan passes the now quiet bundle to Emma who places the infant on the bed, nestled in her mother's arm. Fanny is already dozing. He leans over touching his lips gently to her forehead and whispers, "And, I shall always call her Fanny."

Ethan stands, returns to his office and completes his journal entry…"Frances Margaret Allen to be known henceforth and always as Fanny." He gently shuts the book, placing it at the back of his desk. "Time to toast the babe!" Ethan exclaims to no one. "Let's offer up a round to the boys in Green." Ethan gestures a spirited if imaginary, toast to the empty room and easily fancies the burning taste of rum on his tongue. He hurries out the door, down the hall, taking the stairs two at a time, and burst into Mr. Follett's tavern. In his loudest voice, and with a wide, proud sweep of his arm, Ethan proclaims, "Drinks all 'round. A salute: to my newest Fanny and to her mother, my fairest wife!"

Fanny Margaret sleeps in her cradle; Fanny's foot rhythmically taps the rocker keeping the two-month old infant swaying gently. Ethan sits, working at his desk. Only Fanny's hands show her agitation. Ever since this morning, she's been planning how to approach Ethan. Taking a deep breath and keeping her eyes focused on her handwork, she speaks. "Ethan, I saw Dr. Huntington this morning." Her fingers move back and forth with her needle.

"Mmm." Ethan continues to write.

"He happened to mention some monies due him for his services to Mary and Lorraine."

Ethan places his pen in the holder and turns to look at his wife. "Due him? I don't understand. Levi said he'd take care of that."

Fanny's foot begins to tap more rapidly; the baby sighs in her sleep. "And so he has, Ethan. He's paid off one of Dr. Huntington's debts. I've been led to believe my own use of his services has an outstanding debt."

"Well now, that could be true. There are quite a lot of bills I've been unable to attend."

"Are there still funds in my letter of credit, Ethan? We can't have spent it all." Her tapping gains in momentum. The baby momentarily opens her eyes as if to discern the cause behind the frantic rocking.

"You've expensive habits, m'love." Ethan turns to pick up his pen again, hoping to end this conversation before it accelerates.

"Not my habits alone, Ethan. Your tavern bill is quite extraordinary."

"Now, Fanny, you know I've had to advance the printer money on the *Oracles* and Ira has needed funds for our new homestead. Watch yourself or you'll tip the babe right out of her cradle."

Fanny takes her foot from the cradle rocker, letting it gradually slow before she speaks again. Her anger shows in her reddened face and shaking fingers. She stands, perhaps somehow trying to gain more power for her next thrust. She stomps across the braided rug to stand face to face with Ethan; her eyes now level with her seated husband.

"This is my money and my reputation you're playing with, Ethan. Your Green Mountain cohorts may forgive you your sloppy negligence in paying debts, but I'm accorded no such leniency— nor do I want to be. Mr. Follett's been hinting that we're over due on our lodgings."

Ethan stands, towering over his wife. "Surely, that can't be. I'll search my ledger to set this straight. Now you're not to fret your pretty head about such things. You've a babe to attend to; that should keep you busy enough." Ethan bends to pick up Fanny Margaret and hands her to Fanny. "You know that Ira, Levi, and I own more land than anyone else in this republic. I am a wealthy man." Ethan's voice rises, "And I only use your inheritance to pay current indebtedness."

"You seem forgetful even in that. I will not be shamed, Ethan!"

"There is no shame in owing, Fanny. That is how business functions. Here in these mountains, our word is our bond that debts will be settled. The baby is awake; best you tend to her. I cannot work with a squealing infant in the room."

Fanny shifts the baby to her shoulder and begins to pat the tiny back. Her body sways from side to side in an effort to soothe her daughter. Fanny can feel her own tension ooze into the small body as if the two were one in this argument. She looks up at Ethan defiantly. "I demand you give me an accounting each week of how you spend my money. We must gain control of our expenditures."

"You demand? I think not. No one places demands on Ethan Allen, not even his wife!" He returns to his desk and reseats himself. "Take Fanny Margaret; I need to get back to my writing."

Fanny gathers up her handwork, cradles the baby in her left arm and moves toward the door. Without turning, she says, "I will expect your first accounting on Monday next." She slams the door behind her and scurries down the hall to her own room. With the door closed she flops on the bed holding Fanny Margaret next to her breast and bursts into sobs. The baby joins in the lament with her own shrill, hiccupping wail.

Ethan scoops little Fanny Margaret from the floor as she scurries toward him, her knees catching on her cotton skirt. "You've become quite a crawler while we've been gone, little mistress." Ethan nuzzles his nose into her neck and the baby delights him with uncontrollable giggles. He gains a firmer grasp on her wiggling body. Whispering, he asks, "Did you miss mama and papa? We've been gone almost three weeks. Did Emma and the girls take good care of you, hmmmm?"

Fanny smiles at her husband and daughter. It's been a good trip, a special time with Ethan and she's almost sorry to see it end. Turning to Emma, Fanny laughs, "She certainly seems happy and well cared for. Where are the older girls? I've lots to show them." Turning to Ethan, she adds, "Here, give me my precious little girl. Would you please see that Master Follett has the crates and boxes brought up to the suite? The girls will be so excited." Holding Fanny Margaret and standing on tiptoe in her new silk boots, she tries to kiss Ethan under his chin but can't quite reach. "And on your way, stay out of the tavern, dearest. Ask that our evening meal be brought to the rooms. That way we can regale the family with stories of high society in the big city." She laughs as Ethan rolls his eyes in response and strides toward the door.

Fanny hands her daughter off to Emma as Lucy and her sisters burst in the room. She hugs each one in turn, delighted at the return response she receives.

Pamelia squeals in delight as her stepmother reaches into her silk brocade bag and removes a small package tied with pink ribbon. "You first, Pamelia," Fanny says as she hands the gift to Ethan's youngest. The sisters crowd around as the little girl struggles to untie the ribbon.

"Oooh! How very beautiful," whispers Pamelia. "Look, Lucy, Mary Ann!" Pamelia holds up a dainty silver looking-glass set with sparkling red jewels. She stares at herself in the mirror, twisting this way and that, smiling at herself.

Reaching into her bag once again, Fanny pulls forth two more gifts identically wrapped and hands them to the older two. "One for each of you."

Mary Ann tears the ribbon and paper from her gift and lifts the mirror to her chest. No words will come.

"Look," exclaims Fanny. "Yours is just like Pamelia's only with blue stones." Turning to Lucy, she adds, "And yours is green, to match your eyes." Lucy unwraps hers slowly. Since Fanny Margaret's birth seven months before, she has become more tolerant of her stepmother, but still, she doesn't want to seem overeager or dependent on Fanny's largesse.

"Thank you, oh, thank you. It's just too beautiful for words." Mary Ann gushes. Turning to her older sister, she adds, "Let me see yours."

Lucy holds her mirror up for all to see and smiles at Fanny. "It is truly quite exquisite. I didn't know such things existed."

Fanny hears a polite knock and moves to the door. Master Follett's servant has stacked several crates and boxes and asks permission to bring them into the Allen quarters. Granting him entrance, Fanny asks, "Where is General Allen?"

"In the tavern, I think Mistress. He was ordering your meal, I believe." The young man moves the boxes from the hall into the room, gives a slight bow, and backs out the door.

"Was he raising a quaff?" Fanny watches the young man carefully. When he does not answer but looks down at the floor, Fanny says, "Very well. Please tell the General his family awaits his presence to begin opening all of this." She gestures grandly toward the stacks.

Fanny and the girls sip tea while Emma holds Fanny Margaret in her lap. Emma listens attentively to her mistress. She doesn't want to miss even a small portion of the telling.

"There were so many parties, you couldn't believe how many we attended in those two weeks in New York. Mother

Buchanan was most gracious and held an elegant supper in our honor. All my old friends were there." Fanny takes a long sip from her cup before continuing. "They loved your father; welcomed him like he was a Loyalist."

Lucy gasps and Fanny laughs. "Your father was quite taken with the company we were keeping. We even had a whole afternoon tea along with M. Saint Jean de Crevecœur. Your father was fully in his element expounding away to the Frenchman. M. de Crevecœur is writing articles about the new America; published all over Europe. He's promised to write one whole piece about your father and Vermont. They've become fast friends, it seems. The man wants to buy land from your papa."

"And I shall sell it to him," laughs Ethan. So intent upon listening to Fanny, no one has seen him enter quietly.

"Papa!" All three girls scream and jump at once, rushing to be the first to their father. His arms are long enough to embrace them all. Little Fanny Margaret, not to be left out, squirms and raises her arms. The sounds she emits resemble "da da da." Feeling ignored, she lets out a screech that gains everyone's attention. They guffaw simultaneously and Ethan gathers his youngest into his arms and sits down in the large arm chair beside Fanny.

"I see Fanny is telling our secrets." Ethan turns to smile at his wife. "Indeed, we had quite a time. How will we ever be content in bucolic Vermont again?" His chuckles come from deep within. "Now! Shall we see what wonderful things Fanny has found in New York for our favorite girls?" He leans sideways to plant a quick kiss on Fanny's cheek struggling to keep hold of the energetic baby.

Fanny gains a sniff of whiskey and sighs inwardly. Aloud she says, "Little Fanny Margaret hasn't gotten anything yet. Ethan, can you find the box with her silver teething ring? I think it's the one marked in red."

Ethan pries open crate after crate while fanny unties twine from boxes. Luxurious fabrics drape to the floor. There's lace for Lucy, a gold chain for Mary Ann, dolls for Pamelia; even a new bonnet for Emma. Soon all the boxes save one are open and enjoyed.

"What's in the last crate, Papa?" Mary Ann points.

"Those are Fanny's books and artist paraphernalia. She had as much fun shopping for those as for your elegant luxuries."

"Even more," laughs Fanny. "It's been so long since I've been able to read the latest books from England and France. I've enough to last me until midwinter. We'll use some to add to your studies. Won't that be fun?"

"So much; you brought so much," sighs Lucy.

Ethan moves to hug his oldest daughter. "Since you couldn't make the journey with us, we thought we'd bring the city to you."

† † †

Through the slightly frosted pane, Fanny watches the snowflakes flutter and dance in the light wind. "The first snowfall is always the best for me." Fanny speaks to Emma as she fits the fine woolen to Fanny's expanding body. "There's an excitement one can't contain. I don't think on the endless, dark days of midwinter or the difficulties in getting the sleds through the drifts in January. I think only of the caprice of those tiny flakes; the unscripted ballet they perform—a performance seemingly just for those of us with the proper lenses to see."

Emma runs her needle in a quick basting stitch and responds with only a vague, "mmm." She knows Lucy will soon bring Fanny Margaret in from her afternoon nap and any opportunity to sew will be lost. The almost one-year-old girl demands full time attention and Emma will have to put off finishing Fanny's dress until only the candles bring light. She looks up as she hears a quick rap on the door.

"I'm entering bearing gifts, ready to receive me or not!" Ethan bursts through the door carrying a package carelessly wrapped in his own scarf. "My dearest, you look ravishing!" He bends to kiss Fanny on her lips and pats her stomach affectionately. "Tis a boy this time, I know it. I simply know it." He hands Fanny his gift with another kiss. "I give you this in celebration of this boy who grows within you."

150

Emma keeps her needle working. Her curiosity is a compelling as her need to complete the task.

Removing the scarf, Fanny holds up a cloth bound book. "Oh, Ethan, it's done. At last the Oracles are reality."

"You, my dearest, have honors of the very first copy."

Fanny studies the title: *Reason the Only Oracle of Man, or Compenduous System of Natural Religion.* Further the page expounds, "Alternately adorned with confutations of a variety of Doctrines incompatible to it; deduced from the most exalted Ideas which we are able to form of the Divine and Human Characters, and from the Universe in General." She thinks to herself, "From what I've already gleaned, the text is quite as tedious as the title indicates." Aloud, she exclaims, "You must be so proud. This represents years of your thoughts."

Ethan takes the book, turns the page and points, "Look here at what I've written."

Fanny takes back the book and looks at Ethan's own handwriting.

"This Book is a present from the Author to his Lady------
Dear Fanny wise, the beautiful and young,
The partner of my joys, my dearest self,
My love, pride of my life, your sexes pride,
And partner of Sincere politeness,
To thee a welcome compliment I make
Of treasures rich, the Oracles of Reason.

"Oh, Ethan!" Fanny leans into his chest; her tears dampen his weskit. "You can be so thoughtful."

Emma snips her thread, gathers her sewing and rises. "I'll get your gown later and finish this evening." She curtsies, hiding her smile. She closes the door quietly as she leaves. "That woman turns to porridge when the Master offers her cream," she giggles as she walks down the hall to her own room.

Ethan turns Fanny around and lifts the unfinished gown over her head. As he works, he continues his chatter. "I've sent out a few copies; one to Stephen, of course. One to Benjamin Stiles; he wanted to read my persuasions right away. The man delights in debating my ideas. And then, I had another sent to de Crevecoeur;

he's back in Paris, you know. There are 41 copies ready to be distributed, and more to be completed by our contract."

Fanny watches her husband finish his breakfast. She's eaten earlier with the girls but she enjoys these moments with Ethan. They've developed a pattern. Fanny rises early and supervises the baby's feeding now that Fanny Margaret eats from the table and not from the breast. Ethan also is up and about, usually at his desk, but when weather permits, he strides about Bennington, chatting with early shopkeepers and whomever else he encounters. By nine o'clock his hunger demands attention and he returns to a sturdy meal in their quarters. Fanny joins him and they talk of whatever strikes them. These days, deep into her second pregnancy, Fanny often sneaks bites from Ethan's plate. Her hunger is insatiable; her plump cheeks reflecting an inability to control her gulosity. This morning, Fanny listens only halfheartedly as Ethan speaks of the wrath his book has engendered among the clergy and some scholars. She's tired of Ethan's impotent railings yet she discourages him from publicly attacking his detractors.

"...these clergy, so filled with their power to corrupt, do not use their brains..."

Fanny hears the rushing footsteps before Ethan who is somewhat mesmerized by his own words. She reaches out, touching his arm, to silence him.

Bam! Wham! The door shakes from the brutal pounding. Ethan leaps from his chair, knocking it to the floor in his haste. Fanny pushes her bulk from her seat and follows Ethan to the door. He pulls it open just as Master Follett is about to pound anew. The blow hits Ethan in mid-chest.

Follett and another fellow, covered with dirt and soot, speak almost as one. "Fire! There's a fire; you must come!"

"Here?" screams Fanny. "The children; get the children!" She shoves past Ethan but Master Follett restrains her.

"No. Not here; at the printers!"

Fanny's knees give way and Ethan grabs at her to keep her from falling. He half carries her back to her chair, yelling as he moves. 'Emma! Come quickly, Emma! Lucy!" Having safely seated his wife, Ethan turns and follows the dirty fellow whom he now realizes is David Russell, one of the printers. He shouts over his shoulder to Emma, "Take care of Fanny. There's a fire at the printer's." He's down the stairs, leaping three at a time, his mind having left his family and turned fully to those partially printed volumes, the major musings of his spiritual connection.

Emma holds Fanny's head to her breast, trying to calm her mistress' sobs. "I thought we were going to die—my babies, the girls!"

"Now, now," soothes Emma. "You've had a mighty scare. We're safe, all of us." Emma gently rocks her own body against Fanny's working to slow her own pulse as well as that of the now hiccoughing Fanny. "Let me take you to your bed. We don't want to rush that little boy into this world too soon." Her adrenalin back under control, Fanny pliantly allows Emma to lead her to bed.

Lying beneath the comforter, a cool, damp cloth on her forehead, Fanny has quieted her body but not her mind. "Is this some kind of revenge against Ethan's words?" she ponders. "The attacks on his books have become so volatile; would they dare such an act?" She feels the child move within her and places her hand over the pulsating bump in her abdomen. Unconsciously, she tries to quiet the infant by gently rubbing the spot caused by a nervous foot in utero. Fanny's thinking takes another twist. "We've paid for the printing. Will there be nothing to show for our investment?" Her sobbing begins anew.

Hours later, just before suppertime, Ethan enters Fanny's dark room to find her quietly dozing. He drops his weary body into the chair Emma had occupied throughout the day. His head bows and he hold his face in his palms. His breathing is ragged as he tries to stifle his own sobs. The unexpected sounds raise Fanny from her light sleep. She calls out, "Ethan? Is that you?"

"Yes," he manages but the word sounds stretched and taut, like a bowstring.

"Tell me Ethan, what was saved?" Fanny struggles to sit. She reaches out and tenderly strokes her husband's hands still covering his face. "Was anyone hurt?"

"No. Thankfully, all are safe. The same cannot be said for my volumes."

"Dearest," Fanny pulls Ethan's trembling hands down onto her belly. "Dearest."

"All is lost, Fanny. Even the bound copies are charred beyond use."

"How did the fire start? Does anyone know?" Fanny leans over her bulk to kiss Ethan's forehead.

"The apprentice arrived this morning to find a small area of flames in the back room. Stupidly, he did not strive to extinguish the flames, but ran for Russell and Haswell instead. By the time they arrived the whole back room was afire. There seems no reason for the fire. Russell and Haswell are careful with their inks, storing them properly to prevent ignition." Ethan raises his head and looks into Fanny's eyes. "There are rumors about, Fanny."

"Rumors? What kind of rumors?"

"Some say a group of clergy paid Russell and Haswell to set fire to 'Satan's work'."

"Do you believe them, Ethan?" Fanny touches Ethan's cheek, brushing away a single tear making its way down a crevice between two wrinkles.

"Russell and Haswell are honest men. I know they've not approved of my work, but I trust their integrity as tradesmen. My trust of the clergy is far less. But even they seem incapable of such heinous crime. Is this new country of ours not founded on the ideal that every man is allowed to voice his opinion without fear of retribution?"

"True," nods Fanny. "But, if they think you satanic, the rules change Ethan."

"There is no Satan, Fanny. There is no such entity to steal our souls and drag us into a fiery hell. It is all the rantings of clergy aimed to frighten people into obeisance. Such theology is made of Man, not of God." His broad, powerful shoulders shudder in Fanny's comforting embrace.

The two cling to each other, each with different thoughts. Ethan frets about the loss of his labor of love, *Oracle of Reason*, while Fanny's fears grow quickly about the state of their finances. Ethan has used all her inheritance to fund the printing. What remains of their resources seems to rest only in Ethan's land holdings, with little cash to provide for daily life. Fanny sighs deeply as she removes herself from Ethan's embrace.

Ethan brushes his lips across Fanny's furrowed brow and then loudly whispering into the air, manages, "I'm going out to see if anyone is willing to speak to this willful horror. Why don't you rest; you look exhausted and you're so close to birthing."

Fanny looks at him, grabs his hand and pleads, "Ethan, please, please stay out of the tavern."

Ethan sighs and heads for the door.

Chapter 21

Mr. Follett stands beside the shay holding the paper up to Ethan. "General Allen, there still remains this balance due on your lodgings. I demand payment."

"You know I'm good for it, Follett. I'll send a letter of credit when I reach Burlington and have received the funds from Ira. Thank you for your kindnesses; we are most grateful."

Ethan flicks the whip over the horse's head and the small caravan of wagons slowly begins the journey north to Burlington. The October air carries a chill and Ethan has wrapped Fanny in a wool blanket and insisted she wear her winter bonnet. Fanny had little strength to object and now she'd settled as comfortably as possible into the padded shay seat.

Fanny silently ponders this new phase in their life. They had sold much of their fine furniture, porcelain, and silver to pay debts and to lighten the load for the journey to the Burlington farm. The girls had fretted about the move with Lucy demanding to stay behind. Ethan had allowed his daughter this privilege declaring her old enough as long as she resided with his friends, the Butlers. They'd agreed to welcome her and promised Ethan periodic reports on Lucy's adventures. There was much of Ethan in his second oldest daughter, and Fanny wonders what challenges will befall the Butlers.

Ethan's voice rouses Fanny from her thoughts. "Are you excited, m'love? We're off to our very own home. You'll love Burlington; it's a growing town with new commerce and new people arriving daily. You'll be the queen of it all!"

As Ethan chuckles at his jest, Fanny rallies to a noncommittal response, "Hardly a queen, Ethan. More a mother in homespun." She bites her lip to keep from saying more. No need to start this new venture with a fight that might last all the way to Burlington. Besides, her thoughts were more heavily focused on keeping the child in her womb, until they reached their new home.

Ethan turns his head to check on the three wagons stretched out behind the shay. In the first wagon, Emma holds Fanny Margaret securely in her lap while Mary Ann and Pamelia sit on the back bench gawking at the brightly colored maples. Fanny had given each of the girls paper and ink to record the journey and to draw what most appealed to them. As Ethan eyes the last two wagons containing their remaining household furnishings and clothing for the journey, he is confident that all is secure. His dream to become a simple farmer in his beloved Vermont unfolds in front of him. If only Fanny shared his enthusiasm with equal zest.

✝ ✝ ✝

Fanny is restless, pacing back and forth in the Collins' parlor. Bessie and John have been most hospitable but Fanny aches for their own house to be finished. Each day, Ethan offers a new estimate for completion of the structure. They've been encroaching on the Collins family for over two months and patience is wearing thin on both sides, albeit with some humor and little anger.

Fanny gasps. "My God, it can't be. I've not my own bed yet." She grabs her stomach and stumbles to the nearby chair, knocking it to the floor. Emma, in the kitchen, hears the clatter and rushes to Fanny's side. "Mistress! Is it the baby?" Fanny nods with a grimace and groan.

Bessie Collins, noting the commotion, dashes in behind Emma. "Quick, start the kettle boiling, Emma. Fanny, take hold of my arm. We'll use my bed; it's quieter in there." Turning her head, Bessie shouts, "Mary Ann, quickly! Help Emma. Your new brother or sister is beginning its arrival. Pamelia, go tell John to fetch Ethan at the farm." Bessie, clearly in charge, brings order amidst the chaos of excitement. She thinks to herself, "There hasn't been a bairn in this house for many a year. But I remember; I still remember!"

Having settled a groaning Fanny in her bed, Bessie goes for bedding, towels, and the cottons they've been preparing for this very event. Emma and Mary Ann arrive with pitchers of hot water and a bowl filled with clean rags. Mary Ann, flushed with excitement, giggles loudly.

157

"'T isn't funny," screeches Fanny as she tosses from side to side looking for something, someone to grab onto.

"Mary Ann, go, hold your mother's hand; sing to her!" urges Bessie as she begins preparations with the cottons and towels.

Fanny releases a piercing scream, grabs Mary Ann's arm as if to twist it awry. Mary Ann glances at Bessie for encouragement. Receiving none, she takes a damp rag and begins wiping Fanny's brow, grateful for the feeling returning slowly to her arm.

"This is too fast," pants Fanny. "Fanny Margaret took so long to come. Is something amiss, Bessie? Is the baby safe?"

"Everything seems in order, m'dear, but I can't tell yet. The crowning has just begun. Be thankful for a quick birthing, m'dear." Bessie watches closely as the infant begins to emerge.

A shriek, a groan, and then a loud scream. Shoulders appear and Bessie takes hold gently, cooing as she encourages the infant—and mother. Seconds more and the baby is half way through the birth canal. "One more really strong push, Fanny, and the bairn will join us fully. Go at it, girl!"

Needing no instruction, Fanny bites on the rag Mary Ann holds to her mouth and pushes with all her might!

"Tis a boy!" Chuckles Bessie. Ethan has his boy! A beautiful, healthy boy!"

"Thank god," declares Fanny. "Perhaps now there'll be peace." She sinks back into the pillows exhausted. She does not hear the commotion below as John and Ethan come crashing into the house.

Bessie greets the two men at the door with her finger to her lips. "Shhh, Fanny rests now. But, here, Ethan, here is your new son."

Ethan takes the boy from Bessie, cradling him to his chest. Quietly he crosses the room, leans over Fanny and kisses her on the forehead. "Thank you, m'love, thank you." Fanny manages a faint smile and drifts back into rest.

Ethan, grinning widely, hands the babe back to Bessie. "Here, Bessie, you know much better than I what needs doing for this little fellow. I shall go record the event in my journal."

Taking the stairs two at a time, Ethan strides into the parlor where John has already prepared the celebratory libation. The two toast the newborn. . .and, Fanny. . .and, Bessie. . .and. . .

Ethan settles his journal on the table, inkstand at the ready. He takes the quill, dips it in the ink and writes "born this 24th day of November in the year 1787, is Hannibal Montresor Allen, son of Ethan and Frances Allen. Great joy fills my heart." Turning to John, he shouts, "Fill the tankards again, man! There's much to celebrate!"

Baby Hannibal is but three weeks old when Ethan moves his family into their new farmhouse sitting on the 400 cleared acres of their 1400 acres, total land. What furniture they had left had been stored in their new barn but moved into the house waiting to greet the new occupants. Ethan had appointed Emma to set up all their belongings in the two story, 24 foot by 40 foot structure. Fanny had been left somewhat weakened by Hannibal's arrival and spent much of the last weeks lying beneath a down comforter in the Collins' house. Bessie was a good companion but Fanny was deeply depressed and often cried while Bessie comforted her with tea and stories.

Many of Fanny's thoughts focus on her changing lifestyle. She reflects on past balls, travel, and the luxuries of fine satins and jewels. Much of this finery has been sold or given away. Jewels paid debts, and there were so very many of those to be discharged. Ethan spent more and more time in the taverns, drinking and discussing past battles. Fanny lacked energy and couldn't grasp just where to recover her passions.

Moving day proves stressful for all. Ethan, Emma, Fanny Margaret, and the older girls go ahead in the wagons while Fanny wraps Hannibal in several blankets, dons her winter bonnet, embraces Bessie tightly, then steps firmly into the shay. Her new life falls before her and a slim enthusiasm begins to creep through her heart. "After all," Fanny thinks, "so deeply to I love Ethan, our togetherness means more than what we've left behind. Or, at least I plead so."

The shay stops at the front door of the new farmhouse. Fanny draws a deep breath, brushes a kiss on Hannibal's forehead, and struggles to alight with some dignity. Ethan throws open the door, a wide grin across his face. He grabs Fanny and Hannibal, lifting them both over the threshold while laughing with delight.

"Welcome, dearest Fanny and beloved son to our new home. Great things shall happen here. Farmers at last! What could be more wonderful!"

"You're the farmer, Ethan, not me." Fanny tries to keep the hurt from her voice. "While you work the earth, dear one, I shall be a mother. And, if there are still any paints, charcoal, and paper left, I shall indulge my passions."

The winter of 1787/88 proves difficult. The northern Vermont weather crowds in around the farmhouse, leaving ice and snow clinging to eaves and small window panes, blocking much of the daylight. Inside, the occupants struggle to create a routine in the small space. There are but four rooms on the first floor and two above. Fanny and Ethan's room, the largest, taking up the south end of the building also accommodates baby Hannibal. The small utility room to the west houses the spinning wheels, loom, and washing supplies. The kitchen, almost equal in size to Fanny and Ethan's room, fills the north end. The huge fireplace constantly blazes for both cooking and heat. The front door, to the east enters into the tiny parlor. Life hovers in the kitchen.

Emma and Fanny Margaret's room sits directly over the adult bedroom while Mary Ann and Pamelia share the room over the kitchen, benefitting from the heat rising from the fireplace below, heating the chimney stones as well. Good planning on Ethan's part has the privy located but fifty feet from the back door in the utility room, making Emma's job of emptying the chamber pots less hazardous.

Ethan bored with no physical labor to be done, visits the taverns when he can urge the horse through the deep snow. Often he arrives home after Fanny has fallen asleep. He stumbles about, waking Hannibal and irritating Fanny. Yet, he swears he's absolutely uninfluenced by the drink.

One morning in mid-February, Fanny offers Ethan an ultimatum. "You say you are sober, Ethan. You will need to prove it to me. I have placed a nail high in the wall above your side of the bed. When you arrive home you must hang your watch fob on that nail. If you fail to do so, I will know you are inebriated."

"Fanny, dammit, you've no right!"

"Indeed, I do have a right, General Allen. Our children are under this roof and you are responsible for their well-being. You cannot provide such when you are under the influence of rum or ale."

As April melts the snows, Ethan puts aside his writing, and begins to tend the land he has so long yearned to work. Activity has heightened his attitude and Fanny begins to relax and enjoy the tranquility. Ethan spends most of his waking hours planning, physically digging post holes, or walking behind the plow while hired hand, Newport, guides the ox over the rough, rock-laden terrain. There is little time for reveling at the tavern and Allen domesticity has returned to everyone's relief.

Fanny expects much of Emma and the older girls. Emma's day is long with her cleaning, cooking, and child care responsibilities. The older girls spend time at their studies as required by Fanny. Little Fanny Margaret and Baby Hannibal are often at Fanny's feet as she draws and paints. Fanny is determined to paint one of every single plant in this north country. The spring season brings many specimens to delight Fanny's eye, some of which she had not seen in lower Vermont. When Fanny completes a new painting, she gives the flowers to Fanny Margaret who likes to pinch and sniff the petals.

This sunny, late April afternoon, the aroma of fresh lamb roasting on the spit fills the whole house. There will be potatoes and carrots that had been kept in the root cellar. Fanny wanders outside to see, if perhaps, any wild mint has begun to sprout. "Would add a spark to the lamb," she muses aloud. When she finds none, she wanders slowly back toward the house, waving to Ethan in the far field. The smell of dank, fresh earth fills her nostrils and she breathes deeply to savor the aroma. It's as if she can feel the new plants pushing hard against the soil to burst forth and catch the sunbeams. Her cotton skirts sweep across the ground, capturing mud on their hems. Fanny removes her shawl and waves it in the air. Her muddy shoes demand to dance and Fanny succumbs to temptation, twirling about humming to the beat of her heart.

"This feels so right," Fanny thinks. "Only great things can come from this good earth."

Exhilarated from the fresh air, Fanny's step is light as she skips back to the house. Emma collects clothes from the drying line. She looks at Fanny and asks, "Where's little Fanny Margaret? I thought she was with you."

"No, might she be hiding in the barn again? I'll check." Fanny's heart gives a quick little leap as she calls through the barn door. "Fanny Margaret? Stop playing games and come on inside with me." No answer. "Fanny Margaret?"

Fanny turns to Emma. "Check the house. Quickly!"

Emma disappears through the kitchen door and just as quickly returns. "Not here!"

Fanny's heart sinks. She turns towards the fields and screams. "Ethan. Ethan. Newport! Come quickly. Fanny Margaret is missing."

The two men come running, leaving the horse in the field still attached to the plow. When the men reach the shaken women, Ethan starts giving orders. "Newport, head to the barn and check the loft. She loves to play there. Emma, check the house thoroughly, she may be hiding to tease us. Fanny, you come with me; we'll search toward the river."

Ethan grabs Fanny's hand, giving it a reassuring squeeze. "She's fine, Fanny, I'm sure of it. She's fine." His words were to calm himself as much as to ease Fanny's fears. They head toward the river, eyes searching through the newly greening pastures.

"There she is," shouts Ethan, letting go of Fanny's hand and running toward his young daughter. Fanny lifts her skirts and follows as quickly as her shorter legs can move.

Ethan grabs Fanny Margaret up into his arms. "You're soaking wet little one. Are you all right?" He holds his daughter

162

close to his chest to quiet her shivering. Fanny grabs at Ethan, tears coursing down her cheeks.

"Darling! What happened. How did you get so wet?" weeps Fanny.

"I fell into the river, Mommy. I was so scared. I couldn't breathe. Then this man saved me. He pulled me out of the water and said, 'you'll be all right, little one, you'll be fine.'"

"Who was this man, Fanny Margaret? Do you know him?" asked Ethan.

"No, Papa. I've never seen him. He was so very kind though, and gentle."

Ethan hands his daughter to Fanny saying, "Take the little one back to the house and get her dry and warm. I'll look for this man and thank him; offer him a reward."

Fanny carries the shivering child back to the house. Once inside, she calls to Emma to heat some water for a bath. Emma chatters away as she waits for the water to warm on the stove.

"You silly, silly child. 'Tis too early to go swimming. Oh, I'm so glad you're safe, precious one!" She can't stop talking, and repeats herself over and over in her own guilt for not keeping a closer eye on her charge.

Even little Hannibal adds his crying to the emotion-dripping room. Fanny clothes her clean and dried daughter in a warm nightgown, and wraps her own shawl around the little shoulders. Fanny pulls a small stool close to the fire and sits the little girl firmly on the seat.

Just then, Ethan sticks his head in the door to report. "No sign of any stranger in the area. I checked up and down the river banks and no one has seen such a man." He turns to Fanny Margaret, "Did you make up that story about the man so you wouldn't get scolded, young lady?"

"No, Papa. I would never tell a lie to you. He was a really nice man with a white beard and lots of white hair. I promise."

Ethan shakes his head and rolls his eyes at his wife before he leaves to go back to the fields where Newport has returned to continue the plowing.

The sun still sets early, before the church tower chimes six. Ethan and Newport have quit for the day, feeding the livestock as the last chore. They wash up in the back room while Emma puts the meal on the table. As Ethan readies to seat himself, he staggers and grabs the back of the chair. He gasps for air and turns somewhat gray. Fanny and Newport grab for Ethan and help him to his seat.

"Ethan did you carry rum to the field?" scolds Fanny.

"No ma'am," says Newport. "He's not had a drink all day. I swear! I thinks he's sick."

"I'm fine," manages Ethan. "Just one of those little spells I have now and again."

"Spells?" gasps Fanny, grabbing the back of the chair.

"I'm fine, I tell you—just fine!" A pinkish glow returns to Ethan's face and he seems fully in touch with his faculties once again. "Sit, everyone, I'm famished. Smells delicious, Emma. You feeling better, missy?" as he turns to his daughter.

Hardly anyone speaks during the meal. Ethan offers some occasional words on crops or cattle, but mostly everyone stares at their plates and methodically plies food into their mouths. Ethan is. . .well, Ethan is indomitable. No one has ever contemplated Ethan as anything but hearty, healthy, and gregarious. Can Ethan become sick? Ethan is a man beyond human weaknesses such as illness and death. "Ethan controls his own universe," observes Fanny silently.

Spring turns into summer. Fanny Margaret's little adventure is mostly forgotten. The grass grows slowly and the garden vegetables seem well tended but prospering slowly under Mary Ann and Pamelia's care. The Black Flies come in late May and disappear by July. August is especially dry in 1788, leaving many hay fields withering before their time. September brings a sparse harvest for most of northern Vermont. In October, the normally bright reds, golds and oranges are somewhat lackluster this year. Men gather in the taverns to discuss winter predictions and wonder how they will make it through to spring. Women, to their spinning, speak of partially filled root cellars and poor fleece on the sheep. There is concern afoot most everywhere.

In late December, Fanny finds herself pregnant once again. She is not pleased. Ethan, however, is delighted with himself. At 52, he can still father a child. This spectacular information raises Ethan's spirits to certainty the world is indeed good. Winter will pass and the earth rise to production once again. Surely, 1789 will be a fine year—both for the farm and for his family.

In early February, Ethan realizes there is not enough hay and grain to feed the already thinning cattle. He writes askance to his cousin Ebenezer for some fodder for his herd. Ebenezer has had a good crop due to his location to the south in Hero. On February 11th, Ethan and Newport head out for Hero with a team of oxen pulling the sled across the ice on Lake Champlain. Fanny warns Newport to keep Ethan from the taverns and he agrees.

The next day, fully loaded with hay and grain, Ethan and Newport head north toward home. About an hour into the journey, Ethan starts to shake and spittle drips from his mouth. Newport tries to comfort him but Ethan loses consciousness. Newport urges the oxen on. It seems an endless journey until they at last pull into the farm. Newport carries the unconscious Ethan into the house, placing him on his bed.

Fanny runs screaming from the room. "I told you to keep him from the drink!"

"He's sick, ma'am, not drunk. Can't stop shaking. He's been this way for several hours. He's mighty sick, ma'am."

Fanny returns to the bedside, taking hold of Ethan's cold hand. She murmurs his name over and over. Tears drip unnoticed down her cheeks. Mary Ann and Pamelia join Fanny at Ethan's side. Emma fixes strong tea for all and finds she too has tears trickling from her eyes.

Newport excuses himself and heads for the door. "I'll fetch Master Ira!"

"He's down to Manchester," sobs Pamelia. "Uncle's down to Manchester."

The moon rises, reflecting on the river waters outside the Allen homestead. All is mostly quiet; only the sobs of four women stirring the warm, pungent air of the bedroom.

Ethan twitches, tries to mutter something indistinguishable; he shudders. A strange rattle escapes from his lungs up his throat and out his lips. Ethan breathes no more.

Fanny throws herself across Ethan's body. She kisses his eyelids shut; caresses his cheeks. She lays her face on his chest where only moments before Ethan's heart was thumping. "My darling, darling Ethan! What shall I do without you? You brought my life to the joy of true love. Ethan. Oh, my Ethan."

Newport races to the barn, saddles a horse, and rides hell bent for the nearest tavern. Rushing in, Newport shouts, "The General is dead! General Allen is dead!" He turns and rushes back out the door, mounts on the run and heads south on the road to Manchester. He stops at many taverns along the way, spreading the word of the hero's death. He wonders how he will find Ira, but is positive someone will know his whereabouts. After all, who is more famous in all of Vermont than Ethan and Ira Allen.

✝   ✝   ✝

Ira is exhausted after his hard ride home beside Newport. He goes first to Ethan's house to soothe Fanny before returning to his own bed. His knock on the heavy wooden door is answered by a tearful Emma.

"How is Fanny? The girls?" pants Ira.

"Asleep, mostly. Mistress is stretched out beside the general, refusing to leave his side."

"Fix me a tankard of tea, heavy with the rum. I'm needing some warmth for my body as well as my heart." Ira turns and quietly moves into the bedroom, careful not to let the door bang behind him. Fanny is curled in a fetal position with Ethan's now rigid hand tucked between her breasts. Ira approaches the bed, stares at his brother lying still and grey, and swallows a cry before touching Fanny gently on the shoulder.

"Fanny, I'm here now. Let me help you clean and prepare Ethan's body."

Startled, Fanny gasps, then turns on the bed toward Ira. "Oh, Ira. What will we do? How shall I ever manage? Why has he left me?" Fanny breaks into sobs, hiccoughing between spasms.

"First, let's go into the kitchen and get something hot to drink. We can discuss our plans for the burial." Ira reaches out, helping Fanny to her feet. She's a heavy weight on his arm, belying her tiny body. "We'll shut the door behind us, and give Ethan some private time."

"Do you really believe Nature extends a body's life?" Fanny manages between sobs.

"Well, I'm never quite sure about Ethan's ideas on that, m'dear. What we do know now is there's a funeral to plan and the weather is moving in fast. Feels like snow, I'm afraid.

Emma has tea ready, having poured a fair share of rum into Fanny's tankard as well. The three sit at table in front of the blazing fire. Finally, Fanny is the first to speak. "A small gathering here at the farm, I think. We'll bury him on the farthest edge of the south field, near the river."

"Fanny, I heartily disagree. Ethan's wish has always been to be buried under a volley of arms with the Vermont emblem swishing in the wind overhead. There are so many people who hold honor for Ethan, we cannot deny them a grand farewell."

Fanny's sobs return as she begins to speak, "How difficult for the girls, Ira. Grief is a strange bed partner and I don't want to subject them to public scrutiny."

"Leave them home, then, Fanny. It's the General the public wants to see, not his children." Ira pauses for a deep swallow of tea before continuing. "As for a location, we must find an appropriate spot. Ethan is a hero, Fanny. A monument will soon arise, I'm sure, to his glorious leadership. Let me take care of this."

"Deny his children a final farewell. Never! Ethan loved his children. He would want them at his burial."

"Then we must put both your desires and Ethan's together. You're a strong young woman, Fanny. You will hold the children to your side, and all of you will stand tall for the sake of Ethan's wishes. Time for me to leave and return to Jerusha. I'm sure she's heard the news by now and will be expecting me. I'll call tomorrow." Ira places his tankard resolutely on the table, touches Fanny on the shoulder and moves to leave.

Fanny reaches out to grab Ira's arm. Looking up at her brother-in-law, she nods slightly before saying, "I await news of your plans." As the door closes behind Ira, Fanny exhales, "as you say, Colonel!"

Emma speaks up, "Shall we clean the General's body and dress him? Now is a good time while the girls are asleep and Hannibal is comfortable in his cradle? I've prepared some cloths.

Fanny sighs in response. "I hope I'm up to the task, Emma. My pain is so deep, thoughts flee and only loneliness remains."

The two women go about their task, nary a word between them. Clothing Ethan is difficult as *rigor mortis* has set in. Finally finished, both Fanny and Emma climb the stairs to sleep. Fanny can no longer bear to share a bed with the dead Ethan. She will crawl in beside the girls.

Newport waits in the parlor until everyone has gathered in the kitchen for breakfast. Even though no one is hungry, Emma needs to fill her mind with cooking and serving. "Ma'am," speaks Newport, "Mister Ira has instructed me to move General Allen to his house. Two gentlemen outside will help me. Do you wish to be in the room while we carry him out?"

Fanny looks at the girls who begin to cry again. "I think not, Newport. Thank you for your thoughtfulness. Will Ira be coming here today or does he wish us to come to his house?"

"He said he would visit you before evening after he has begun recruitment of troops. I, myself, will return shortly in order to care for the animals. You can count on me, Mistress Fanny."

Fanny wanders about the house, now quiet with grief. She desperately needs comfort but must stay strong for the children. Tears come, then vanish. The pain in her heart is deep. "I need Maggy," she says aloud. "Where is my beloved doll?" Ethan filled that space Maggy had held for so long. "Where is she. I must find her!" Fanny begins a frantic search for the ragged doll, digging through drawers and trunks. Finally! There she was, tucked between folds of a cherished old shawl Mother Margaret had given her years before.

"Maggy, oh Maggy. I need you so," weeps Fanny. She clutches the doll to her breast. "Help me, Maggy, help me!" Fanny tucks the doll into her apron bib where she carries her throughout the next days, not wanting to be parted from her as she had been parted from Ethan.

The next days are filled with tears and memories. What dresses should be worn? Will the weather hold? Will the river ice hold a procession of mourners to the burial spot? Should Fanny offer a barrel of reserve rum for the condolence gathering? Ethan won't be needing it any more—on the other hand, Fanny might sell it for much needed cash. So many decisions, so little energy to rise to the tasks. The new babe stirs in the womb. The movement brings more tears to Fanny's already drained eyes.

The day of the funeral, northwest winds rush across Lake Champlain. Dark clouds loom between sun and snow covered earth. The huge crowd mulls restlessly, waiting for the family to arrive so the procession can begin. A whole regiment has arrived with a special platoon out in front. Today each of these former militiamen will honor their beloved General.

The front door of Ira's house opens and the Allen family emerges. First comes Ira and Jerusha who holds Fanny's arm to keep her steady. The girls follow, Mary Ann holding tight to Fanny Margaret's hand. Emma, with Hannibal in her arms, walks close behind. Levi's family comes next, followed by faithful Newport whom Fanny insisted should be included. A hush palls over the gathered as the family walks slowly up to the coffin that holds General Allen. A bugle blows and the procession moves forward one slow step at a time. They cross the river above the dam, each praying the ice will hold strong 'til everyone has crossed safely. Upon reaching the hilltop, the platoon circles the gravesite while the regiment lines up behind them. The family circles opposite the platoon. Ira steps forward to speak a tribute. The wind blows his words into the clouds.

Fanny doesn't want to hear Ira's words. Her mind focuses on the day Ethan shared his dream of the magnificent white horse. "At least he has his mountain top." Tears trickle silently down to her bonnet strings, turning to icy dots as they land.

The sound of gunshots and cannon snap Fanny from her tearful reverie. Fanny remembers little of what happened next. She spoke to so many people, thanked them for their sorrow, and tried to keep her children from being lost in the crowd. Sometime later, long after nightfall, Newport has driven them all home. That first night back in her own bed, she finally cried herself to sleep, holding tight to Maggy for comfort. She knew she could not continue to live in this house without Ethan.

In the next months, Fanny finds lodging for the family at Widow Lawrence's. Her husband had just died in April and needed both the companionship and the rent. The two widows take to each other for comfort. Fanny sold many of the household pieces but left enough furniture, pottery, and utensils for Newport and his new wife to use. Fanny has insisted Newport stay on at the farm and tend to the animals and fields. Newport is to receive a portion of the profits—if there are any--as his own. At the very least he will be fed and housed safely. Ira, in charge of Ethan's small estate, has agreed this a capital move.

In early October, Fanny takes to her bed, depressed and distraught. The doll, Maggy, is her constant companion. Fanny talks to her doll when she won't speak with anyone else. She feels the baby's shift in her belly and knows she is about to give birth to Ethan's final gift to her. Emma and the older girls try to comfort her to no avail. As the sun crests the eastern mountains on October 24th, Fanny feels the first twinges of labor. Sadness fills her heart. "When this child is born, I shall no longer have you inside me, my beloved husband," Fanny sobs quietly.

As the morning progresses, Emma and Mary Ann prepare for the birthing, each trying to find the right words to comfort Fanny. Before the evening meal hour, Fanny has born a son. She holds the infant close to her breast, rocking back and forth crying silently. "Oh, Ethan, my Ethan, if only you were here." Fanny falls asleep exhausted. In her dreams she sees a magnificent white stallion looking down on her from the mountaintop. A peaceful sigh escapes her lips heard only by Emma who was sitting watch. Emma reaches out and lifts the newborn, Ethan Alphonso, from his mother's limp arms.

Chapter 22
THE PENNIMAN YEARS
1793 - 1810 and Beyond

Ethan Alphonso's birth adds challenge to an already over-crowded household. Fanny still finds it difficult to rise from her bed and tend to her tasks. Emma has taken over total responsibility for the children. Their schoolwork goes un-programmed with Mary Ann uninterested in bringing the children to their studies. Widow Lawrence, compassionate to Fanny's plight, still feels the strain. She ponders how to best approach Fanny with her concerns.

Ice crystals coat the small windows as Widow Lawrence carries her single candle toward Fanny's room. The moon has risen, its light making the crystal formations dance with color. Widow Lawrence takes a deep breath as she raises her arm to knock on Fanny's door.

"Come in," is all Fanny can muster. Seeing Widow Lawrence, Fanny raises herself on her pillows, pulling her shawl tightly around her shoulders. "Please, dear friend, come sit by my side. Here, put Baby Ethan in his cradle. He's sleeping soundly, I think; not likely to wake."

Having placed the candle on the bedside table and tucked the babe into his cradle, Widow Lawrence sits next to Fanny on the bed. She takes hold of Fanny's hands. The two women sit silently for several minutes. Mistress Lawrence finally breaks the still air, "Fanny, dearest, we've become such good friends. We've helped each other through some difficult months. I need to say how very honored I am to have General Allen's family in my house. The time has come for both you and me to make some decisions."

Tears well up in Fanny's eyes. "You have been so kind to us. We're grateful for your patience and caring. I know how such a house full of people must impose on your good will. I want you to know that I've been writing Mother Margaret and Stephen Bradley asking them to find housing for us in Westminster. I'm hoping to hear from them soon. I'm a bit worried about traveling during these winter months with Ethan so young. . . but I feel such a strong need to return south to my family."

The two women embrace, clinging to each other. "You will be sorely missed, dearest Fanny, but you are making a good decision. Friends are helpful but family can be so comforting. Please don't feel you need to rush but know I'm willing to help you all I can."

Widow Lawrence rises, still holding Fanny's hands. "Let me know when you have news from your family. Now rest easy while Baby Ethan slumbers."

As she closes the door behind her, Widow Lawrence sighs gently, relieved she didn't have to suggest the Allen's find other living accommodations. "A dear family, the Allen's, but oh, so many of them," she thinks to herself.

A fortnight passes. Fanny seems a bit rejuvenated after confessing to her landlady that she will be leaving. Emma has taken Fanny Margaret and Pamelia to the nearby general store for some potatoes to add to the dinner kettle. Fanny sits by the parlor fire drawing on her precious paper. Much stomping and laughing explodes outside the door. The three come in shaking snow from their cloaks.

"Ma'am," laughs Emma. "Fanny Margaret has a surprise for you. Go ahead, little one, give it to your mother."

Fanny Margaret, proud to be in charge of something, darts to her mother's side and thrusts a folded, sealed paper into her lap. "For you, Mama, for you!"

Instantly, Fanny recognizes the perfect script of her mother's hand. She flips over the letter, breaks the wax seal and unfolds the fine paper. Fanny's eyes rush over the words and a smile creeps into her lips. "Good news! My darlings, such great news," as she looks at the expectant girls. "Here, let me read it to you."

Hearing the noise, Widow Lawrence joins the excited group. Fanny takes a deep breath and begins to read:

Dearest Fanny,

Of course we welcome you home to Westminster. Patrick has agreed you will stay with us on the farm until Stephen can find appropriate dwelling for you and the children.

We all look forward to meeting the two young boys and having Ethan's girls with us. Fanny Margaret must be quite a fine little girl by now. Emma, too, is certainly part of your family and welcome. We know how valuable she must be to you.

Now, to tantalize you, we have a surprise awaiting your arrival. Not a tot more shall I say.

We await word of your departure date. With deepest love,
Mother

The girls jump up and down though Fanny Margaret isn't quite sure of the reasons behind such enthusiasm. Mary Ann comes dashing into the room, long hair hanging unbraided. "Such excitement! What's it all about," she asks above the gleeful noise.

"Here, darling, read for yourself!" Fanny hands the letter to Mary Ann.

Mary Ann reads the letter carefully, then folds it and hands it back to Fanny. For a moment she remains silent. Then, tears welling in her lids, she speaks. "Dearest Mother Fanny, I do love you so, but I cannot move south with you. I beg you, allow me to go be with Lucy. Please." Mary Ann drops to her knees, laying her head in Fanny's lap.

The journey south has been long and cold, producing minor accidents along the way. Pamelia cried for several days, missing Mary Ann's comfort. Fanny's temper has frayed, startling them all, even tiny Ethan. At last, after ten days of bumpy rides, skids, and unspeakable meals, the travelers arrive at Patrick's farm on the outskirts of Westminster. Already dark in the late afternoon, Fanny spies candles lit in the frosty windows of the farmhouse. She lets out a loud whoop startling the horses and making them jump sideways, almost tipping the wagon. The farmhouse door flies open and Mother Margaret rushes out ignoring the snow and cold. Patrick, close behind, grabs the horses' reins to prevent further mishap.

"Oh, my dearest, you're home at last!" Tears stream down Mother Margaret's cheeks. "Here, let me help you."

Fanny, with a jolt of energy to her sore limbs, leaps from the driver's seat, enfolding her mother in her arms. The two stand in tight embrace, weeping, totally unaware of those around them. Onncie comes to the door; mother and daughter still connected move to include her in their embrace. Emma, having handed Ethan to Pamelia, helps Hannibal alight; a somewhat difficult task as he was wrapped tightly in a sheepskin with a thick wool cap pulled down almost to his nose.

Patrick calls for the farm hand to come stable the horses and roll the wagon into the barn. Time enough later, to unload. Better, now, to bring out the sherry and hot tea. He herds the women and children into the house and securely latches the door against the wind.

Fanny, her mother, and Onncie still cling to each other. Patrick moves about helping to remove outer garments and greeting his grandchildren for the first time. He pulls small pieces of peppermint candy out of his weskit pocket, as he hugs each one. He offers a piece to Emma who shakes her head and drops a slight curtsy. Baby Ethan has quieted as he surveys the excitement. Emma carries him close to the fireplace sinking into the nearest chair. She is exhausted and wonders how much longer she can hold this babe without nodding off. The heat from the fire, while welcome, does nothing to keep her alert.

The housemaid, acting quickly in the excitement, has put on the kettle and heated mugs. Whether or not the vessels shall contain sherry or tea matters not. She carries a mug filled with tea to Emma. "Here. This will help. You must be exhausted. Shall I take the baby from you while you sip your tea?" She reaches out and takes Ethan from Emma's arms and is thanked with a weak smile, all that Emma can manage.

Later, gathered around the large dinner table, everyone chatters excitedly, several different conversations going on at once. Onncie holds Ethan while she eats, not wanting to put him down for a single second. Pamelia jabbers away with Patrick, who is totally smitten with Ethan's youngest daughter. Young Hannibal focuses more on his food than on his surroundings. Fanny Margaret regales her grandmother with stories of the journey from Burlington, emphasizing her mother's skills at commanding the horses. "She even used words I'd never heard before," she whispers close to Mother Margaret's ear.

"Fanny, why didn't you hire transport for such a long, dangerous trip?" asks Mother Margaret, staring hard at her daughter.

"Truthfully?" Fanny looks down at her food.

Mother Margaret sighs, "Yes, truthfully."

"There quite simply were no funds to hire anyone. Purchasing the wagon and horses was the best I could do. All of us, including the horses, ate quite simply along the way. We mostly slept in the stables with the animals."

Mother Margaret puts down her spoon, turns to her daughter to hug her tightly once again. "I had no idea! No idea."

Fanny returns the hug and then, straightening her back, speaks up. "Mother Margaret, you promised a surprise upon our arrival. I am ready to learn this great enigma."

Margaret looks at Patrick as if to encourage him to speak. He shakes his head indicating the news is his wife's to share.

"Fanny, we have found Crean's daughter, and she is here in Westminster!"

Chapter 23

Fanny shivers as she raises her hand to the knocker on Stephen Bradley's door. This is a meeting she excitedly anticipates while, at the same time, being anxious about how this stranger, Crean's Irish daughter, will accept her. Determinedly, she raises and lowers the knocker twice. Momentarily, the door opens and she is greeted with Stephen's smiling face. The two embrace on the threshold, the wind swirling past them. Stephen pulls Fanny into the house, stretches his arms and looks her full in the face before he speaks. "You are just as pretty as ever! Come in, my dear; let's sit by the fire. Tea is ready."

Stephen shouts gleefully, "Merab, bring the tea, our Fanny is here!"

Merab burst through the door to the kitchen, laughing and crying at the same time. "Oh, Fanny, how I've missed you." The two hug and prance a bit in pure delight, almost knocking over Cook carrying the tea.

Still laughing, Merab drops into a fireside chair and exclaims, "Where are the children? Didn't you bring the children?"

Fanny smiles, answering, "Another time—soon, Merab. I thought perhaps this meeting would go more easily without children darting about and interrupting."

As if right on cue, the sound of the door knocker stops the conversation. Fanny looks expectantly at Stephen. "You'll like Elizabeth, Fanny. Truly, you will. She's a lovely woman." He moves to answer the door.

Both Fanny and Merab stand, waiting to greet Crean's daughter. Merab takes Fanny's hand giving it a quick squeeze of encouragement.

Stephen ushers Elizabeth and a tall, handsome man into the parlor. He speaks gently, "Fanny, may I introduce Elizabeth, and her husband Thomas."

Elizabeth moves quickly toward Fanny, reaching out to hug her. Startled, Fanny hesitates, and then accepts the warm greeting.

"Fanny, you are more beautiful than everyone has proclaimed. Isn't it marvelous that we sisters finally meet?"

Fanny's first thought surges "no blood runs between us." She quickly averts her disquiet and responds aloud, "Elizabeth, you are a dream come to life." Turning to Thomas, she extends her hand. "And, you Thomas, are a most welcome surprise. No one has told me about you." She softens the words with a smile.

Each finds a seat as close to the fire as possible and Merab begins to serve tea. Fanny relaxes as she listens to Stephen explain the latest developments in his efforts to retrieve Elizabeth's share of Crean's estate.

"As you well know, Fanny," Stephen reaches out to touch her hand to protect her from the pain of what is to follow. "As you know, Crean's land, Elizabeth's share of his estate, was confiscated during the . . .the struggle. Thomas has appointed me to appeal for its return to proper ownership." This will probably take years to accomplish, but I'm confident we will be successful in the end."

Fanny cringes inwardly, remembering Ethan's role in grabbing her father's land to help fund the patriot's army. Outwardly, she smiles to reassure Stephen she will not bolt.

Thomas joins the conversation. "Meanwhile, we've taken a house on River Street and are quite enjoying this charming new country."

Elizabeth, more into the excitement of the meeting, interrupts. "Your children, Fanny, I can't wait to meet your children. Mother Margaret and Mareb often speak of them, especially after receiving letters from you." We must get together as a family as soon as possible. My own son is excited to meet cousins."

Stephen nods to Thomas and they quietly rise and leave for the study where some stronger drink awaits. The women bend in toward each other enthusiastically sharing domestic details, laughing, and enjoying their tea.

✝ ✝ ✝

Elizabeth and Thomas issue an invitation to friends and Brush family members for a gala "soon-to-be-spring" party. Snow still blankets the hillsides around Westminster, yet spirits are eager for the annual sound of ice cracking on the Connecticut River. The high pitched snap of ice breaking apart, followed by the surge of rushing water bring hope of warmer weather and bluer skies.

The Normans have chosen a residence that welcomes visitors, with plenty of room for entertaining on a scale quite grand for Westminster. Apparently, Elizabeth has inherited her father's love for lavishness. For days, the servants have been preparing for "the party," mulling cider, baking enough scones and cakes for a militia gathering. Kettles emit rich aromas of braising meats mixed with spirits and herbs. Deep dishes of baked squashes sit on the large, wooden kitchen table, covered in cloths to prevent any invasion of insect or pinching fingers. Young Henry is remarkably skilled at purloining goodies from right under cook's piercing gaze. With cook so busy, Henry samples a bit of everything, particularly enjoying the cider laced with rum.

"Henry!" Elizabeth calls from the front of the house. "Henry, come here—NOW!"

Cook turns to glare at the boy, shooing with her arm. "Git, boy! Don't want missus in here looking for you. Got enough to do without having to watch you get a scolding. Now, git!"

Henry darts down the hall to skid up behind his mother fluffing her hair in front of the silvered glass. "Here, Madam. Present and accounted for." He offers her a staunch salute.

"Sassy boy! Let me look at you. What's on your mouth? Wipe it off quickly. They'll all be arriving any moment and you don't want to meet your cousins with a dirty face. Here, let me help."

Henry steps back quickly to avoid his mother's help. He wipes his mouth on his sleeve cuff encouraging his mother to snort loudly.

Sleigh bells jingle as several shays pull up in front of the house. Thomas steps from the parlor to open the door. No time to wait for the houseman.

Fanny and Patrick help the children climb down from the first shay, while Mother Margaret manages the order of dismounting from inside the vehicle. Pamelia is the last to jump down, disdaining any assistance. Emma, in the second shay, carries baby Ethan, almost invisible in his blankets. Patrick reaches up to grab hold of Onncie, who moves cautiously, somewhat intimidated by the step height and the slippery ground.

Arriving just as Onncie steps to the ground, Stephen and Merab, laugh aloud as he helps her down. Czar follows with a swagger common to those closing in on manhood. Already, he has spotted Pamelia and thinks to himself, "This gathering won't be so dull after all." He moves quickly to greet "Aunt" Fanny, just brushing against Pamelia. "Oh, pardon me, young lady, please forgive my clumsiness. I'm Czar Bradley and just who might you be?"

Straightening her skirts, Pamelia looks up, straight into the young man's eyes. "Pamelia. Pamelia Allen, daughter of the great General Ethan Allen."

Taken aback by her boldness, Czar stutters some additional apology and moves away. Fanny smiles, and rolls her eyes at Mother Margaret. "Guess we'll be seeing a lot more of this behavior in the coming months." Margaret chuckles inviting Pamelia to stick out her tongue at her mother and grandmother. They move quickly into the warmth of the brightly candle-lit house.

Soon the house is filled with people moving about, sipping cider or spirits. Fanny Margaret and Hannibal find a safe place, close to the parlor fire, out of the way of social traffic. Watching this one and that, the two siblings make comments to each other, often laughing but never overtly pointing. Mother would be sure to see such rude behavior and the consequences dealt out later would be appropriate.

Fanny glides into the library for a break from the need to smile incessantly. The room is already occupied by a man and woman standing close to each other. Fanny starts to retreat with an apology for intrusion when the gentleman turns to face her.

"My god! Mistress Fanny?" The man moves quickly towards her.

179

Fanny braces herself, wondering who this might be. She breaks into a broad smile, just as he identifies himself. "Cooper! I can't believe it. What a wonderful surprise. I didn't know you were still in Westminster." She reaches out and gives him a big hug, brushing her lips across his cheek.

"Let me introduce you to my wife, Sarabella." He turns, taking his wife gently by the arm, pulling her close.

"My dear, how nice to meet you." Fanny smiles as she notices the extended belly and flushed face. "Sarabella, you have married the most wonderful friend in all the kingdom. Congratulations." She embraces them both. Fanny steps back. "Cooper, you must tell me what you've been doing, how you met Sarabella—just everything since we've last been together." She leads them to seats by the fireside.

"What a long time that's been!" Cooper helps his wife to a chair. "Where to begin. . ." He looks up to see a gentleman standing in the doorway. "Jazeb, please, come in."

"I've no wish to intrude into what seems a joyous reunion. We can speak later."

"No, please. Let me introduce you to my dear friend, Mistress Fanny Brush Buchanan. Excuse me, Fanny Allen. She was still a Brush-Buchanan when last we saw each other."

The gentleman approaches Fanny, bowing deeply before speaking. "Most pleased to meet you Mistress Allen. This humble physician is honored to meet the widow of General Allen. You are certainly well known throughout this region. Jazeb Penniman at your service, madam."

Fanny smiles. "Dr. Penniman, I do hope you mean my reputation is golden, and not filled with cracks and pitfalls."

"Indeed, madam. Indeed, it is so. I hear the music starting. It would be my honor to enter this first dance with such a beautiful, renowned lady." Jazeb bows and takes her hand.

Fanny rises with a smile. Jazeb turns to Cooper, "So sorry to take Mistress Fanny from your company. I shall bring her back later so you can continue your reunion."

Cooper looks knowingly at Sarabella who winks at her husband. "My! Jazeb moves quickly, I must say."

180

Cooper smiles. "At least we know he's not after her money—not that she has any these days, so I've heard."

Chapter 24

Fanny gazes out at the river as she sets up her easel in the newly greening meadow. The first of the spring flowers are just bursting their buds. She's anxious to sketch these little blossoms with their paler colors. Fanny Margaret and Hannibal romp barefoot through the sprouting grasses, squealing in delight. Emma sits on a blanket nearby watching little Ethan stretch and squirm as he tries to creep toward some fascinating object unseen by his caretaker.

Fanny takes up her pens and begins to sketch. Her mind wanders; her hand pauses. There is so much to consider about her future and that of her children. Concentration on nature is superseded by life's realities. A shadow appears on her easel and she looks up to see Jazeb standing there with a blanket and a basket covered in linen. "Jazeb, what a surprise. We didn't expect your today."

Jazeb smiles down at her, spreads his blanket and places the basket squarely in the middle. "Too pretty a day to spend it in the dispensary, and aside from spring fever, the local population seems free of diseases today. A small holiday as it were."

Smiling, Fanny turns toward the children and calls, "Come here, you two. The treat man has arrived." The children turn to see Mama's new friend and recognize the basket will be filled with goodies. Fanny Margaret grabs Hannibal's hand and they scramble toward their reward.

Jazeb uncovers the basket with a flourish and removes a plate filled with shortbreads dipped in chocolate. The children's gasps explain their delight. Jazeb motions to Emma. "Come join us, Emma. There's plenty for everyone, even little Ethan."

Emma gathers up the baby and her blanket, and walks toward the little group. "Thank you, Master Penniman; how kind to include me. I'll take one with me as wee Ethan could do with a nap." She curtsies and heads toward the farm house. Thinking to herself, "I don't need to watch himself court Mistress. No help, I'll be!"

Jazeb watches Emma's back, thinking to himself, "Fanny relies on Emma's support. They seem almost like sisters in some small way. I do wish she was more friendly toward me." Turning back to Fanny, they begin idle chatter about the vista before them. The children have returned to their playful searching.

"Fanny, my dear," Jazeb switches topics, gently taking Fanny's hand. "Fanny, I'm sure you must realize I've fallen in love with you."

Startled, Fanny gently removes her hand from his and looks into his eyes. "Jazeb, you are a dear, dear man. I treasure your company. Yet, Ethan is dead only a year and a half. He still occupies my heart. I don't know that there'll ever be room for another. You are so special to me yet I cannot promise you deep, abiding love. Perhaps that comes but once in a lifetime."

"I understand, Fanny. Truly, I do; and I honor your love for Ethan." Jazeb takes Fanny's hand again and she does not resist. "I am concerned for your welfare, for the children, their education, and all the realities that life imposes upon us. I can willingly provide all of life's necessities for you with my adoring heart thrown in. Promise me, Fanny, you will at least consider my proposal."

Fanny sits silently for several moments, her hand still in Jazeb's. "You know I cannot give you my heart, at least not yet. You are quite generous to understand. I will at least promise to carefully consider what you offer me and the children."

"Thank you, dearest Fanny. I shall cherish that promise and pray for more to come."

After supper, the children tucked into bed, Mother Margaret and Fanny sit by the fireside, sipping sherry. Patrick has gone to check on the livestock so the two are alone. The two women sit silently, staring at the dancing flames. Onncie joins them from the kitchen and the three feel as one. Fanny speaks first.

"Jazeb has offered me a proposal." Silence.

After a few moments, Mother Margaret speaks softly. "What does he offer?" More silence while each sips sherry.

"To provide for the children and for me."

"Anything else?"

"To earnestly love me."

"Does he drink?" mutters Onncie.

"Shush!" scolds Mother Margaret, but Fanny just smiles, remembering the challenges of Ethan's tottling. "That seems a welcome proposal, my dear."

"Indeed!" Fanny remains silent before continuing. "Jazeb is truly a kind and generous man. Yet, I cannot shake Ethan from my heart. Somehow it seems cruel to take so much from Jazeb without giving much in return."

"Hmmf," grunts Onncie. "You are quite a gifted and beautiful woman. You are strong and Jazeb will need a strong woman beside him as we watch these times unfold."

"Are you having visions, again, Onncie?" Fanny asks with a grin.

"No. Just common sense! Think carefully, Mistress Fanny, you need a stable life for the children and for yourself."

More silence until Fanny speaks, "I miss the love, Onncie. Mother Margaret. I miss the love in my heart."

Margaret gently pats her daughter's hand. "You have many whom you love and who love you, dearest, but loving a man is a different species entirely. Practicality is needed now, not love."

Silence hovers in the room. All three women stare into what are now only glowing embers.

Sleep evades Fanny. She cannot free her mind even as she holds tight to her doll, Maggy. What Mother Margaret said is quite true and probably based partially on the overcrowded farmhouse and the demands on her own resources. Fanny knows neither Patrick nor Mother Margaret would ever ask her to leave. However, her own three children, Pamelia, and Emma take up a great deal of space and produce more noise than this house has ever sheltered. Quite simply, they cannot stay here forever and options are limited. Still…Ethan. How her heart aches for Ethan. "Oh, Maggy, I miss him so. What am I to do. Tell me, Maggy." The doll's eyes remain open and blank.

Chapter 25

Jazeb arrives at the Wall farm to pick up Fanny for a lively evening at Stephen and Mareb Bradley's home. The leaves have just begun to change colors and the sugar maples are bright red ahead of the birches lingering clutch to green before becoming yellow. Fanny opens the door herself and grabs Jazeb by the hand, pulling him into the parlor.

"Look! Look! Finally, I'm done with the first volume of flora paintings. I'm ready to search for a printer!"

Jazeb genuinely admires her paintings, knowing how much these mean to Fanny. After closely examining several of the pieces, he smiles, turning to Fanny. "These are magnificent, dearest, even as I've seen many of these as you've worked on them. We must leave now or Mareb will be cranky if we're late."

Jazeb helps Fanny with her cloak and leads her to the carriage. The horse starts off in a trot and Jazeb takes hold of Fanny's gloved hand. "We're going to stop here for a moment, dearest, as I must speak to you." He pulls on the reins and the horse stops.

Fanny's heart clutches, suspecting the next few moments will require a decision. She looks into Jazeb's eyes as he begins to speak.

"Fanny, you know I love you; have loved you for what feels like eons. It's been over two years now since Ethan died. We've become good friends; shared joys and sorrows. It's time for me to press my proposal. I pray you will say 'yes'!"

Fanny sighs, dropping her eyes to her hand held by a nervous Jazeb. She looks up, smiling. "You have been so patient with me. I must admit you have taken over a space in my heart. If you can understand that Ethan will always share my heart with you, I will joyfully accept your proposal."

Jazeb pulls Fanny to his chest and breathes deeply. "Oh, Fanny, I thought you'd say no once again. I am now the happiest man in the world." He plants a kiss on her forehead, following her lead as she pulls his lips down to hers.

"Shall we let Stephen and Merab be the first to know," asks Jazeb, finally extricating himself from a deep embrace.

"That seems right, but we must tell Mother Margaret and Onncie as soon as you take me home." Fanny rests her head on Jazeb's upper arm with a fleeting thought of why she'd chosen two such tall men in her life.

Fanny more or less drifts through the evening's entertainment, her mind on the decision she'd made earlier in the evening. Stephen and Mareb are excited for her and toasts offered all around. Later, in the parlor, Mareb asks a single, important question, "When do you plan to marry?"

"Oh, I hadn't yet thought," mutters Fanny. "It's still a very new idea to me." Fanny sits quietly a moment until tears dribble down her cheeks. "What would Ethan think, Merab? Am I disloyal to his love?" She wipes her eyes with the linen tucked into her sleeve cuff.

"Ethan would be delighted, dearest. What Ethan wanted more than anything was for you to be happy." Mareb reached over to touch Fanny's arm. "And to be well cared for. You need this, Fanny. Be happy for your good fortune. Jazeb is a generous and kind man."

Fanny is anxious to get home and share the news with Mother Margaret and Onncie. She finds Jazeb in the library with Stephen. "Perhaps it is time we leave. Those at home will be anxious."

Stephen smiles as he looks at Fanny. "I suspect you're the anxious one. You'll be wanting to spread the news with your family, I'm sure. How wonderful it was to celebrate with you two this evening." The two men rise, each hugging Fanny as they prepare to leave.

Fanny remains quiet during the ride back to the farm. Jazeb hums to himself. He's quite certain their news will be received well. At sight of glowing windows at the farm, Jazeb slows the horse to a walk. "Are you ready to share our news, dearest? Shall I ask Patrick for you hand?"

"I'm ready, yes. I'd like to tell the news, if you don't mind. Loving Patrick as I do, he is not my father. I am truly a woman on my own, though I've certainly the love and support of my beloved family. I must decide whether to wake the children or wait and tell them in the morning."

"No longer are you a woman alone, Fanny. Together we'll build a strong new bond; one only broken by death."

"Indeed. Death. Death often comes too soon." Fanny exhales a long, deep breath. "Shall we go in?" She leans over and kisses him quickly on the cheek.

Only Patrick looks up as the two enter the parlor. Margaret and Onncie bend over their needlework, conscious of a new energy in room. Margaret slyly glances at her companion, who barely manages to restrain a smile.

"Good evening." Jazeb greets the gathered as he helps Fanny remove her cloak. "You all look comfortable by the fire."

"Come, sit," offers Patrick who stands, pulling two chairs closer to the fire.

"Patrick, might we have some sherry?" Fanny smiles up at her step-father. "Jazeb and I have something to tell you."

It is Margaret who answers. "Of course, my dear." Onncie puts down her needlework and heads for the kitchen to bring the spirits. Patrick raises his eyebrows but remains silent.

Warmed sherry delivered, all turn expectantly toward Jazeb. Fanny smiles and begins the conversation. "I have made a decision; one long in the making, yet made with my heart. You all are aware Jazeb has been asking me to marry him for a long time, over two years. Tonight, he asked me again. This time I said yes." She reaches over and takes hold of Jazeb's hand.

Patrick lets out a whoop! Margaret shushes him with, "You'll wake the children."

"How wonderful!" Margaret rises to hug her daughter and Jazeb.

Pamelia, having heard the noise, clatters down the stairs to learn what has brought about such enthusiasm. Fanny leaves her chair to greet her stepdaughter. "Jazeb and I are to be married. Are you happy?"

"Oh, yes, very happy!" Pamelia moves to hug Jazeb. Looking into his eyes, she enunciates each word. "I am still the daughter of the great General Ethan Allen."

Everyone laughs. Jazeb responds, "Indeed, you are and so you shall remain."

The increased jubilation brings Fanny Margaret and Hannibal to the parlor where they are joined from the kitchen by Emma. Laughter, congratulations, and embraces abound.

Much later, Fanny lies in her bed cuddling her beloved doll to her chest. "Oh, Maggy! I do so hope I've done the right thing." The doll remains mute. "Ethan, Ethan, forgive me. I must think of the children. I must take care of myself."

Chapter 26

Fanny has insisted their wedding be simple with no great celebration. Jazeb, somewhat disappointed, agreed. Just gathering the family requires a large space. Stephen and Merab have offered to host a small, simple supper following the ceremony. October 28th arrives brisk and sunny. Mother Margaret, Onncie and Emma hustle the children together, making sure their bows are straight and their shirt tails tucked inside their pants. Fanny is alone, dressing slowly, talking with her doll Maggy.

"I'm sure this is best, Maggy. We'll be fine, won't we? All of us?" Fanny places a single pearl earring in each lobe; the last of Ethan's gifts which Fanny has refused to sell over the years. Running a final hand through her hair to straighten any strays, Fanny breathes deeply, stands straight, and walks toward whatever tomorrow will bring.

The Bradley home is full to bursting with the Walls, the Allens, the Norman trio, Onncie and Emma along with Cooper and Sarabella. The judge arrives as the town clock strikes one. Jazeb takes Fanny's hand and they enter the Bradley library. Pamelia and eight-year-old Fanny Margaret come to stand by Fanny's side, each holding a small bouquet of fall flowers. The judge begins.

Suddenly, Fanny feels faint. She's just realized that almost nine years ago, she stood in this very same room, marrying Ethan. She's about to swoon. Jazeb puts his arm around her waist, steadying her. Fanny hardly hears what the judge is saying. Pamelia pokes her, "Say yes, Mama. Say yes." Fanny manages to nod her head in assent. The next words she hears: "Jazeb Penniman and Frances Allen, you are now married."

Mareb, disregarding Fanny's orders, has prepared a lavish feast, music, and dancing. Rum and sherry flow generously. Fanny has allowed herself to relax. She finds dancing with Jazeb quite exhilarating. Perhaps it's the spirits, but Fanny enjoys every moment.

Long after the tower clock has chimed nine times, Margaret and Patrick with the help of Onncie and Emma, round up the children to take them back to the farm. Fanny and Jazeb are still dancing when the family quietly exits the Bradley's. At last, only Stephen, Merab, and the wedding couple remain. The musicians have all left; the servants have retired to the kitchen to clean up. Jazeb whispers in Fanny's ear then turns to Stephen.

"Thank you both so much for this wonderful party—a beautiful beginning to a long and happy marriage. It seems timely to take our leave now. Thank you once again."

Fanny smiles, then hugs Mareb as she whispers, "Thank you so much. I wouldn't have made it without you."

Jazeb places Fanny's cloak around her shoulders and they wave goodbye as he helps her into the carriage.

"Be careful with those instruments, they're quite fragile." Jazeb speaks to the houseboy as he packs up the last of the medical instruments and supplies. "It looks like we'll have to add an additional wagon if we're to get all of Fanny's belongings and the children's acquisitions."

Fanny and Emma check off the last item on their list to be packed for the move to the Burlington farm. Pamelia, now quite a grown up young lady, locks the lid of her own trunk. She can't quite decide how she feels about the return to the farm. Suitors in Westminster are far grander than they might be further north. She'll miss Czar and his stumbling, fumbling attempts to engage her in courtship. Just maybe, the devil you know is better than the devil you've not yet met.

Fanny carefully packs her portfolios into the special leather case Jazeb has had made for them. Fanny gently rubs her fingers across the embossed initials FAP. Her husband had been quite thoughtful in not omitting Ethan's surname from the set of letters. A faint smile crosses her face as her fingers pause on the A. Jazeb has kept his promise these last few years in allowing Ethan's spirit to remain in the midst of the Penniman family household. Jazeb's openness to the Allen legend has truly endeared him to Ethan's children. With the addition of two Penniman siblings, Udney and Hortensia, the household is now quite large. Emma has her hands full caring for the four youngest children. Young Fanny Margaret is now nearly the same age as her mother was when she married John Buchanan.

Fanny walks to the window and stares down at the Connecticut River; a view she wants fixed in her mind. The old doll, Maggy, rests on the sill. Fanny reaches for her beloved doll. "Maggy, we're off on another adventure. I'm not sure how I'll feel having Jazeb in Ethan's house. You've been with me the whole journey, dear Maggy, don't leave me now." Fanny unlocks her precious leather case and tucks Maggy in with her treasured paintings then refastens the latch. She lets out a deep sigh, takes one last look out the window, lingering on the treasured view. Sighing, she turns and leaves the room.

It seems like everyone has come to see the Pennimans off. Mother Margaret, Onncie, Patrick, the three Bradleys, the Norman family, Cooper, his wife and their two young children. Elizabeth secretly slips a sealed note into Fanny's hand. "For later, when you might need it," whispers Elizabeth. Hugs and advice are in abundance as each offers their best wishes for the long journey through the mountains. The hired driver of the lead carriage gives a sharp whistle, letting everyone know it's time to climb aboard. Time's a-fleeting and there's a good distance to travel before nightfall.

Chapter 27

Fanny stamps her foot in frustration! "All you children, out the door! Now! Emma, make sure you're available when the new cook comes. You'll have to make certain she can handle this family. Something I can't seem to do. Has this house grown smaller or are there just too many people in it? That's not a question, Pamelia, so wipe that smile from your face and help Emma." Fanny's flushed face proves to all they best do what they're told.

Jazeb comes in from the barn, a light sweat on his brow, just as the younger children shove past him out the door. Hannibal manages a semi-polite "pardon me!" and turns to make sure the door closes behind him. No need to make Mama any angrier.

"Newport says they'll be fine in the barn for a while at least. I do hate to evict them but there seems no alternative. He and I discussed the possibility of building a medical office between the road and the barn. Seems impractical, though. My next option is to look for office space in town. Tomorrow, I'll go in search for something suitable." Jazeb swats at his neck. "Damn May flies. Hateful beasts!"

Fanny shouts, "Well, look for a bigger house while you're at it. This is quite impossible. Oh, and have you seen Fanny Margaret? She seems to have made herself absent from all that needs to be done."

"Thought I saw her heading down towards the river a while back. Don't be too hard on her, Fanny. This must be difficult both for her and Pamelia. This was their father's house and he's not here."

"Well, it's hard on me as well!" Fanny turns, stomps out the front door, slamming it behind her. She trots toward the river in search of her daughter. Halfway, Fanny yields to her memories. She drops to the newly greening grasses and begins to sob. Visions of Ethan and her searching for the young Fanny Margaret and the bearded man who saved her. Ethan, himself, so present here on the

193

farm. Then, memories of him lying there, dying in his bed. "It's a mistake to have returned to the farm. I shouldn't have let Jazeb persuade me." Still the sobs will not cease.

Fanny Margaret comes up the hill to find her mother collapsed in the grass, face wet with tears, breaths coming in gasps. She drops to her mother's side. "Mama. What is it? Are you all right? Shall I get Jazeb?"

Fanny takes hold of her daughter's hand, pressing it to her cheek. "No, no. I'll be fine. The memories just raged; I couldn't contain them. This shall pass, I'm sure. What I'm not sure of is all of us is living here in such cramped quarters. Too many of us; we get in each other's way. There's no quiet space for anyone."

"I know, Mama. It's not the same without Papa here. Jazeb is so good to us but he's not Papa!" The two hug each other, wiping the tears from the other's cheeks. Finally, Fanny Margaret speaks. "Come on, Mama. There's so much to do and we all need you to lead the way."

The two help each other stand, checking to make sure the other's face is clear. Both smile and turn toward the house arm in arm. Their pace is slow as if to prolong this precious time between the two—or to stave off returning to the midst of chaos.

New cook has done well with her first meal made from stores available after the journey northward. Emma suggested the four younger children eat earlier in order to accommodate the rest at the large table. They have eaten and are outside enjoying the lengthening days. Emma joins the remaining family at their meal, something she has done since her first days of employment with the Allens.

The usual casual chatter is interrupted by Fanny Margaret. "I have something I'd like to say."

Everyone stops eating and looks at Fanny Margaret. Jazeb ventures, "Well, let's hear it."

"I want to become a nun." She holds up her hand to protest any interruption. "I know this sounds weird but down by the river today, I felt this urge, so strong I could not shake it. I know in my heart of hearts I want to be a nun." Fanny Margaret looks around the table as if daring anyone to oppose her.

"Do you even know what a nun is, dearest?" Fanny smiles at her daughter. "You never get to see anyone but the other nuns. You have to spend a great deal of time on your knees praying. You have to know about God, something not often talked about in our family. Do you even believe there is such a thing as God?"

"Papa said God was in nature. In the natural order of things. I can believe in that." Fanny looks squarely at her mother.

Pamelia joins in, "I've heard nuns have to wear funny clothes and cover their heads at all times."

Jazeb, who has returned to his meal, looks up. "Nuns are Catholic, Fanny Margaret. They're Catholic."

Fanny adds, "There are not many Catholics here in Vermont. Mostly, they're up in New France. That would mean you'd have to leave us and I don't know if I could stand that."

"I know, Mama. I know those things. Yet, it's something I cannot escape. I don't know how to explain it any better." Fanny Margaret returns to eating. The meal ends without further conversation.

Later that night, Jazeb and Fanny lie together in the new bed Fanny has insisted Jazeb buy. The candle burns on the bedside table. The sound of Emma's footsteps up the stairs intrudes on their silence.

"Jazeb rolls to his side, touching Fanny's cheek before he begins to speak. "I've been thinking, dearest, about Fanny Margaret's…uh, shall we say, 'calling.' Why a Catholic nun? She knows nothing of their ways or beliefs. She's never even been exposed to religious beliefs of any kind. What if we send her to a religious school so she gains some experience? There's an excellent seminary run by the Anglican order. She would learn how it is to be away from family, could immerse herself in theology, at least some reasonably familiar religious thought. Then she could make an educated decision before a permanent commitment."

Fanny kisses his fingertips then smiling, says, "Jazeb, you have such foresight, something I've never seemed to have." To herself she thinks, "Neither had Ethan!" Aloud, she continues, "Let's remain quiet for a while. Perhaps this phase will pass with

Fanny Margaret. In the meantime, you can explore your educational idea—right after you find your office space."

Fanny rolls into her husband's arms and the two drift off to sleep.

† † †

Newport, with the help of young Hannibal, manages to get the timothy and corn planted before Jazeb finds a suitable place for his dispensary. Now, all hands are needed to transfer equipment and medicines to the new office in Burlington. Pamelia bounces with excitement thinking there just might be some handsome young men hanging around. Her hormones have been on hold while limited to the farm. Newport and his wife, after helping the older three children climb aboard the loaded wagon, mount to the front seat board. Jazeb urges his horse to a trot and the procession is on its way. Fanny and Emma wave goodbye, each expressing relief in a deep, extended sigh. There's no shortage of work for them here at the farm, but the enduring commotion will subside if only for a few hours. Emma urges cook to peel her potatoes in the dooryard so she can watch the three younger children at play. Emma pours boiling water over the precious tea leaves in the porcelain pot, places it on the table and plops into a chair. She signals Fanny to do likewise. Both women stare at the teapot as if wishing it to steep faster.

Emma speaks first, so deep is their friendship. "Master Jazeb seems truly sorry he couldn't find a suitable house in town. You wanted so much to have more comfortable quarters for all of us."

Fanny slowly pours two cups of tea before answering. "It's more than the comfort, Emma. I've tried so hard to adjust to Ethan's absence but he's everywhere here on the farm. He's in the woodwork that he cut and nailed. He's in the fire bricks that Newport made and Ethan laid. The very air breathes Ethan's image and voice. Jazeb understands in some ways but thinks I've been moping about too long now. His very look says, 'Straighten up, Fanny. It's you and me now with all these children to care for. Straighten up!' Pamelia and Fanny Margaret seem to have settled in all right, don't you think, Emma?"

Emma reaches out to take Fanny's once lovely hands, now cracked and raw with work. "They'll be fine, Fanny, just fine." The two sit silently, sipping their tea, listening to the children's laughter as they romp in the sunshine.

Young Ethan bursts through the door reintroducing exuberant energy into the kitchen. Fanny smiles at Emma, "Time to get on with the laundry. Reverie time has now passed."

Having helped Emma with the endless wash, Fanny hums as she hangs clothes on the extra line Newport hung to accommodate the increased need. She bends to examine the blooming laurel bush when she hears the sound of wagon wheels coming up the lane. Sighing, she stands and waits for the wagon to come 'round to the barn. The remaining damp clothes remain in the basket.

Hannibal is asleep in the wagon; the girls chat with each other seemingly unaware they're home at last. Jazeb rounds the house, his horse anxious for the barn and feed. Fanny smiles and waves, sighing inwardly.

"All settled into the dispensary?" asks Fanny. "You must be exhausted. Come on girls, you're not too tired to hang the rest of the laundry." She helps them alight and laughs at their pouting faces. "A woman's work is never done, they say, my sweets. Get to it."

Later, at supper, Jazeb pulls a folded, paper from inside his weskit. "There is a surprise, everyone." All eyes focus on Jazeb. "Yep, thought that would get your attention. This surprise is especially for Fanny Margaret." He unfolds the paper and reads of Fanny Margaret's acceptance to Middlebury Seminary.

Fanny gasps, covering her mouth with her hand. Fanny Margaret laughs uncertainly. Everyone else claps. Jazeb continues, "there is a condition, my dear."

"What might that be?" Fanny Margaret is hoping it's a condition she'll be unable to meet.

"Within six weeks of beginning your studies, you must receive the Rite of Holy Baptism into the Anglican community."

"But I want to become a Catholic, not an Anglican!" Fanny Margaret attempts to rise but her mother firmly takes her arm preventing the departure.

"First things first. You need to know something of religion before you take such a drastic step into a nunnery." Fanny lets go of her daughter's arm.

No further conversation ensues until Jazeb excuses the children from the table. "And so, that is that!" smiles Jazeb.

Chapter 28

The sun sets over Lake Champlain while Fanny and Jazeb relax in the dooryard as the day winds down. Fanny reaches for her husband's arm and leans into his shoulder. "So, what will you do?" she asks.

"It's a silly offer, Fanny. I'm a physician not a government agent."

"Think seriously, Jazeb. The appointment by President Jefferson is quite an honor, even in these confusing times."

"Fanny, you know the offer comes to me because of you and Ethan. The president thought well of Ethan, and thus of you. Did you ever meet him?"

Fanny smiles, "Once, very long ago it seems. Quite a gracious man."

"Really, what do I know about supervising goods going in and out of Lake Champlain and the Northeast Kingdom? Nothing, absolutely nothing!"

"US Collector of Customs is a title, Jazeb, not an albatross around your neck. Consider accepting the title and then hiring someone to do the work for you. You can still devote your time in the dispensary."

"Certainly an idea I've not considered." Jazeb remains quiet. Fanny does not interrupt his silence. Finally, Jazeb continues, "there is so much confusion learning to be a state and a country. Just look at the new paper currency. Already counterfeiters are afoot even here in Vermont. One must be diligent in all directions."

"Custom agents don't have responsibility for fake money. Think about it, please, Jazeb. We don't want to offend President Jefferson." Fanny kisses him on the cheek as the last of the sun disappears in the horizon. "Time to go in before we take a chill."

The next morning Jazeb rises early and leaves for the dispensary without eating any of the barley cereal cook has hot in the pot. He needs to think seriously about the President's appointment before any patients appear on his doorstep. By the time he's taken his horse to the town stable, he has made a decision. He sits at his desk and pens an "acceptance with pleasure" to President Jefferson. He never imagines how this move will affect his life.

Fanny's life has changed drastically since the family's move from the farm to a larger house in Swanton. The move had been necessitated with Jazeb's acceptance of President's Jefferson's appointment and required yet another relocation of his dispensary. Both Mother Margaret and Onncie have died, bringing deep grief into her life—almost as destroying as Ethan's death had been to her spirit. Only her children and Jazeb's deep devotion have kept her from spiraling into oblivion.

Fanny ponders these past two years as the family heads to Middlebury to attend Fanny Margaret's Baptism. At 45, Fanny still emits an elegant presence though her garments are no longer silk and her jewels are long gone. She stands tall with a strength only imagined by others.

The carriages pull up in front of the Seminary chapel where they are greeted by the Rev. Daniel Barber. He's not looking too pleased as he ushers the family into the narthex. "Welcome, Dr. Penniman, ma'am. May I speak privately before we begin the Service?" The three step to the side. The Rev. Barber looks long at the floor before speaking. "Sir, Madam, I'm not sure your daughter takes this Rite of Baptism very seriously. I shall continue because of your personal commitment to her religious education. However, I remember quite clearly her father's opposition to the Church. I suspect your daughter follows her father's pathways."

"Thank you, Mr. Barber, for your consideration." Fanny almost curtsies but thinks better of it. "Shall we begin, then?"

The family gathers in the front pews, quietly waiting for this new experience to begin. Fanny Margaret is escorted from the Sacristy to the Baptismal Font just in front of the prayer rail. The Rev. Barber indicates for all to stand, then begins to read from the Book of Common Prayer. Fanny Margaret starts to giggle. The priest stops, raises his eyebrow, then frowns. Fanny Margaret turns to look at her mother who widens her eyes in distress. The Rev. Barber continues. Periodically, Fanny Margaret giggles audibly. Fanny cannot help but scold Ethan in her mind. "Go away, you devil spirit!" A smile creeps across Fanny's face.

As the Service comes to an end, Fanny Margaret laughs, "And now I have completed my obligations. Shall we have tea?" The Rev. Barber scowls and stomps into the Sacristy where he records this disgraceful abomination.

Hannibal hugs his sister, whispering in her ear, "A fine display, Missy! You've done Papa proud."

Fanny Margaret whispers back, "That wasn't for Papa, silly, that was for the Catholics!"

Jazeb sits at his desk reading the new Embargo Act imposed by President Jefferson, declaring that American goods shall remain in America and not shipped beyond its borders. As the nation is expanding, Jefferson's altruistic thinking is the need is far greater to have resources for its citizens than to gain monies from outside its borders. Jazeb thinks this creates quite a conundrum for Vermont. The three main marketable products available in the Green Mountain State are timber, potash, and rum. The closest large U.S. outlets for these products are Boston and New York. Vermont's terrain makes transportation to these cities impractical and profits negligible if any at all. Vermont's only feasible markets are Montreal and Quebec. Jazeb thinks to himself, "Life is about to change for me. I should never have taken that Customs appointment." He lifts his head as he hears a tap on his office door, "Come in."

Fanny peeks her head around the door jam. "Doesn't look like you're very busy right now and I've brought some lunch. May I come in?"

"Of course, my dear, always." Jazeb stands to hug his wife. He takes the basket and places it on his work table. "Here, Fanny, come sit and we'll talk while we eat your fine smelling offerings."

"And, what shall we discuss that isn't about children. I am consumed by the needs of our children!" Fanny smiles as she lifts a morsel of corn cake to her mouth.

"Well, this embargo business is a good place to start. I've just been reading it and I feel doom approaching."

"Doom? Really?" Fanny looks puzzled.

"Vermonters are a close knit group; they'll support one another, no matter what comes. When folks become aware they can't sell to New France, there will be hell to pay and some will wish we'd never become a United State." Jazeb cuts a piece of pie from the pan.

"They will continue to sell to Montreal from here and to Quebec from the Northeast Kingdom, won't they?" asks Fanny.

"And that's where my difficulties begin. As Collector of Customs I have the responsibility to call out the militia when infringements occur—and they will occur."

"You may be a bit behind the news, Jazeb. I've heard talk already. Even Hannibal and Young Ethan have heard the rumblings. Your nose is always here in the dispensary."

"What rumblings? Tell me." Jazeb finishes the last bite of his pie.

"I've heard that the business men are making a deal with the militia."

"What deal?" snaps Jazeb.

"Stay calm, husband!" Fanny touches Jazeb's outstretched hand. "What I hear is that if the militia spot Vermont goods leaving the State for New France, they will look away and fire their shots into the air."

"That's treason!" gasps Jazeb.

"I'd call it good commerce," retorts Fanny. "Difficult times require difficult actions."

"My, but you've become a great Patriot over the years. One could almost call you a Green Mountain Girl. Ethan must have taught you well."

† † †

Smuggling has become a way of life in Vermont. There are entrepreneurial smugglers and there are the militia assigned to prevent the activity; sometime even both in the same person. The pact between the two groups works perfectly most of the time. Timber and potash are brought down the rivers to Lake Champlain, put aboard small vessels and transported north to New France. When a militiaman spots such activity, he yells loudly and shots are fired, skyward. Skirmishes ensue, but the smugglers just laugh and keep on their way.

Jazeb has told his deputies there must be some accountability for the Federal authorities. Sometimes, the militia must apprehend smugglers. So, occasionally, smugglers are caught. Trials are held; sentencing is light, often with the culprits being released immediately following the trial. It is a system that benefits everyone in Vermont. However, it is a system kept secret from those beyond Vermont's borders. And, so it was, on the night of August 3, 1808, the system falls apart.

Eager to obtain a more expansive delivery, New France has sent their own larger ship, the *Black Snake*, to pick up potash. In the bow is a Wall Gun (a 75 lb. flintlock musket) with a pile of ammunition close at hand. The night is quiet, very little wind, and the *Black Snake* is able to sneak along the eastern shore of Lake Champlain, up the Onion River to the assigned destination. Just as the captain lowers anchor, shots are fired from shore. Having been promised no legal interference during the delivery, the captain's surprise leads him to retaliate with musket fire.The militiamen change their aim from the sky to the ship.

The battle escalates quickly and more militia arrive, led by Jazeb's appointee, Lt. Daniel Farrington. The militia now outnumber the *Blake Snake* crew and are able to board and capture them. The conflict is not without loss of two militia and a bystander. The *Blake Snake* is secured on American soil and the prisoners, including some Vermont smugglers, are marched to Burlington.

Chapter 29

Fanny sighs as she flicks the whip above the horse's back. Fanny Margaret sits rigidly beside her. The two women barely speak as wrapped as they are in their own thoughts.

The arguments had been endless and futile. Fanny Margaret was adamant, the nunnery or nothing! Jazeb finally convinced his wife that nothing was going to change the young woman's mind and to let her chart her own course in life—even if it went against everything Fanny believed. When Jazeb accused her of protesting on behalf of Ethan, Fanny stormed from the room but issued her permission for entry to the Montreal convent.

"Thus," thinks Fanny, "we are now on our way to Hôtel-Dieu de Montréal for Fanny Margaret to begin her novitiate, studying to be a nurse. At least I understand the nursing half of my daughter's stubbornness." The ride is pleasant this September, 1808; the leaves on the maples are just beginning their transition to bright red and the birch's yellows respond to the symphony of color along the roadside. Both women remain silent for most of the trip.

Upon arrival in Montreal, Fanny maneuvers the carriage through the narrow streets. She stops to ask directions to the convent hospital and at last pulls up in front of a large but not ornate building. A young boy jumps from the steps to grab the horse's reins and then helps the two women dismount. Fanny places a coin into his hand and he quickly drops his knee. "Merci. Merci, madam."

Fanny Margaret strides up the steps, shoulders straight but taut, and raises the heavy knocker. Almost immediately the door is opened by a young nun who ushers the two women into the entrance hall.

"You must be our new novitiate. Welcome. Mother Superior is expecting you and will be here to greet you in a few minutes. She's in the ward at the moment." The young nun smiles and leaves the hall.

Fanny Margaret gasps. "Oh. Oh."

"What is it, dear? Are you ill? Have you changed your mind?" Fanny asks hopefully.

Fanny Margaret can't seem to speak, only point to the portrait of a white-bearded man hanging on the wall. One hand covers her mouth and tears well from her eyes. Her hand shakes as she continues to point.

Fanny looks at the portrait and then at her daughter. "Tell me what it is."

"It's him!" Fanny Margaret continues to point.

"Him? Him who?"

"The man who saved me from the river!" Fanny Margaret turns and buries her face in Fanny's cloak.

"Don't be silly, dear. That's a saint of some kind. He's been dead for centuries." Fanny gently loosens her daughter from her shoulder, looking her full in the face. "Are you sure you don't want to go home?"

"No. Definitely not. This is a sign from God; it must be." The two stand staring at the painting.

Mother Superior arrives quietly, watching the two, wondering what emotions are at play at this mother/daughter parting. She walks silently to Fanny Margaret's side. "God's blessings, young lady. Welcome to our convent." Looking at Fanny, she adds, "You, too, are most welcome. This is a challenging moment as one's daughter leaves your life behind and lives only to serve God. Our prayers are with you."

Since Mother Superior spoke in French, Fanny responds likewise. "Yes, it is a difficult moment, but one we respect. Will you please tell me who the man is in this painting?"

"That is St. Joseph, husband of the Blessed Mary. Our Patron Saint here at the hospital."

Almost uncontrollably, Fanny Margaret tells the story of being saved years ago by this man. She is absolutely sure it is the exact person who intervened in her drowning scare.

"Child, if this is the case as you say, it is surely God's sign to bring you here to us. God has a purpose for you and truly it must be here at our hospital." Mother Superior, gently takes hold of

Fanny Margaret's arm. "Come child, it is time to enter our doors. Give your mother a blessing for her return journey and we shall grant her leave."

Fanny Margaret gives her mother a long, tight squeeze, kisses her on the cheek before issuing, "Go in peace; safe journey." She turns and leaves the hall with Mother Superior.

Fanny stands for a moment watching her daughter's back as it disappears through the private doorway. She blows a kiss from her fingertips as Fanny Margaret turns for one last look at her mother. She shudders slightly, takes a final look at St. Joseph, and leaves the convent. The young boy stands quietly, petting the horse to keep him calm. Fanny offers him another coin and climbs into the carriage. Tears fill her eyes as she urges the horse into the crowded street. To fight her sadness, she forces herself to think of her next big challenge. "Now back to all this abominable *Black Snake* business. How will we manage to weather this storm?"

† † †

Fanny and Jazeb sit across from one another while Emma pours some strong tea. Fanny takes a hold of her husband's hand, speaking softly. "Jazeb, we will figure out this mess. There is no way you bear any responsibility for these ridiculous accusations." Emma recognizes it is time to go about her chores and heads to her neglected spinning.

Jazeb watches Emma leave before speaking. "I am the Customs Collector and thus my duty to make sure smugglers are apprehended. There is so much opposition to the embargo act, I have admittedly, turned a blind eye to much of the illegal trade. Though I have been adamant with my officers about confiscating smuggling goods."

"You know, Jazeb, how critical this trade is to Vermont economy. We've seen political thought rapidly move from Democratic-Republican to Federalist. Vermonters support what puts food on their tables."

"Oh, if that were the only issue. Ormsby, you remember, was killed in the scuffle at the *Black Snake*. You also know that

I'd sold part of the homestead to him and that Ira is suing him for return. Ira is persistent to continue suit with the heirs. My popularity, if it ever existed, plunges with those associated with Ormsby." Jazeb finishes his tea and walks to the window.

Fanny studies the few leaves floating in her tea. "I hear there are to be three separate trials and that they brought in judges Tyler, Galusha and Herrington. I'm not sure I trust Herrington's point of view, but Tyler and Galusha are open minded and true Vermonters. They understand our economy and our loyalties. Juror selection will begin before long. Have you heard anything about that?"

"You have a more devoted ear to that, Fanny. I focus more on my patients, who, by the way, seem to be dwindling of late. This is beginning to worry me more than the trials."

Fanny rises to stand beside her husband. She tucks her hand into his arm. "Do you think the two are connected? The trials and the practice, I mean."

"I pray not. People can be quite fickle."

The *Black Snake* trials have brought hundreds of visitors to Burlington, many as witnesses, some simply as gawkers. Excitement remains high throughout the initial hearings and abundant political ploys. Vermonter Samuel Mott's attorneys claim injustice on the grounds that Mott was used by both sides of the issue—promises from the smugglers and militia alike, each offering significant monies for his services. Many think, if Mott takes this plea, others on trial can do likewise. Vigorous debate occurs at many a supper table around northern Vermont.

Taverns are full at the ends of the days, clientele eager for news of the trials. Not since the days of the Green Mountain Boys' sorties in the last century have the taverns been so prosperous. The earliest and best news is to be found in the taverns nearest the courthouse.

Jazeb and Fanny have stayed away from the center of controversy; he tending to the few patients that now attend his dispensary, she to domestic chores and her garden. This day, neither have much to occupy their time or thoughts. Fanny has suggested a walk along the river path to enjoy the crisp autumn breezes and the emerging colors among the foliage.

Fanny tightens her bonnet strings as the winds increase along the river. She tucks her arm into Jazeb's and smiles up at him. She knows how deeply he is worried about his personal consequences of this awful smuggling scandal. "Jazeb, it's almost a year now since Fanny Margaret has joined the convent. Wouldn't it be a nice treat to go to Montreal for a few days and make a surprise visit to my daughter?"

Jazeb is quick to catch the exclusion of parenthood in his wife's words. He breathes deeply before responding. "Yes, Fanny dearest, I too miss Fanny Margaret. She is like my own daughter, as you well know." Not wanting his remarks to sound overly critical, he quickly continues. "You are quite right in suggesting a few days away from this madhouse of skullduggery. It would do well by both of us, almost like an elixir I might prescribe—only you're the physician in this case." He leans in to kiss his wife quite gently on her cheek.

Smiling, Fanny replies, "Udney and Hortensia are quite capable of taking care of themselves though Emma will have to keep a firm hand on that boy while we're gone. He'll not make a run around her! She'll have Hannibal and Ethan, Jr. to rein him in if she can't handle it. I swear that boy has the devil in his genes."

"Remember, dearest, you speak of my heir, though I do admit he's quite a handful." Jazeb chuckles and squeezes Fanny's arm.

"So, it's settled then. We'll make a holiday of it. I'll put Emma on alert when we get back to the house."

In the five days following their decision, both Fanny and Jazeb work to make preparations feasible for their time away. Their chores keep their minds off the increasing frenzy in Burlington. Finally, the two set off in the carriage wrapped in warm lap robes. With each mile, they become more relaxed. They chatter about the sites along the roadway, both deliberately staying away from talk about the trials. Jazeb steers the horse up to the rail at the first tavern he spies on the outskirts of Montreal. Leaving Fanny in the carriage, he enters the tavern to inquire about a decent inn where they might stay. Unfortunately, the tavern keeper speaks only French and Jazeb has to seek Fanny's interpretation skills.

Before Fanny can even speak, the tavern keeper begins a barrage of expletives about *foreigners* who arrest honest French tradesmen and bring them to trial. "We spit on you!" He exclaims as he ends his tirade.

Fanny turns to Jazeb, "We're obviously not welcome here. There's no need for any conversation. Just leave." The two turn and push through the oaken door. Loud laughter follows them through the portal.

"Well, so much for escaping those blasted trials!" Fanny grimaces as Jazeb helps her into the carriage. "I suggest we ask for assistance further from the border."

Finally, having found accommodations reasonably close to the convent, Jazeb and Fanny enjoy a delicious meal provided by their hosts. Fanny asks the innkeeper if he might send someone with a note to the convent. Being assured it would be a pleasure, Fanny returns to their room while Jazeb relaxes with a fine glass of port wine.

Digging into her portmanteau, Fanny pulls out a very ragged Maggy. "I couldn't leave you at home, Maggy. I knew I'd need your support upon visiting Fanny Margaret. You never fail to comfort me." She sits Maggy on the table while she pulls out some writing paper, quill and ink wrapped carefully in deerskin. She pens a request to Mother Superior asking to visit her daughter the next day, folds the paper and seals it with a few drops from the dripping candle. She picks up Maggy, holds her tight to her breast before replacing her on the table top.

Jazeb stands as his wife returns to the inn dining area. "Done?" he asks. As Fanny nods, he signals the innkeeper. Fanny hands their host the note with a slight curtsy and a smile. "Merci, monsieur."

By noon the next day, Fanny is nervous because there has been no response from the convent. She and Jazeb had spent the morning strolling the narrow streets around the inn, popping into shops, visiting the Sailor's Church, and just plain enjoying their escape from the turmoil at home. Returning to the inn, Fanny had questioned the innkeeper of any response that might have arrived. He suggests she and Jazeb enjoy some fruit and cheese while he sends his son to the convent to request a reply. Accepting the kind offer, Jazeb asks for an ale for himself and tea for his wife. Eternity passes through Fanny's emotions as she sips the hot brew.

Within 20 minutes the son returns with a sealed note he takes directly to Fanny. Her hands shake as she opens the missile. A smile lights her face, "Mother Superior says we may call at four o'clock for tea." She takes hold of Jazeb's hands as tears roll from her eyes.

Much relieved, Jazeb hugs Fanny. "See, no need for all that worry. You've exhausted yourself for naught. May I suggest a nap to refresh you for the visit? I'll just chat with the innkeeper or look for a local apothecary to see what's popular here in Montreal."

"Yes. Oh, yes. You'll wake me in time to get ready?" Receiving assurance her husband will not fail her, Fanny returns to their room, takes Maggy from the table and falls onto the bed. Sleep overtakes her almost immediately. Maggy stares blankly into space, held tightly in Fanny's arm.

True to his word, Jazeb returns by three o'clock giving plenty of time for them both to prepare for the visit. Fanny takes extraordinary time with her hair and rouging her cheeks. Adding a little powder, Fanny asks Jazeb, "do you think I've overdone it a bit with the rouge?"

"You're always beautiful, dearest," Jazeb responds tactfully. "Fanny Margaret won't care what you look like. She'll be so thrilled to see you."

During the short carriage ride to the convent, Fanny holds tight to Jazeb's arm. "Careful or my arm will turn blue," he jokes. Fanny smiles weakly, but says nothing. Arriving at the convent Fanny sees the same boy of a year ago, grown taller by inches. The young fellow takes the reins and bows. Jazeb drops a coin into his hand.

"You knock, Jazeb." Fanny trembles as she holds on to her husband.

"I've never seen you so frightened before, Fanny. What could possibly be so horrifying seeing your daughter?"

The door opens and a young nun greets them. Fanny stares at the face, hoping to see Fanny Margaret. Instead, this strange face smiles and ushers them into the hall. "Mother Superior and Sister Allen await you in the refectory. I'll show you the way."

Their heels click on the stone floor as they follow the nun. Fanny still clings to Jazeb, almost panting. The nun opens the door into the refectory where Fanny sees Mother Superior and Fanny Margaret standing by the table. Fanny rushes to hug her daughter but Fanny Margaret steps quickly aside.

"You'll forgive your daughter, Madam, but we discourage family embraces while in the novitiate. It makes parting more difficult. Please, come sit. We have prepared tea."

Fanny feels her heart thumping in her chest. What? She cannot hug her own daughter! Why then has she come? Outwardly, Fanny smiles and nods. All she can think of to say is, "You look pale dearest. Are you unwell?"

Fanny Margaret looks at the floor as she answers, "I'm quite well, thank you. We work very hard here with our patients. Thank you for inquiring."

Jazeb thinks to himself, "this is not going as Fanny had hoped. I suspect our visit will be quite short; something Mother Superior is adept at planning."

The conversation quickly becomes superficial and of little satisfaction to Fanny. The tea finished and the oat scones devoured, Mother Superior stands signaling the end of their visit. Fanny Margaret rises, crosses herself and offers a blessing, "May God grant you safe journey and a long life of fulfillment." Fanny, unable to speak, stares at her daughter as she leaves the refectory. Mother Superior also offers a blessing, signaling the young nun to escort the couple from the convent. Fanny is aghast at the impersonal visit and clings to Jazeb's arm. She thinks she might faint.

During the ride back to the inn Fanny sobs uncontrollably. Jazeb encircles her shoulders with his left arm while managing the reins with his right. Neither speaks.

211

Later that night, the two lie in bed. Fanny's head rests on her husband's chest; her eyes puffy and red from hours of crying. Jazeb tries to find comforting words but none seem to work.

Hiccoughing, Fanny tries to bring reason to her feelings. "I understand visiting makes it harder for the novitiates, but at least an embrace wouldn't hurt," she manages between sobs.

"At least you know she's safe and doing exactly what she begged for over the years." Jazeb hands Fanny a handkerchief to wipe her running nose.

"You're right, I know, but it hurts."

"The pain will pass, dearest. A cliché I realize, but true."

"I want to go home!" Fanny grabs Maggy and turns away from Jazeb, lying awake even as she eventually hears him snoring.

† † †

The Sheffield, Mott, and Mudgett trials are over. Sentences have been set and the convicted now reside in jail awaiting sentencing. Fanny and Jazeb have stayed away due to angry, protesting crowds. In Swanton, hecklers manage to locate the Penniman house and pelt the property with trash. Jazeb closes his dispensary, worrying that any patients he might still have could find themselves in harm's way. Emma occasionally receives disparaging attention when she ventures out to shop for essential goods.

Fanny sits near the kitchen fire, embroidering. Jazeb comes in from the outbuildings, shaking the few snowflakes from his coat. "Brrr. Looks like more snow tonight. I'm wondering if we should change our plans to go to Burlington for the Dean trial."

"Mmmm," mutters Fanny pushing her needle up through the linen. "We need to go, I think. Ethan has been selected for the jury and we need to support him. Besides, you owe Cyrus Dean some loyalty."

"I do? How's that?" Jazeb pulls a chair up to the fire, warming his hands.

"Both of you know the importance of the timber and potash trade. You both strove to keep commerce alive. The difference is only that you had a federal role as well. What I can't understand about this whole thing is what was Cyrus Dean doing on the *Black Snake*?"

"He was guiding the French up the river to the rendezvous location." Jazeb pokes haphazardly at the fire logs.

"So, then he knows the cues for safe transport. Why does all the shooting start? And, even more, why would he shoot his fellow Vermonter and militiaman Ellis Drake?"

Jazeb stares into the fire for moments before answering. "I don't think it was deliberate. That Wall Gun isn't very accurate. The two weren't exactly friends, but Cyrus made fine profits from his potash. Ellis was true militia, with no ties to the smugglers. He was one of the few that didn't row on both sides of the boat."

Fanny smiles and puts her handwork on the candle table. She reaches over to take her husband's hand. "It seems you rowed with two oars as well, dearest. I'm sorry I ever talked you into taking the Federal appointment. I know how deeply you support life here in the mountains."

"I'm no longer upholding the federal perspective. I fear my time will come for trial."

"It's important, I think," replies Fanny as she picks up her handwork again. "Important for you to show strength and courage to those involved. We can stay with Levi and Nancy while we're in Burlington. That way, we'll only move in public during the sessions."

"You're right. Right, as always." Jazeb smiles and rises to kiss Fanny's forehead. He heads to the cupboard for some rum. "The trial begins next week; shall we leave on Friday?"

Crowds have increased considerably. Occasional fights break out between the two factions—those cheering on the smugglers and those supporting federal law. Cheering and jeering take place as prisoners are escorted to and from the courthouse.

"Here comes Dean!" A voice rises from the street corner. Pushing and shoving accelerate, everyone hoping to catch a glimpse of the prisoner.

"Guilty! Guilty!" Someone shouts.

"Hero!" claims another.

Fanny and Jazeb seize the opportunity to walk unseen into the courthouse and find a seat in the gallery. Mostly they are ignored by other onlookers but one man seems determined to be uncivil.

"You've got your nerve, showing up here. Penniman, you're as guilty as Dean. And, you lady, do a disservice to General Allen."

Fanny's face flushes as she appears ready to rebuke the heckler. Before she can speak, Jazeb takes her arm and leads her several seats down on the bench. "Let him be, Fanny. Let him be."

Onlookers grow silent as the prospective jurors are brought into the courtroom and seated in the jury box. Attendants rise as Judge Royall Tyler enters and takes his seat behind the podium.

"Attention, the murder case of Cyrus Dean will now begin. Please be seated." Tyler taps his gavel.

Fanny gasps! "Murder? I thought this was a smuggling trial." She grabs Jazeb's arm and leans forward, peering over the gallery railing. No one else seems surprised. "Jazeb, did you know?"

He does not reply; simply stares at the judge.

Lawyers begin to question potential jurors. Fanny watches intently as Ethan's turn begins.

"Are you related to the late General Ethan Allen, sir?" asks Dean's attorney.

"Indeed, sir, I am his son."

"Then surely you are an acceptable juror." Responds Dean's representative, seating himself, waiting for State's Attorney, William Harrington's next move.

Harrington rises and approaches the jury box. "Master Allen, it is a pleasure and an honor to meet you. You are a true Vermonter, are you not?"

Ethan smiles, "I am my father's son and, as such, steeped in the tradition of justice and truth. A loyal Vermonter, yes!"

"Hmm, yes, the truth. Let's address the truth. How old are you?"

"Nineteen, sir."

"Is it true you are about to enter West Point?"

"Yes."

The military academy demands truth and honor from its cadets, does it not?"

"Indeed, it does, sir."

"So, as General Allen's son, a Vermonter, and a soon to be West Point cadet, you are committed to the truth."

"Correct."

"Then, tell me, Master Allen, what do you think of the Embargo Act?"

Ethan momentarily shifts in his seat before answering. "It is a Federal Law to be upheld. However, it is a law that impinges on Vermont's commerce."

"Move to dismiss this juror!" Harrington turns to the judge.

"On what grounds?" shouts Dean's attorney.

"Mr. Allen shows inclination towards smuggling. As such, he will not be an impartial participant on this jury."

"Dismissed." Judge Tyler bangs his gavel. Ethan is escorted from the jury box and out of the court room.

Fanny sinks back in her seat. She can't believe that Ethan Allen's son has been so dismissed.

Dean's trial continues for almost two weeks. The final verdict: guilty of murder. Dean is sentenced to hang, along with his cohorts. Fanny and Jazeb attend most of the trial but on days when the crowds seem most agitated, they prefer to stay in Levi's house out of public view. A week before the scheduled hangings, all but Cyrus Dean receive commuted sentences.

Fanny refuses to attend the hanging and insists that she and Jazeb return home as word spreads about the verdict. No one in Vermont has ever been publicly executed. Citizens appear drawn to this morbid event.

On November 11, 1809, 10,000 people gather in Burlington to witness Dean's death.

215

In Swanton, Fanny, clasping Maggy in her arms, partakes of some of Jazeb's port. Her hand trembles as she raises the goblet to her lips. Feeling the bite of the wine and then the warmth it provides, Fanny swallows the rest and pours another. Jazeb spends the day locked in his dispensary trying to keep visions of the execution from pounding in his head.

Chapter 30
THE FINAL HOURS
1834

Fanny lies in her bed, too weak to rise. Jazeb sits by her side, holding gently to her hand. Maggy sits upright on the highest pillow, staring down at Fanny. Her hair is faded, her right eye long since missing, her clothes more rags than not. Still, the doll and Fanny are inseparable. The maid knocks, wishing to enter with some tea laced with laudanum—Jazeb's prescription.

"I'm dying you know," Fanny manages a whisper.

The rims of Jazeb's eyes dampen as he speaks. "Yes, dearest. I am still the doctor. You're becoming weaker each day. My heart is breaking to watch you suffer so. The tea will bring some comfort, I think. Let me help you." He gently lifts Fanny just far enough to allow her to sip some of the brew.

"There is so much to remember in my long life. How long have we been in Colchester now? I can't seem to put a good number to the years."

"Well, we moved here in 1813 so that makes it just about 21 years. Does it feel like a very long time, Fanny?"

Fanny takes a moment to gain her breath. "It may not seem like a long time in some ways, but it does mean I am a very old woman." She tries to laugh, but hasn't the strength.

Jazeb chuckles, "So much has happened during our years in this house. I've left my medical practice behind though I've managed to serve the community well. From doctor to judge, a mighty leap."

"You're old, too, Jazeb." Fanny manages a smile. "Think of all who have died while we have lived."

"Who do you miss the most, dearest?" Jazeb offers her another sip of the laudanum tea.

"Unfair! How can one choose between one's children? First Hannibal during that awful war. I thought I'd die myself after that." Fanny takes another drink that her husband suggests. After a few minutes, she's able to continue. "Ethan would have been so proud of his sons, both to graduate from that military school."

"West Point, dearest." Jazeb gently pushes back a few locks of gray hair that have drifted on to Fanny's forehead."

"Then, of course, was Fanny Margaret's death, so unpredicted. In September, uhm, 1819, wasn't it? Even now, I can't stand to remember it. I'll never forgive that convent for preventing me from visiting her." Tears trickle down through the wrinkles on Fanny's face.

"Don't upset yourself, dearest. Here, let's finish this tea and maybe you'll get some rest."

"But they never even told me she was sick—sick enough to die!" Fanny closes her eyes trying to stop the river of tears. Her breathing settles and she appears to rest.

Then, after a deep gasp, and without opening her eyes, Fanny speaks again. "And, Emma, dearest Emma. More like a sister than a servant. Oh, how we all missed her for so long. It's hard isn't it, Jazeb, to grieve for loved ones?" Fanny sobs quietly.

Jazeb senses she has drifted off and rises to leave. Before he reaches the door, Fanny begins speaking again—softly, struggling for each word.

"Hortensia. Oh, my, Hortensia. Not quite 30 years and leaving behind those little ones. I so regret being that far away as they grew up." Her body shudders slightly.

"Thank goodness we still have Ethan and Udney." Jazeb adds as he reseats himself.

Fanny manages another smile. "They might as well be gone; we never see them. Only two left out of five. Doesn't seem natural, somehow. Sadly, Ethan's girls, all three, are gone. Don't you wonder sometime why we're still here?" Fanny appears to drift off once again.

Jazeb decides to wait to make sure she's finally under the influence of the medication. He checks his pocket watch, noting supper hour is not far off. He's feeling a bit hungry, noting he hasn't eaten much of late as he's spent so much time by his wife's side. He hears her stir again.

Fanny barely opens her eyes; her words sound fuzzy. "So much forgiveness to accomplish—for both of us."

Jazeb leans close. "Between us, dearest? There is nothing to forgive between us."

"No. I'm pleased there is no forgiveness necessary for the two of us together. I do believe, though, we both need to forgive those judges and the government that did you so wrong."

"I've no need to forgive them. I got what I deserved. Smuggling is illegal and I turned a blind eye believing it was better for our State. I took my sentence and was done with it. No prison, just restitution for my pay, and forbidden from Federal service ever again."

Jazeb sits quietly, reliving much of his trial in his mind. The condemnation of the judges; the anger of the crowds; the loss of his medical practice. What hurt most, he thinks, was the disgrace for Fanny as they were hooted at and scorned as they left Swanton after the trial. He is startled to hear Fanny speak again.

"I think we both need to forgive Ira." Fanny pauses a moment to catch her breath."When he sold Ethan's property, it broke my heart. It was if the last of Ethan was gone. I couldn't believe you won the law suit against him."

"Indeed, that was a painful time. Ira, Ethan, and Levi had spent so much of their resources building up the Onion River company. They felt Ethan's property was as much theirs as co-partners."

Fanny tries to raise herself on her elbow but falls back into the pillow. She rests a moment before continuing the conversation. "Truly, I believe Levi, and particularly Ira, never quite forgave me for my early Loyalist stances." She manages a soft chuckle.

Jazeb adjusts the pillows for his wife. "Did it hurt you as much when I sold the property to Van Ness?"

"No, it didn't." Fanny shakes her head with great effort. "I don't know why. Perhaps, I'd just had enough of it all. The pain came again when Ira died that year. Poor Jerusha, how ashamed she felt at all that family discord."

Both were silent for several moments as if they were enacting forgiveness in their hearts.

"I'm feeling so sleepy. I think your tea is working. Hand me Maggy, please." Fanny slips into sleep holding her beloved doll.

Jazeb tiptoes from the room and heads toward the kitchen. He needs a tout of rum. As he pours the liquid into his mug, he hears a cry from Fanny's room. Without setting down his mug, he dashes to her side. As he enters the room he sees Fanny half upright in the bed, holding Maggy with her left arm, pointing at the ceiling with her right.

Quite clearly she speaks, "Thank God, he's come at last! My Great White Stallion has come for me at last." A glorious smile lights her face and she sinks back into the pillows, quite still.

Jazeb closes her eyes and still carrying his rum, walks to his office. He pulls out his journal and writes: "October 13, 1834, Frances Montresor Brush Buchanan Allen Penniman, my beloved Fanny, returns to her one true love in death."

ACKNOWLEDGEMENTS

When it takes almost 20 years to write a book, there are many people to thank for their assistance and encouragement. I don't want to forget anyone, but it will happen.

Sara Tamplin dutifully and lovingly read the rough manuscript with an eye to grammar and content. She has a sharp pencil and I'm so grateful for her teaching skills. If you find grammatical holes in this story, it's probably because she fell asleep reading into the wee hours of the morning. Thank you, dear friend.

Millie Curtis, author of 14 books, did me the honor of reading for continuity, story line, and character development. Her comments helped me sharpen the story. I'll never look at adverbs the same way again!

Pat Lincoln got in on the ground floor of this project. She traveled around Vermont with me, pouring over journals, ledgers, and any memorabilia we could find. She's probably responsible for 35% of the reference notes in my file boxes. I thank her for her patience and enthusiasm.

Ron Reaves kept prodding me and encouraging me to finish what I'd started so many years ago. I might have given up if it weren't for him.

Piper Leo and Esther Munro Swift, both now deceased Vermont scholars, kept feeding me clues on where to look for more information. They were excellent sounding boards.

George Chafee, our family genealogist, was most helpful in researching the Allen and Norman family histories.

Then there were those whose names I never knew or no longer remember. The two wonderful women at the Westminster Court House. (Retired by now, no doubt!) They let us spend hours, days even, pouring over old records, making copies, and cheering us on. The staff at the Ethan Allen Homestead, members of the Center for Research in Vermont, all were generous with their information.

Photo of Francis Montresor Brush debut portrait courtesy of Wikipedia.

Most of all, I give great thanks to Fanny, herself. What a woman!

ABOUT THE AUTHOR

History, women's history in particular, has claimed Micki Smith's enthusiasm much of her adult life. Owning an inn in Vermont provided opportunities to explore local stories that never made it into history books. Once Micki "met" Fanny, she was hooked.

Writing was integral to her professional life and her volunteer activities. Several of her short stories have been published. She's taught creative writing to children and adults. In retirement, she focuses on the fiber arts and writing. She lives in rural Virginia, where she designs and makes one-of-a-kind fiber items sold under her company name: Brazen Sheep.

Author's photo by Sara Tamplin